Muriel Barbery is the author of *The Elegance of the Hedgehog* and *The Gourmet*. She has lived in Kyoto and Amsterdam and now lives in the French countryside.

Alison Anderson is a translator and author. She has translated numerous novels from French, including *The Elegance of the Hedgehog* and *The Gourmet* by Muriel Barbery.

THE LIFE OF ELVES
Muriel Barbery

THE LIFE OF ELVES
Muriel Barbery

Translated from the French by Alison Anderson

Gallic Books
London

A Gallic Book

First published in France as *La vie des elfes*
by Éditions Gallimard, Paris

Copyright © 2015 by Éditions Gallimard, Paris
English translation copyright © Europa Editions 2015

First published in Great Britain in 2016 by
Gallic Books, 59 Ebury Street, London, SW1W 0NZ

ISBN 978-1-910477-21-2

Typeset in Fournier MT by Gallic Books
Printed and bound by
CPI Group (UK) Ltd, Croydon, CR0 4YY

2 4 6 8 10 9 7 5 3 1

For Sébastien
For Arty, Elena, Miguel, Pierre and Simona

CONTENTS

LIST OF CHARACTERS

Burgundy

On the Hollows Farm
Maria Faure
André Faure, her father, a farmer
Rose Faure, her mother
Eugénie and Angèle, André's aunts
Jeannette and Marie, Rose's first cousins once removed

On Marcelot's farm
Eugène Marcelot, known as Gégène, a farmer
Lorette Marcelot, known as La Marcelotte, his wife

In the village
Father François, the priest
Jeannot, the postman
Paul-Henri, known as Ripol, the blacksmith
Léon Saurat, a farmer
Léon and Gaston-Valéry, his sons
Henri Faure, known as Riri, the forester
Jules Lecot, known as Julot, mayor of the village and head of the
    roadmenders
Georges Echard, known as Chachard, the master saddler

Abruzzo

At the presbytery
Clara Centi
Father Centi, her adoptive father, the priest of Santo Stefano
Alessandro Centi, the priest's younger brother and friend of Pietro
    Volpe
An old housekeeper

In the village
Paolo, known as Paolino, a shepherd

Rome

At the Villa Acciavatti
Gustavo Acciavatti, the Maestro
Leonora Acciavatti, his wife, née Volpe
Petrus, a strange servant

At the Villa Volpe
Pietro Volpe, an art dealer, Gustavo Acciavatti's brother-in-law
Roberto, his father (†)
Alba, his mother
Leonora, his sister

At the Villa Clemente
The Clementes, wealthy patricians
Marta, the older daughter (†), Alessandro's great love
Teresa, the younger daughter (†), a virtuoso pianist

The Capitol of Rome
Raffaele Santangelo, the Governor of Rome

The World of Mists

The Head of the Council of the Mists (appearing as a grey horse /a
    hare)
The Guardian of the Pavilion of the Mists (appearing as a white horse
    /a wild boar)
Marcus and Paulus, friends of Gustavo Acciavatti and Petrus
Aelius, the leader of the enemy

BIRTHS

THE LITTLE GIRL FROM SPAIN

The little girl spent most of her hours of leisure among the branches. When her family were looking for her, they would go to the trees, the tall beech to start with, the one that stood to the north above the outhouse, for that was where she liked to daydream while observing the activity on the farm; then it was the old lime tree in the priest's garden beyond the low wall of cool stone; and finally—most often in winter—among the oaks in the combe to the west of the adjacent field, a hollow planted with three of the most majestic specimens in all the region. The little girl would nestle in the trees, all the hours she could steal from the village life of book-learning, meals, and mass, and not infrequently she would invite a few friends to come along, and they would marvel at the airy spaces she had arranged there, and together they would spend glorious days in laughter and chat.

One evening as she sat on a lower branch of the middle oak, while the combe was filling with shadow, aware that they would soon be coming to take her back to the warmth, she decided for a change to cut across the meadow and pay a visit to the neighbour's sheep. She set out as the mist was rising. She knew every clump of grass in an area extending from the foothills of her father's farm all the way to Marcelot's; she could have closed her eyes and known exactly where she was, as if guided by the stars, from the swelling of the field, the rushes in the stream, the stones on the pathways and the gentle incline of the slope; but instead, for a particular reason, she now opened her eyes wide. Someone was walking through the mist only slightly ahead of her, and this presence tugged strangely at her heart, as if the organ were coiling in upon itself and bringing curious images to her: in the bronze glow of undergrowth she saw a white horse, and a path paved with black stones gleaming under foliage.

Who was that child, on the day of this remarkable event? The six adults who lived on the farm—father, mother, two great-aunts and two grown-up cousins—adored her. There was an enchantment about her that was far from that found in children whose first hours have been mild, that sort of grace born of a careful mixture of ignorance and happiness; no, it was, instead, as if when she moved she carried with her an iridescent halo, which minds forged in pastures and woods would compare to the vibrations of the tallest trees. Only the eldest auntie, by virtue of an abiding penchant for anything that could not be explained, thought to herself that there was something magical about the little girl; but one thing was certain: for such a young child she bore herself in a most unusual way, incorporating some of the invisibility and trembling of the air, as a dragonfly would, or palms swaying in the wind.

Otherwise, she was very dark and very lively, rather thin, but with a great deal of elegance; two eyes of sparkling obsidian; olive, almost swarthy skin; high Slavic-looking cheekbones flushed with a round rosiness; finally, well-defined lips, the colour of fresh blood. She was splendid. And what character! Always running through the fields or flinging herself onto the grass, where she would stay and stare at the too vast sky; or crossing the stream barefoot, even in winter, to feel the sweet chill or biting cold, and then with the solemnity of a bishop she would relate to all assembled the highlights and humdrum moments of her days spent out of doors. To all of this one must add the faint sadness of a soul whose intelligence surpassed her perception and who—from the handful of clues that, although weak, were to be found everywhere, even in those protected places, however poor, in which she had grown up—already had an intimation of the world's tragedies.

Thus, at five o'clock it was that glowing, secretive young sprig of a girl who sensed the nearby presence in the mist of an invisible creature, and she knew more surely than the existence of God proclaimed by the priest that this creature was both friendly and supernatural. Thus she was not afraid. Instead, she set off in the direction she had determined shortly before, towards the sheep.

Something took her by the hand. Something like a large fist wrapped in a soft warm weave, creating a gentle grip in which her own hand felt lost. But no man could have possessed a palm that, as she felt through the silky skein, had hollows and ridges that might belong to the hoof of a giant wild boar. Just then they made a turn to their left, almost at a right angle, and she understood that they were heading towards the little woods, skirting round the sheep and Marcelot's farm. There was a fallow field, overgrown with sleek serried blades of grass, rising gently to meet the hill through a winding passage, until it reached a lovely copse of poplar trees rich with strawberries and a carpet of periwinkles where not so long ago every family had been permitted to gather wood, and would commence with the sawing by first snowfall; alas, that era is now gone, but it will not be spoken of today, be it due to sorrow or forgetfulness, or because at this hour the little girl is running to meet her destiny, holding tight to the boar's hoof.

And this on the mildest autumn evening anyone had seen for many a year. People had delayed putting their apples and pears to ripen on the wooden racks in the cellar, and all day long the air was streaked with insects inebriated with the finest orchard vintage. There was a languidness in the air, an indolent sigh, a quiet certainty that things would never end, and while people went about their work as usual, without pause and without complaint, they took secret delight in this endless autumn as it told them not to forget to love.

Now just as the little girl was heading towards the clearing in the east wood, another unexpected event occurred. It began to snow. It began to snow all of a sudden, and not those timid little snowflakes that bob about in the gloom and scarcely strive to settle, no, heavy snowflakes began to fall, as big as magnolia buds, and they fell thick on the ground, forming a thoroughly opaque screen. In the village, as it was nearing six o'clock, everyone was surprised; the father in his simple twill shirt, chopping wood, Marcelot warming up his dogs over by the pond, Jeannette kneading her dough, and others who, on this late autumn day that was like a dream of lost happiness, were coming and going about their business, be it leather, flour or straw; yes, they had all been surprised and now they were closing the latches tightly on the stable doors, calling in the sheep and the dogs, and getting ready for something that brought them almost as much well-being as the sweet languor of autumn: the first evening they'd spend clustered around the fireside, when outside there was a raging snowstorm.

They were preparing, and thinking.

They were thinking—those who remembered—about an autumn day some ten years earlier, when the snow had suddenly begun to fall as if the sky were peeling away into immaculate white strips. And it was at the little girl's farm in particular that they were thinking about it, for her absence there had just been discovered, and the father was pulling on his fur cap and a hunting jacket that stank of mothballs from a hundred metres away.

"They'd better not come back for her," he muttered before disappearing into the night.

He knocked on the doors of the village houses where other farmers were to be found, along with the master saddler, the mayor (who was also the head roadmender), the forester, and a few others. Everywhere, he said the same thing: *the wee girl has gone missing*, before he set off to the next door, and behind him the man of the house would shout for his hunting jacket, or his thick overcoat, and he'd put on his gear and hurry into the tempest towards the next house. And eventually there were fifteen of them gathered at the home of

Marcelot, whose wife had already fried up a panful of thick bacon and set out a jug of mulled wine. They polished it off in ten minutes, calling out their battle instructions, no different from the ones they reeled off on the mornings they went hunting—but a wild boar's trail was no mystery to them, whereas the little girl, now, she was more unpredictable than a sprite. Only, the father had his opinion on the matter, as did all the others, because in these parts no one believes in coincidences, where legends and the Good Lord go hand in hand and where they are suspected of having a few tricks city people have long forgotten. Around these parts, you see, it's a rare event to turn to reason in a shipwreck; what's called for are eyes, feet, intuition, and perseverance, and that is what they mustered that evening, because they remembered just such a night only ten years earlier when they'd gone up the mountain pass looking for someone whose traces led straight to the clearing in the east wood. Now the father feared more than anything that once they got up there the lads would be bound to open their eyes wide, make the sign of the cross, and nod their heads, just as they had done that time when the footprints came to a sudden stop in the middle of the circle, and they found themselves staring at a carpet of snow as smooth as a newborn's skin, a place of pristine silence where no one—and this all the hunters were prepared to swear—no one had set foot for at least two days.

Off they go, up through the blizzard.

As for the little girl, she has reached the clearing. It's snowing. She's not cold. The creature that brought her here is speaking. It's a majestic, tall white horse, its coat steaming in the evening air, spreading a light mist in every direction on earth—to the west, where the Morvan is turning blue; to the east where the harvest was brought in without a single drop of rain; to the north where the plain stretches for miles; and to the south where the men are struggling through the snow up to their thighs, their hearts twisted in fear. Yes, a fine tall white horse with arms and legs, and dewclaws too, a horse that is neither a horse nor a man nor a wild boar but a combination of all three, although not wholly assembled— at times the horse's head turns into a man's while its body expands and is fitted with hooves that shrink to little trotters then grow again until they are those of a wild boar. This goes on unendingly, while the little girl contemplates the dance of essences greeting and mingling as they trace the steps of knowledge and faith. The creature speaks gently to her and the mist is transformed. And she sees. She does not understand what he is saying but she sees a snowy evening just like this one in the same village where she has her farm, and on the porch there is a white shape against the whiteness of the snow. And she is that shape.

Who can help but recall the event whenever they meet that little girl, as full of life as a chick whose pure vitality you can feel beating against your shoulder and within your own heart. It was Auntie Angèle who, when the time came to go and round up the hens, found the poor thing staring at her with her all-engulfing black eyes and her little amber face, so visibly human that Angèle stood poised with one foot in the air, until she got a hold of herself and began to shout *a child in the night!* and lifted her up to take her inside, this little girl whom the snowflakes had spared even though it was still snowing a blizzard. Not long afterwards, that same night, the auntie would say: *'Twas as if the Good Lord was speaking to me*, then fall silent, troubled by the sensation that it was impossible to describe how the shape of the world had been distorted by the discovery of the infant swaddled in white, the dazzling splitting of possibilities into unfamiliar pathways howling in the snowy night, while time and space retracted, contracted—but still, she had felt it, and she left it up to God to understand it.

One hour after Angèle had come upon the little girl, the farm had filled with villagers who stood deliberating, and the countryside with men who were following a set of footprints. They were tracing the solitary footprints that left the farm and went up to the east wood, scarcely sinking into the snow, although the men were in up to their hips. What happened after that, we already know: once they reached the clearing, they stopped their tracking and headed back to the village, their minds heavy with dark thoughts.

"So long as …" said the father.

No one added anything but everyone was thinking about the poor woman who, maybe … and they made the sign of the cross.

The tiny girl observed all of this from deep within the fine cambric swaddling decorated with a sort of lace unknown in these parts: there was an embroidered cross, which warmed the hearts of all the old ladies, and there were two words in a foreign tongue, which terrified them. They all focused their attention on those two words, in vain, until the arrival of Jeannot, the postman; because of the war, the one from which twenty-one of the village men did not return, and the reason for a monument opposite the town hall and the church, he had once descended deep into that territory they called Europe—which was located nowhere else, in the mind of the rescuers, than in those pink, blue, green and red patches on the map in the community hall, for what might Europe be when strict borders separated villages only three leagues from one another?

So this Jeannot, who had just come in with his hair covered in snow, and had been served a coffee with a big splash of brandy by the mother, now looked at the embroidered inscription on the satiny cotton and said, "Upon my word, it'll be Spanish."

"Are you sure?" asked the father.

The lad nodded vigorously, his nose glowing with brandy.

"And what's it mean?" asked the father.

"How am I supposed to know?" answered Jeannot, who didn't speak barbaric tongues.

They all nodded, and digested the news with the help of another encouraging shot of brandy. So the little tot came from Spain? Well, I never.

Meanwhile, the women, who weren't drinking, had gone to fetch Lucette. Lucette had recently recovered from her confinement and was now nursing two little ones nestled against her bosom as white as the snow outside, and all those present looked without an ounce of spite at that bosom as fine as a pair of sugarloaves—they could just lap it up!—and they felt that a sort of peace had come over the earth because there before them were two little babies clinging to those nourishing breasts. After she'd had a good feed, the little lass let out a sweet little burp, as round as a ball and clear as a bell, and everyone burst out laughing and gave each other a fraternal tap on the shoulder. They relaxed, Lucette buttoned up her bodice, and the women served up some hare pâté on big slices of bread reheated in goose fat, because they knew that this was the priest's favourite and they'd got it into their heads to keep the young miss in a Christian home. What's more, it didn't cause the problems they'd have had elsewhere if a little Spaniard suddenly showed up just like that on some fellow's porch.

"Well, well," said the father, "I'm of the opinion that this little girl is at home," and he looked at the mother who smiled back at him, he looked at every one of the guests, whose satiated gazes lingered on the infants settled on a blanket to one side of the great wood stove, and finally he looked at the priest who, in a haze of hare pâté and goose fat, stood up and went over to the stove.

They all got to their feet.

We shall not repeat here the country priest's blessing; all that Latin, when in fact we wish we knew a bit of Spanish, would be too confusing. But they got to their feet, the priest blessed the infant, and everyone knew that the snowy night was a night of grace. They recalled an ancestor who had told them the story of a cold spell in which you could just as easily have died of fright as of frost; it was during the last campaign, the one that left them victorious and forever damned to remember their dead—the last campaign, where the columns were advancing in a lunar twilight and the ancestor himself no longer knew whether the paths of his childhood had ever existed, and that walnut tree in the bend in the road, and the swarms of insects around the time of Saint John's Day, no, he couldn't remember a thing, and all the men were just like him, because it was so cold there, so cold … it's hard to imagine such a fate. But at dawn, after a night of misery in which the cold struck down those brave souls the enemy had missed, it suddenly began to snow, and that snow … that snow was the redemption of the world, because among their divisions it would not freeze again, and soon on their brows they felt the miraculous warmth of the flakes signalling the thaw.

The little girl didn't feel the cold any more than the soldiers of the last campaign, or the lads who had reached the clearing and who were gazing at the scene, soundless as pointer dogs. Later, they could not recall what they had seen clear as day, and to each question they would reply with the vague tone of someone searching within for some confused memory. Most of the time, all they said was, "The little lass was there in the middle of a bloody blizzard, but she was warm and alive as could be and she was talking to some creature that made off afterwards."

"What sort of creature?" asked the women.

"Ah, some creature," they replied. And as in these parts where legends and the Good Lord, et cetera … they stuck to that reply and went on watching over the child as if over the Holy Sepulchre itself.

A singularly human creature, that's how each of them had sensed it, looking at vibrations as visible as matter whirling around the little girl, and it was an unfamiliar sight that gave them a strange shiver, as if life were suddenly splitting open and they could look inside it at last. But what do you see when you look inside life? You see trees and wood and snow, perhaps a bridge, and landscapes slipping by before your eyes have time to grasp them. You see the toil and the winds, the seasons and the sorrows, and you might see a tableau that belongs to your heart alone—a strap of leather in a tin box, a patch of meadow where the hawthorn blossoms run riot, the wrinkled face of a beloved woman and the smile of the little girl telling tales of tree frogs. Then, nothing more. The men would recall that the world suddenly landed back on its feet in an explosion that left them weak and drained—and after that they saw that the mist had been swept from the clearing, that it was snowing so hard you could drown in it, and the little girl stood all alone in the middle of the circle where there were no other footprints save her own. Then they all went back down to the farm where they sat the child in front of a bowl of scorching hot milk, and the men hastily stored their rifles, because there was mushroom stew with brawn and ten bottles of wine in the cellar.

There you have the story of the little girl who held the hoof of a giant wild boar tight in her hand. Truth be told, no one can really explain what it all means. But there is one more thing to say, about the two words embroidered on the edge of the white cambric in an elegant Spanish with neither object nor logic, and which the little girl would learn about once she had already left the village and set in motion the wheels of fate—and before that there is one other thing to say: we all have the right to know the secret of our birth. This is how you pray in your churches and your woods and how you go off to travel the world—because you were born on a snowy night and you inherited two words that came from Spain.

Mantendré siempre.[1]

_____

1. I will maintain.

THE LITTLE GIRL FROM ITALY

Anyone who doesn't know how to read between the lines of life need only remember that the little girl grew up in a remote village in Abruzzo cared for by a country priest and his old, illiterate housekeeper.

Father Centi lived in a tall building, and below the cellar was a garden with plum trees where they would hang the laundry in the early hours so that in time it would dry in the wind from the mountains. The house was halfway up the village, which rose straight up to the sky in such a way that the streets twisted round the hill like the strands of a tightly wound ball of wool, dotted with a church, an inn, and just the right amount of stone to shelter sixty souls. After a day spent running around outside, Clara never went home without first slipping through the orchard, where she would stop to pray to the spirits of enclosure to prepare her for her return within four walls. Then she went to the kitchen—a long low room adjoining a pantry that smelled of plums, the old jam cupboard, and the noble dust of cellars.

From dawn to sunset, the old housekeeper recounted her stories. She had told the priest she'd inherited them from her grandmother, but she told Clara that the spirits of the Sasso mountain had whispered them to her while she slept, and the little girl knew that this shared secret must be true, because she had heard Paolo's tales, and he got them from the spirits of the high mountain pastures. But if she valued the figures and turns of speech of those tales, in truth it was for the velvety chanting of the storyteller's voice, because that coarse old woman, whom only two words rescued from complete illiteracy—all she knew was how to write her name, and the name of the village, and at mass she could not read the prayers but recited them, rather, from memory—that old woman had a manner of speaking that contrasted with the modesty of the remote parish on the escarpments of the Sasso; in actual fact, one must imagine what Abruzzo was like in those days, in that mountainous region where Clara's protectors lived: eight months of snow interspersed with storms over the massifs set between two seas where it was not uncommon to see a few snowflakes in summer. Add to that real poverty, the poverty of regions where people till the soil and raise their flocks, herding them at the peak of summer to the highest point on the gradients. Not many lived there, consequently, and even fewer when the snow came and everyone left with their beasts for the sunshine in Apulia. The only ones who stayed in the village were those who were tireless workers, growing their dark lentils, for lentils only grow in poor soil, and valiant women who in the cold weather looked after the children, the farms, and their attendance at church. But while the people of this land might have been sculpted into jagged rock by wind and snow, they were also fashioned by the poetry of their landscape, which made shepherds compose rhymes in the icy fog of the high pastures, and storms give birth to hamlets that dangled from the web of the sky.

Thus, the old woman, whose life had unfolded within the walls of a backward village, had a silkiness to her voice that came to her from the splendour of the landscape. The little girl was sure of this: it was the timbre of this very voice that had awoken her to the world, even though people assured her she was only an infant at the time, lying in hunger on the top step outside the church. But Clara did not question her faith. There was a great void of sensations, an absence festooned with whiteness and wind; and there was the melodious cascade that pierced the emptiness and which was there again every morning when the old housekeeper wished her a good day. The little girl had learned the Italian language with miraculous speed, but Paolo the shepherd had grasped that it was something other than her facility with Italian that had left a scent of prodigy in her wake, and one evening he whispered to her, *It's the music, little one, isn't it, it's the music you hear?* In response, she looked up at him with her eyes as blue as the torrents from the glacier, with a gaze in which the angels of mystery sang. And life flowed down the slopes of the Sasso with the slowness and intensity of those places where everything requires effort but also takes its time, in the current of a bygone dream where humankind knew languor interwoven with the bitterness of the world. Labour was intense, and prayer along with it, and they protected a little girl who spoke the way others sing, and who knew how to converse with the spirits of the rocks and the combes.

*

One day in June, late in the afternoon, there came a knock on the door of the presbytery and two men strode into the kitchen, wiping their brows. One was the priest's youngest brother, the other was the carter who had driven the large twohorse cart all the way from L'Aquila; on the cart was a massive shape secured with blankets and straps. Clara had watched the convoy making its way along the northern route as she stood after lunch on the steep path above the village; from there the view encompassed both valleys and, on a fine day, Pescara and the sea. When the cart had almost reached the final uphill stretch, she scampered down the slope and arrived at the presbytery, her face glowing with love. The two men had left the cart outside the church and climbed up to the plum garden where they were greeted with hugs and a glass of the sweet chilled white wine that was served on warm days, along with some restorative victuals, and then, agreeing to some dinner later, they wiped their mouths on the cuffs of their sleeves and went back to the church where Father Centi was waiting.

Two more men were needed to help move the big object into the nave, then they set about freeing it from its straps, and in the meantime the village began to assemble in the pews of the little church; the air held a sweetness that coincided with the arrival of this unexpected bequest from the city. But Clara kept well back, motionless, speechless, in the shadow of a pillar. This was her moment, and she had known as soon as she saw the shape moving along the north road; if the old housekeeper saw on her face the exaltation of a bride, it was because she felt as if she were about to partake in strange yet familiar nuptials. When the last strap was removed and the object was finally visible, there was a murmur of satisfaction, followed by a burst of applause, because it was a fine black piano, as polished as a pebble is by the sea, and it was almost without a scratch, despite having travelled widely and experienced much.

This is the story of the piano. Father Centi came from an affluent family in L'Aquila, but his lineage was declining, since he had become a priest and two of his brothers had died young, and the third, Alessandro, who was now at his aunt's expiating the errant ways of his former dissolute life in Rome, had never got round to taking a wife. The brothers' father had died before the war, leaving his widow with an unexpected pile of debts and a house that was too opulent for the impoverished woman she had become overnight. Once she had sold all her belongings and the creditors had finished knocking at her door, she withdrew to the same convent where she would die several years later, long before Clara arrived at the village. But upon leaving her secular life for her final seclusion in the convent, she had arranged for the only relic of her past glory to be conveyed to her sister— an old maid who lived near the city walls—a relic she had managed to preserve in spite of the vultures: she asked her sister to look after it for the grandchildren she might one day have on this earth. *I will not know them, but they will receive this from me, and now I must go, and I wish you a good life*, the aunt had faithfully transcribed in her own will, bequeathing the piano to whichever of her nephews had children when her time came, and adding: *Do as she wished*.

Thus the notary, who had heard about the orphan's arrival

at the presbytery, thought he was doing the right thing by asking Alessandro to escort the inheritance to his brother's home. As the piano had stayed in the attic during the war and no one had thought to bring it back down afterwards, the same lawyer informed them by letter that on its arrival it would need tuning, to which the priest replied that the piano tuner, who made his rounds through the neighbouring towns once a year, had been summoned to make a detour through the village in early summer.

They gazed at the fine piano that shone beneath the stained-glass windows, and they laughed, talked about it, and succumbed to the cheer of this lovely evening in late spring. But Clara was silent. She had already heard the organ played at funerals in the neighbouring church, where the God-fearing old woman who performed the liturgical pieces was as hard of hearing as she was hopeless as a musician—and anyway, those chords she thumped out, without hearing them, were probably not worth remembering either. Clara preferred a hundred times over the threnody which Paolo coaxed from his mountain flute; it was so much more powerful and true than the fracas from the organ devoted to the glory of the Most High. So when she saw the cart begin its climb up the long road of hairpin bends towards the village, her heart leapt as if to signal an extraordinary event. Now that the object was there before her, that feeling grew all the stronger, and Clara wondered how she would ever be able to bear the waiting, since they had been told, to the regret of those who would have enjoyed a foretaste of the pleasures in store, that the instrument was not to be touched until it had been tuned.

But they respected what the shepherd of their consciences had decreed, and prepared instead to spend a fine evening savouring some wine under the benign gaze of the stars.

And a splendid evening it was. The table had been laid beneath the plum trees in the orchard and Alessandro's old friends had been invited for supper. He had once been a very handsome man, and beneath the marks of time and past excesses you could still see the fine features and proud contours of his face. What was more, he spoke Italian with a smoothness of tone which in no way diminished its melodiousness, and he always told stories about very beautiful women and endless afternoons where people sat smoking under the awning while conversing with wise men and poets.

That evening he began to tell a story that took place in perfumed salons where the men smoked fine cigars and drank golden liqueurs; Clara could make no sense of it, so foreign to her were the settings and the manners. But just as he was about to begin the part about a mysterious thing known as a concert, the old housekeeper interrupted him and said, *Sandro, al vino ci pensi tu?* And the affable man whose entire life had been consumed in just a few years of incandescent, luxurious youth went off to the cellar to fetch a few bottles which he opened with the same elegance he had displayed while ransacking his life, and on his lips he wore the same smile with which he had always faced disaster. Thus, as the light of a warm moon incrementally set portions of the dinner table at the presbytery aglow, stealing them from obscurity, for a brief moment he was the flamboyant young man of his past. Then the ashes of the night veiled his expression, on which everyone had been focusing their rapt attention. In the distance they could see lights suspended in the void, and they knew that others were drinking the summer wine and thanking the Lord for this offering of a warm twilight. There were new poppies all over the mountainside and a little girl whose hair was lighter than the meadow grass, and very soon the priest would be teaching her to play the piano, just like a young lady in town. Ah … There was a pause, and a moment to catch one's breath from the ceaseless toil. It was a special night, and everyone there knew it.

Alessandro Centi stayed at the presbytery on the days that followed the piano's arrival, and it was he who welcomed the piano tuner in the first heat of July. Clara followed the two men to the church and watched in silence as the man took the instruments from his bag. The first notes that came from the untuned keys produced in her the sensation of a sharpened blade together with a delicious swoon, and while Alessandro and the piano tuner talked and joked amid the trial and error of ivory and felt, her life was changing forever. Then Alessandro sat down at the keyboard, placed a score on the music stand and played well enough, despite the years of neglect. At the end of the piece, Clara came and stood next to him and, pointing to the score, motioned to him to turn the pages. He smiled, amused, but something in her gaze struck him, and he turned the pages as she had requested. He turned them slowly, one after the other, then started again at the beginning. When they had finished, she said, *Play it again*, and he played the piece one more time. After that, no one spoke. Alessandro stood up and went to fetch a big red cushion from the sacristy, and placed it on the velvet stool. *Would you like to play?* he asked, and his voice was hoarse.

The little girl's hands were slender and graceful, rather big for a child who had only turned ten in November, and extremely nimble. She held them above the keys in the proper way to begin playing, then left them there for a moment, and the two men felt as if an ineffable wind were blowing through the nave. Then she lowered them to the keyboard. And a tempest swept through the church, a veritable tempest that ruffled the pages, and it roared like a wave that rises and crashes up to the seamark on the rocks. Finally the wave ebbed away and the little girl began to play.

She played slowly, without looking at her hands, and never making a single mistake. Alessandro turned the pages of the score and she went on playing with the same inexorable perfection, at the same speed, and flawlessly, until silence fell again in the transfigured church.

"Are you reading the notes?" asked Alessandro after a long while.

She said, "I'm looking."

"Can you play without looking?"

She nodded.

"Are you just looking to learn?"

She nodded again and they gazed at each other indecisively, as if they had been given a crystal so delicate that they didn't know how to hold it. Alessandro Centi had once been well acquainted with the transparency and dizzying purities of crystal, and he knew both its exaltation and its depletion. But the life he now led no longer resonated with the echo of past moments of exhilaration, other than the trilling of birds at dawn, or the grand calligraphy of clouds. Therefore, when the little girl began to play, the pain he felt courted a sorrow he no longer knew still lived inside him, a brief recollection of the cruelty of pleasure. When Alessandro had asked, *Are you just looking to learn?* he had known what Clara would say.

Father Centi and his housekeeper were sent for, and they came with all the sheet music Alessandro had brought from the city. The priest and the old woman sat in a pew at the front and Alessandro asked Clara to play the piece again from memory. When she began to play, the two newcomers were stunned, as if struck on the head by a hammer. Then the old woman made the sign of the cross a hundred times, while Clara went on playing twice as fast as before, since now she was truly celebrating the nuptials, and she read, one after the other, the scores that Alessandro handed to her. The tale will soon be told of how Clara played, and in what manner the rigour of her execution was not the true miracle of this July union. All one need know for now is that the moment she started on a blue score which Alessandro had solemnly set before her, she took a deep breath which caused the others present to feel as if a mountain breeze had lost its way among the arches of the great vaulted ceiling. Then she played. Tears were streaming down Alessandro's cheeks, and he did not try to hold them back. There was a fleeting image that was so precious it could go through him without him ever forgetting it again, and in the fugitive vision of this face, against the background of a painting where a woman sobbed as she held Christ to her breast, he realized it had been ten whole years since he last wept.

He left again the next morning, saying he would be back in the first days of August. He went away, and came back as he had said he would. One week after his return, a tall, rather stooped man knocked on the door to the presbytery. Alessandro went down to welcome him into the kitchen, and they embraced like brothers.

"At last, Sandro," said the man.

Clara stood motionless on the threshold of the back door.

Alessandro took her by the hand and led her up to the tall, stooped man.

"May I introduce Pietro," he said.

They looked at each other with a mutual curiosity born of opposing reasons: Pietro had heard about her, while she knew nothing about him. Then, never taking his eyes from her, Pietro said to Alessandro, "Will you explain it to me, now?"

It was a lovely, late afternoon and there were people outside their houses as the trio made their way down the street to the church. They stared at the two men: although they knew one of them, both were rather singular, not only in their garb but also in their demeanour, and once they had gone by, some people stood up, the better to follow them, thoughtfully, with their gaze. Then Clara played, and Pietro understood the reason for the long road that had brought him from Rome to these steep and godforsaken escarpments of the Sasso. Just as she was playing the final note, he felt a dizziness of prodigious intensity that left him reeling, before it burst into a spray of images, only to vanish again almost at once—but the last image remained etched on his mind long after he left the village, and he looked respectfully at the frail child thanks to whom the miracle of this rebirth had come about: superimposed on her face was the face of a woman, laughing in the chiaroscuro of a forgotten garden.

She played until nightfall. Then a great silence cloaked the vaults of the church where a shipwrecked piano had come to her in the summer before her eleventh birthday. You see, this is a tale, of course, but it is also the truth. Who can unravel these things? Nobody, in any case, who heard the story of the little girl found in an isolated village in Abruzzo cared for by a country priest and his ignorant old housekeeper. All we know is that her name was Clara Centi and that the story did not end there: Pietro did not go all that way to hear a rather wild little girl play the piano, only to leave again for Rome as if nothing had happened. Therefore, we will say one more thing before we follow them to the big city, where some are now preparing for war; we will repeat what that same Pietro said to Clara in the privacy of the church after she had played the last score:

Alle orfane la grazia.[2]

---

2. May the orphans be blessed.

ARCHERS

the rootless the last alliance

ANGÈLE
The Black Arrows

The little girl, whom they had baptized Maria in honour of both the Holy Virgin and the words that had come from Spain, was growing up on the farm under the protection of four formidable old women. These ladies kept their rosary beads ever at the ready, along with the eye of the Lord, or so people called it when referring to old women who did not miss a thing for miles around, even though they only ever left their homes to bury a cousin or see a goddaughter married, and for as long as anyone could remember, they had never crossed the borders of the region.

Ah, but they were something else again, those old women. The youngest was just recovering from her eighty-first birthday, and respectfully fell silent whenever her elders gave their verdict on the salting of a pig or the way to cook sage leaves. The little girl's arrival hadn't changed much in the routine of their days, devoted to the painstaking, pious activities which, in Christian lands, are the lot of decent women; they simply made sure to have morning milk fresh from the cow for her, and to read her the Sacred History, when they weren't busy drying the mugwort, and to teach her about simples—listing, in order if you don't mind, each one's medicinal and spiritual properties. No, the coming of the little girl did not seem to have changed the configuration of the months and years, filled to the brim with the four staples the people in these parts used as nourishment: devotion, work, hunting and consequently food; but in reality Maria had transformed the hours, and if no one had noticed it at first, it was because her action needed some time to take effect, while her own powers were spreading, becoming seasoned, without her even being aware of it. But there came a wealth of bounteous springs and magnificent winters, and no one ever thought for a moment that they might have something to do with that first snowy night, just as the enhancement of the old ladies' gifts was seen as nothing more than a blessing given to those lands where women pray in abundance; it never occurred to anyone that these marvellous old crones might owe their surfeit of talent to two words in Spanish.

The wariest of the four old women was Auntie Angèle, the sister of the paternal grandmother, from a lineage renowned for its women as tiny as mice but more strongwilled than wild boars surprised by the hunt. Angèle belonged to that same lineage, and she'd even added something of her own to it by cultivating a special form of obstinacy which, had she not been intelligent, might have proven abstruse; but since she was as lively as a stream, her strength of will liberated a surplus of wisdom which she employed to understand the world, without ever setting foot in it. From the very first—and this we know—Angèle sniffed out that there was something magical about the little girl. After the episode with the creature—when the men were so hopeless they were incapable of saying what it looked like, though she could have sworn it was no animal—she had no further doubt, and she even embraced the certainty, enhanced daily with new layers of proof, that the little girl was not only magical but also very powerful. And since they were old women who knew as sure as sure could be—even though their entire acquaintance with the world consisted of two forests and three hills—Angèle trembled at the thought that the child's magical powers made her a natural prey; so every morning before Matins she would say a couple of Hail Marys to herself and an equal number of Lord's Prayers, and out of the corner of her eye of the Lord she kept a close watch over all the child's comings and goings, even if it meant the milk left untended on the stove curdled ten times in a row.

A year had passed since the event in the clearing in the east wood, rolling by as if in a dream, at the steady pace happiness sets. One morning at the end of November, Angèle turned her eye of the Lord to look for the child, whom they had seen at dawn in the storeroom helping herself to a piece of cheese, then setting off like a whirlwind to her trees and her lessons. Those people who have forgotten the life to be had in contact with primitive nature will think of the subtext, and assume that her purpose was merely to go and chat with the neighbours, and in truth the network of acquaintance in our countryside, as tight-knit as the cells of a beehive, has always existed. But the eye of the Lord sees far beyond any village gossip: if anything, it bears greater resemblance to a probe that allows one to make out—as if in semi-darkness—those people or things that are not immediately apparent to the naked eye. Of course, deep down Auntie Angèle would not have been thinking any of this, and if you questioned any of the old women about their vision they would have fingered their rosaries and muttered something vague about the clairvoyance of mothers—for magic is the devil, and they kept well away from it, even if that meant denying certain aptitudes that, however well established, were hardly what you'd call Christian.

The countryside that morning was dazzling. There had been a frost at dawn, and it sparkled from one end of the land to the other; then the sun came up, all of a sudden, above an earth now covered with a cloth that glistened like a sea of light. So when Angèle cast her gaze over the frost-laden fields, and found the little girl almost at once at the edge of a cluster of trees to the east of the farm, she was not surprised by the clarity of her vision, and for a moment, so beautiful was the scene that she was lost in contemplation, because Maria stood out against a background of trees girdled in white that arched above her head like diamond ogives. Therefore to look on such a scene is no sin: it is not idleness but praise of the Lord's work, and it has to be said there was no shortage of such work in those days, in those parts where people lived simply; it was easy to run one's finger along the cheek of the divine, and the divine came from a daily commerce with clouds and stones and the glorious, dripping dawns that shot salvoes of translucent beams towards the earth.

Thus, from her kitchen, as she stared into space, Angèle was smiling at the sight of the little girl at the edge of that lovely copse, ringed by ice as if by a prayer, when she was startled by a sudden realization. How could she have failed to notice? It occurred to her, quite abruptly, that such clarity was not usual, and that the luminous arches and cathedrals of diamonds had concealed the fact that the little girl was not alone and, consequently, that she might be in danger. Angèle did not hesitate for a moment. The mother and the other old women had left earlier for a funeral, and would not be back for a good two hours. At the neighbouring farm there would only be La Marcelotte, because all the men in the village had gathered at dawn for the first of the winter's major hunts. As for the priest, whom she could have gone to fetch from his presbytery, he appeared to her, in all the splendour of his fine goose-fat-filled paunch (she promised to do penance later for this ungodly thought), radically unsuited to combat the dark forces of the universe.

In that time of ignorance as yet untouched by the heat of progress, Angèle wore three bodices and seven skirts and petticoats, to which she added a heavy woollen cape. In this armour, with her coif pulled tight around her remaining meagre strands of hair, she strode out into the treacherous light of that perilous day. In all—in other words, Angèle, along with her eight winter layers, her clogs, her three rosaries and a silver cross upon a chain, not forgetting the coif with its ribbons, over which she had placed a thick felt headscarf—in all she could not have weighed more than forty kilos; hence, her ninety-four summers seemed to fly above the dirt track, so much so that you could not even hear the crunching of wooden sole against frost, and she rushed almost soundlessly, short of breath, crimson-nosed, to the patch of the meadow her eyes had scanned earlier. She scarcely had time to catch a glimpse of the little girl, who was shouting something in the direction of a big grey horse with a coat that glinted like unpolished silver, and she tried to utter a sound that meant to say, *By all the Saints and the great mercy of the Virgin Mary!* but it only emerged as *oh oh oh!*—before darkness fell over the meadow. Yes, a hurricane swooped down upon the little girl and the intruder, and would have knocked Angèle onto her behind had she not held fast to one of her rosaries and, believe it or not, the beads were instantly transformed into a walking stick. A miracle.

The auntie brandished her rosary in the storm, cursing the barrier of opaque swirls that kept her from approaching Maria. She had lost her headscarf and her beribboned coif, and her two white plaits with strands as fine as a spider's web stood straight up on her head, which she shook in frustration at the tumultuous wind. *Oh oh oh!* she said again, and this time it meant, *Don't ye dare come for the little lass or I'll skin yer ugly villainous mugs.* Let it be known that a clog thrown straight ahead by an indignant old granny can part the waters of a downpour, not unlike Moses who may also have had all his robes blown inside out, right down to the last one which was as red as the sea in the Holy Book. When she saw the breach her clog had made in the weather, Angèle hopped into it like a young goat and landed head over petticoat in a furious maelstrom, wind and currents gusting all around her. But the downpour that obscured her view and prevented her from reaching the little girl was now swirling around this magma of energy (this she understood in a flash of awareness which could never be translated into words) and kept it constant, as if in a pressure cooker. Angèle opened wide her short-sighted eyes, and using her rosary stick, tried to get to her feet and tidy her petticoats. Maria's clothing was spinning in the screaming air, and she was shouting something to the grey horse, which had withdrawn to the edge of the trees, because between them there was a black column of smoke that rumbled like thunder and grew thicker as it spun on itself. But the horse, too, was wrapped in a mist that swirled delicately before his noble head; he was a beautiful horse, with glossy nostrils and a coat of shimmering mercury, and his mane was streaked with fine threads of silver. The auntie, for all that she was as blind as a mole, was hardly surprised that at twenty paces she could make out that fine mane (after the business with the rosary, this was small beer). The little girl went on shouting something she couldn't hear, but the black smoke was stronger than the horse's desire to reach Maria, and in the movement he made in her direction, his neck arched with compassion both to reassure her and bid her farewell, she could read sadness but hope, too, something that said, *We will meet again*—and quite stupidly (they were surrounded by lightning, after all) she wanted to weep and blow her nose profusely.

The horse vanished.

For a few seconds the fate of these two souls trapped in their dark maelstrom seemed uncertain. Then there came a terrible whistling, the clouds grew lighter, the black smoke rose skyward like arrows of death then dissipated in a raging splash. In a petrified silence the countryside returned to its finery of gems and salt, until the auntie regained consciousness, and squeezed the little girl tightly enough to stifle her against her heavy woollen cape.

That evening the men were summoned to the farm. The women made dinner, and they waited for the father, who had put in a brief appearance earlier (in addition to bringing two hares and the promise of some fine cuts of wild boar) and heard the others tell of the day's extraordinary events. Consequently he had gone away again to knock on a few doors while the women laid the table for fifteen. Ordinarily they would have supped on soup, bacon, a half-cheese per person, and a smidgen of Eugénie's quince jellies, but instead they were busy preparing a stew and a chanterelle pie: they'd just opened three jars from that year's harvest. On Maria's plate was a big pear drowned in honey fragrant with the thyme the bees had frequented all summer long, and she was silent. They had tried to ask her a few questions, but they'd given up, worried by the feverish gleam in her dark pupils and wondering what she had shouted to the grey horse of the mist. But no one doubted Angèle's story, and the supper began in a great hubbub, talking of rosaries, storms, and days in late November, and through it all Angèle had to tell her story in detail half a dozen times, making it a point of honour not to change a single thing.

An elaborate story, but not altogether complete, or so Maria noticed as she sat unspeaking and thoughtful, eating her pear. She thought Angèle gave her a sidelong glance as she was about to begin a certain part of the story, when the black smoke formed long thin arrows, and when you looked at them you knew they were deadly. You looked at them, and you knew, that was all there was to it. And Maria noticed, for a slew of reasons that offended Angèle's love of truth, that the auntie said nothing of the horror etched in her breast by the baleful vision. All she said was, *And the smoke went up to the sky like that and exploded all of a sudden up there and the sky turned blue again*—and then fell silent. Maria went on thinking. She thought that she knew many things these fine folk knew nothing about, and that she loved them with all the strength a child of eleven can place in a love born not only of early attachment but also of an understanding of others in their moments of both greatness and unspeakable misery.

If Angèle chose not to speak of the deadly force of the black arrows it was in part because she feared her words might turn into a prediction, and in part because she did not want to frighten the little lass—because she didn't know whether the child had seen what she had seen—and in part, too, because once upon a time she had been a fiery woman. While now her auntie might look like a dried-up walnut who fed on immaterial prayer alone, Maria could see—because since her tenth birthday she had acquired the gift of knowing the past through images—that in years gone by Angèle had been a pretty firefly, and that her body and mind had fated her to the winds of freedom. She could see that she had often crossed the river in her bare feet while staring at the sky, daydreaming; but she could still see time and destiny, vanishing lines which never vanish, and she knew that Angèle's fire had gradually retreated inside her, reduced to a point long forgotten. But the discovery of the little girl from Spain on the steps of the farmhouse had revived the memory of the ardour that had once flowed in her veins; now in its second life it was ordering Maria to be free and fiery. Angèle was afraid that if she spoke of the arrows of death, others might think it best to restrain the child in her everyday life, but Angèle thought she could protect her—or at least she hoped she could, keeping the child from being shackled, a child whom one afternoon spent shut indoors would kill more surely than all the arrows a simple rosary had managed to repel.

Maria sat thinking, while the adults conversed. The wine from the *arrière-côte* had loosened up the men, and the black smoke and fantastical creatures no longer seemed quite as threatening, but they were discussing them all the same, to decide whether they should send for the constabulary or the exorcists, or place their faith instead in the ancient wisdom which says that the countryside protects us from evil if our hearts are pure. All the men had to do was look at Auntie Angèle in the rocking chair where the women had firmly placed her; Angèle, her aged countenance aglow with stew and wine, wearing a new coif with ribbons the colour of forget-me-nots, seemed to be sculpted from a fine smooth wood with noble veins, and all the men had to do was glance over at the dear old thing to contemplate the courage with which our lands are blessed. And there were even a few of them who thought that it was these very lowlands that had made the women like this, in their armchairs of old age, women who, in spite of the stove, the garden, the hens, the cows, the remedies, and the prayers, would take up their headscarves and their rosaries without a moment's hesitation to go off and rescue an innocent life in danger. They are good companions to us, thought the men as they sipped their wine, and our land is a fine one. And while the chanterelle pie may have had something to do with their assertion, this did not contradict its basic sincerity, for the men from the lowlands loved their land and their women, and they knew that the land and the women were connected, as surely as they themselves belonged to their acres, as surely as they saw the toil of harvest and hunt as a tribute to be paid to the magnanimity of fate.

The priest, who disapproved of talk of exorcists, and ordinarily did not miss an opportunity to take his flock to task, sensed the battle against superstition was drowning in the honey pear he had been served along with a full glass of excellent wine. But he was a decent sort, who liked fine fare because he was of a kindly nature (whereas others are only tolerant because they are forever indulging in the sins of the flesh), and no sooner had he left the seminary and arrived in the village than he learned that people of the land rarely drifted from their faith, and that a man had to choose his battles if he wanted to find his place among them. So this was exactly how he thought of his ministry: he wanted to be among them, not against them, and this subsequently entitled him not only to the consideration of those he ministered to but also to certain generous secular gifts in the form of the hare pâté and quince jam that Eugénie could transform into food fit for a king.

And so in this pleasant atmosphere, with everyone well imbued with the sweetness of thyme honey and the tannins of our vines, Marcelot broached a topic that seemed timely to him:

"Since the little lass has been here, we've had our finest seasons, wouldn't you say?"

In the well-heated room where the old women were nodding off, and the men were tilting back their chairs as they savoured the evening brandy, and Maria was thinking, looking at no one but noticing everything, there came a long sigh as if the very farm itself were inhaling and exhaling a lungful of nocturnal air before holding its breath in anticipation. A heavy silence fell, filled with the din of fifteen bodies diffusing great waves of alertness and concentration. And yet you could sense a powerful rush of desire in this sudden petrifaction, and you knew that everyone there was only sitting still in expectation of a long-awaited burgeoning. Only Maria seemed to be absent from the events in the room, but the others held themselves as tautly as the bow of a Cheyenne Indian (or so the priest imagined the scene, for he was reading a book written by a missionary in Indian territory) and in that moment of complete tension, you couldn't have said how matters would be resolved.

Finally Marcelot, who didn't expect such a reaction, cleared his throat and looked at the father a touch more insistently. This was a signal for the thaw, and everyone began talking in a feverish jumble of words.

"Eleven summers we've had these golden harvests," said the mayor.

"Snow always comes just at the right time and we've an abundance of game!" exclaimed Jeannot.

And it was true that the forests in the lowlands were the richest in the region for game, so much so that we had trouble keeping the forests to ourselves, because the people from neighbouring regions, deprived of similar bounty, came here regularly to alleviate their frustration.

"And aren't the orchards lovely," added Eugénie, "with peaches and pears like in heaven!"

At which point she glanced nervously at the priest, but that was indeed how she imagined the Garden of Eden, with golden peaches as velvety as the kiss of an innocent being, and pears so juicy that when you cooked them you'd only think to add wine out of a guilty weakness (the true sin of the matter). But the priest was otherwise preoccupied than with the aspect of peaches in paradise according to some old granny, who in any case was so pious that she could have imagined peaches that were blue or gifted with speech and it would have been all the same to him. He saw above all that his flock were still in possession of arguments that tended quite frankly towards magic. And yet he was troubled. He may have been a country priest, but he was unusually cultivated for a man of such modest function. He had a passion for tales of exploration, and he could often be found sobbing under his lamp as he read of the suffering endured by his brothers who had gone to spread the word of God in the Americas. But his greatest passion was medicinal and aromatic plants, and every evening, in his fine seminarian's handwriting, he would note down his observations about desiccation or the therapeutic use of simples, on the subject of which he owned an impressive collection of precious engravings and erudite tomes.

This culture of his, because he was good, and full of good intentions and curiosity, meant he was a man who was capable of doubt, who did not approach every unusual event with a brandishing of his missal but displayed, instead, reasoned circumspection. And when it came to the prosperity of the lowlands over these eleven years, he had to admit that it was fact, and more than just fact, it was enchantment. One needed only to stroll down any of the region's byways to see how fine the trees were, how well tilled the soil, how plentiful the insects as they worked to gather and spread the pollen; and there were ever more dragonflies for Maria to watch in summer, dense vibrant swarms of the sort you would see nowhere else, because this cloud of blessings, this surfeit of amber fruit and superb harvests was concentrated in the village and along its pathways and in its communal woods, and it clearly came to an end at an invisible border that was more tangible to the inhabitants in these parts than any drawn up in a grand European treaty.

That evening they recalled a spring morning two years earlier when everyone emerged onto their front steps and cried out in astonishment and delight at the sight of a huge carpet of violets that adorned the fields and banks with its gossamer drapery; or of one dawn hunt some four winters earlier when the men went out into the frosty air with their thick scarves and their caps with ear-flaps, and were amazed to find the streets of the village packed solid with hares all bound for the woods. It had only happened the one time, but what a time it was! The men had followed the hares to the woods, and no one would have dreamt of firing at them along the way, and then the animals had scattered and the hunt had begun in the normal fashion. But it was as if the creatures had manifested their own abundance before things went back to normal.

Thus, the priest was uneasy. Like a dog sniffing out its prey, a primitive voice inside him could sense that Maria was an anomaly, an envoy from the world that owes nothing to God, and this secret side of himself, which the man of the Church could express only in his pages on the curative decoction of mugwort or the application of nettles in an unguent, also sensed the connection between the appearance of the infant in the snow and the astonishing mildness that had enveloped the region. He looked at the child; she seemed to be sleeping, but he perceived a palpable vigilance in her, and he understood that she could hear and see everything around her, and that her apparent distraction came from one of those states to be found in the trance of prayer, when the mind may be detached from the body yet still registers the world with greatly enhanced acuity.

He took a deep breath.

"There's some mystery here that must be brought to light," he said, raising the little tot of brandy which a charitable hand had placed next to the remains of his honeyed pear. "The little girl has been blessed, and we will find out how."

And after resolving not to lecture these good people, who would have liked to see fantastical creatures spread their mist all the way to the Morvan hills, he also resolved to have a word with Maria when next the opportunity arose. His words produced the desired effect: everyone was quite satisfied that their spiritual authority had acknowledged the mystery; for all they enjoyed stuffing him with brawn, he nevertheless remained above his flock, aloof. They were also quite satisfied that there was something reassuring about his words, because it meant that sooner or later they would find out, and from the Good Lord Himself, what it all meant. So everyone, therefore, was *more or less* satisfied with the conclusion the priest had drawn from a remark they were all relieved had been made in the first place, but no one was *deeply* satisfied, the priest least of all: this was merely an acceptable pause in the enlightenment of the riddle; they would catch their breath and calmly await the next stage, but everyone knew that one day they would have to enter a circle of life that held considerable surprise and commotion in store. True faith, it is a well-known fact, has little regard for chapels, but it does believe in the communion of mysteries, and with its willingness to embrace a range of beliefs, resists the temptations of intolerance.

GUSTAVO
A Voice of Death

At the beginning of September, two months before the events on the French farm, Clara arrived in Rome, escorted by Pietro.

Leaving her mountains behind had been a source of pain, which the glory of the landscapes through which they travelled failed to appease. For as long as she could remember, she had been unhappy when it was time to go home to the presbytery; every time, she would go through the walled garden before opening the door to the kitchen; and as that vestibule planted with magnificent trees was as vital to her as the air she breathed, she dreaded the walls of the city more than any scourge in her nightmares. Clearly, no human being had ever managed to touch her soul the way the mountains had, and therefore the snow and the storms lived inside a heart that was still equally open both to happiness and to the curse of misfortune. And now, the further they went into the city, the more her heart bled. She was discovering not only a terrain that had surrendered to its interment under stone, but also what had been done to the stones themselves: they now rose to the sky in straight, dull walls, having ceased to breathe beneath the onslaught that had defaced them forever. Thus as night fell upon the joyful crowds drunkenly celebrating the return of the warm breezes, Clara saw only a mass of dead stone and a cemetery where living people went willingly to be buried.

The carriage made its way to the top of a hill; here, there were fewer people, and Clara felt she could breathe more easily. During the entire journey, Pietro had attended to her comfort, but he did not try to speak to her otherwise, and she had fallen silent, as she did every day, her mind full of mountainsides, staves, and notes. At last they came to a halt outside a large dwelling with high brown walls, where slender pine trees emerged from an inner courtyard, rising above the walls like a motionless fountain. Honeysuckle cascaded down the walls in perfumed bursts towards the cobblestone street, and in the twilight long, gauzy curtains billowed out from the windows.

They were ushered into a vast vestibule; there Pietro left them, and Clara was guided through gigantic rooms whose walls and surfaces were crowded with paintings and sculptures. Clara looked at them with a trepidation that quickly yielded to hope when she understood that this strangeness might bring consolation for the loss of her mountains. Finally, a door was opened that led to an unadorned white room with a single painting on the wall. They left her alone, telling her they would come back soon to draw her bath and bring her some dinner, and then they would all go to bed early, in view of the tiring journey, and would come again at first light to take her to the Maestro. She went up to the painting, feeling a curious mixture of reverence and fear. *I know you, but I don't know how*. A long moment passed. Then something changed in the air in the room, and a slight trance came over Clara, also enhancing the layers in the painting, which she no longer saw in two dimensions but with a new depth that opened the door to the realm of dreams. She did not know now whether she was sleeping or awake, only that time was passing with the same momentum as the clouds high in a sky of black ink and silver. She must have fallen asleep, because the scene changed and she saw, in a summer garden, a woman laughing in the evening.

She could not make out her face but she was young, surely, and very cheerful; then she disappeared and Clara saw nothing but the shimmering ripples of moving ink before she lapsed into a last visionless sleep.

"We are going to see the Maestro," said Pietro the next day. "He's not an easy man, but you will play, and that will be enough."

The practice room of Maestro Gustavo Acciavatti was located on the top floor of a fine building, with tall casement windows that let the sun transform the parquet floor into a lake of liquid light. The man seated at the keyboard seemed both very young and very old, and when she met his gaze Clara thought of a tree she used to go to when she felt sad. Its roots reached deep into the earth but its boughs were as vigorous as young branches, and it seemed vigilant, which allowed it both to observe and to radiate all around, and it listened, although Clara did not need to speak. She could have described the shape of every stone along her walks, and drawn from memory every branch of every tree. Faces, on the other hand, passed her by as if in a dream before they melted into a universal confusion. Yet this man, who was gazing at her in silence, was as present and alive to her as her trees, and she could discern the texture of his skin and the iridescence of his eyes, so dazzling it almost hurt. She stood before him. *I know you, but I don't know how*. The revelation that he knew who she was flashed through her consciousness then vanished instantly. Suddenly she noticed a form slumped on a chair in the corner of the room. Her eye had detected a movement and she thought she saw a short man who, as far as she could tell, had a little round belly. He had ginger hair and he was snoring, with his head on his shoulder. But as no one paid him any attention, she ignored him, too.

Then the Maestro spoke.

"Who taught you your music?"

"Alessandro," she answered.

"He says that you taught yourself. But no one can learn in a day. Was it the priest who gave you lessons?"

She shook her head.

"Someone else in the village?"

"I'm not lying," she said.

"Adults lie," he said, "and children believe them."

"So then you can lie, too."

"Do you know who I am?"

"The Maestro."

"What do you want to play?"

"I don't know."

He motioned to her to take her place, adjusted the stool, sat down next to her and opened the score that was on the stand.

"Come now, play, play. I'll turn the pages."

Clara's gaze swept quickly and intensely over the two open pages of the score—she blinked, once, twice, three times—and an inscrutable expression settled briefly on the Maestro's face. Then she played. She played so slowly, so sorrowfully, so perfectly, she played with such infinite slowness, such infinite softness and perfection, that no one could say a word. When she stopped, no one could speak. They knew of no adult who could play the prelude in this way, because this child was playing with a child's sadness and pain, but with the slowness and perfection of a mature adult, when no adult knows any longer how to attain the enchantment of that which is young and old at the same time.

After a long silence, the Maestro asked her to let him sit in her place, and he played the first movement of a sonata. At the end he introduced a tiny change. She was staring at a blind spot, far beyond any vision. He asked her to play again what she had heard. She did as he asked. He went to fetch the score. She followed what was written there, and did not introduce the change, but as she was about to play that bar she raised her head and looked at him. Then they brought an entire stack of scores which they spread out before her. She opened them, one after the other, blinked once, twice, three times, and they all died and were reborn with each blink of her eyelids, as if in a downpour of snowflakes from a forgotten dream. Finally, everything seemed transfixed in a heavy, tremulous silence. One single blink and Clara was staring at the pages of a worn red score, trembling, until each of them was trembling and an abyss opened inside them. She went over to the grand piano and played the Russian sonata which had made her giddy; and they knew that this was how mankind must live and love, in this fury, this peace, with this intensity and rage, in a world swept with the colours of earth and storm, in a world washed blue at dawn and darkened by rain.

A moment went by. *I know you, but I don't know how.*

There came a discreet knock at the door.

"Yes?" said the Maestro.

"Governor Santangelo," came the reply.

Clara sat on alone in the room in the company of the fat little ginger-haired man, who had not moved and gave no sign of waking. They brought her some tea, and some unfamiliar fruit with a velvety orange skin, and they gave her still more scores, while insisting that the Maestro had said she was to play only one. The first one seemed like a desecration to her and she immediately closed it, repelled by all the staves— they were like the bombastic effusions of those funeral dirges for the organ. No other score had the same lugubrious effect on her, but she opened a great many of them and did not find what it was that had so enthralled her about the Russian sonata and, in Santo Stefano, about the last piece that Sandro had placed before her in the church. Finally she came to a thin booklet. The first page whirled a new type of arabesque into the air. There were curved lines that took flight like feathers, and that had the same texture as the velvety skin on the lovely fruit. Before, when she had played the Russian sonata, there had been a splendour of trees with silvery leaves, mingled with vast dry prairies where rivers ran and, at the very end, she had the vision of a rushing wind in a wheat field where the stalks were flattened by gusts before springing back up in an animal roar. But this new music brought some warmth to the equation of landscapes, with the sparkle of Alessandro's stories, and she felt that for such lightness to be possible, there must be deep roots. She wondered if she would ever know the smiling canopies where this affability was born; at least now she knew that there were places where beauty was born of gentleness, whereas she had only ever known harshness and grandeur, and she loved this, tasting the unfamiliar fruit that told of the land where it was grown through her encounter with music. When she had finished playing the piece, she sat for a moment dreaming of foreign continents, and she began to smile in the noonday solitude.

An hour had gone by in this luminous reverie when muffled sounds reached her from the room next door. There was some agitation, and among the voices she recognized the Maestro's, accompanying the visitor to the door, then she heard a stranger's voice in reply and, although his words were inaudible, Clara stood up, her heart pounding, because it was a voice of death, sending warnings she heard as a death knell—and no matter where she turned in the tumult of what she was hearing, she felt an icy chill as she watched a shadow looming over an expanse of terror and chaos. Finally, the voice was doubly terrifying because it was beautiful as well, a beauty that stemmed from a former energy, now depraved. *I know you, but I don't know how.*

"You can tinkle those ivories, that's for sure," said a voice behind her.

The ginger-haired man had stood up, with some difficulty, apparently, because he was staggering as he came over, running his hand unsteadily through his hair. He had a round face, a double chin that gave him a childish look, and lively, sparkling eyes, somewhat crossed at present.

"My name is Petrus," he said, bowing to her, and immediately collapsing to the floor.

She looked at him, stunned, while he struggled to his feet and repeated his greeting.

"The Maestro's no easy man, but that scoundrel is evil," he said when he had steadied himself.

She understood that he was referring to the voice of death.

"Do you know the Governor?" she asked.

"Everyone knows the Governor," he replied, puzzled. Then, with a smile: "I'm sorry I'm not very presentable. Our sort doesn't do well with alcohol, it's a question of constitution. But the moscato after dinner was divine."

"Who are you?" she asked.

"Ah, it's true," he said, "we haven't been introduced."

And he bowed for the third time.

"Petrus, at your service. I act as a sort of secretary for the Maestro. But as of this morning I am above all your chaperone."

Then, smiling contritely, "I'll grant you, a hangover does not augur well for our first meeting. But I'll do my best to make myself agreeable, especially as you really do play very well."

And this was how Clara's first days in Rome were spent. She did not forget the voice of death, although she was working relentlessly, with no thought for the outside world. Acciavatti had told her she should come to the deserted studio early in the morning, so that no one would know about the little prodigy he had taken on as his pupil.

"Rome is fond of monsters," he had said, "and I don't want her to turn you into one."

Every day at dawn Petrus came to fetch her from her room and led her through the silent streets. Then he departed again for the Villa Volpe, where she joined him at lunch; after that he left her in the room that opened onto the courtyard, where there was a piano for practice, and she worked there until dinner, which she ate with him and with Pietro. Sometimes the Maestro joined them afterwards, and they worked a while longer, until Clara's bedtime. She was surprised by how indulgent Acciavatti and Pietro were towards Petrus. They greeted him warmly and paid no attention to his strange behaviour. It could not be said, however, that his conduct was at all becoming; when he came to wake her in the morning, he was out of breath, his hair dishevelled and his gaze unfocused; she no longer believed that the moscato of that first day was an exception, because he was forever stumbling on the carpet, and while she was practising he would collapse in an armchair and sleep, drooling; he let out intermittent, unintelligible grunts; when he awoke, he seemed surprised to be there. Then he tried to set the world to rights, tugging with conviction on his jacket or his trousers, but he generally lost his drift and gave up, sheepishly bowing his head. Finally, by the time he remembered she was there and sought to speak to her, he had to start again more than once because what initially came out of his mouth contained no vowels. And yet she did like him for all that, without really knowing what he was doing there in her company. But her new life as a pianist absorbed so much of her energy that she had little left over for other aspects of her life in Rome.

*

Her lessons with the Maestro were not at all as she had imagined they would be. Most of the time, he talked to her. When he gave her a score, he never told her how to play it. But then he would ask questions, and she always knew how to answer, because he did not want to know what she had thought but rather what she had seen. She told him that the Russian sonata had inspired images of arid plains and silver rivers, so he spoke to her of the steppes in the north and the vastness of those territories of willow and ice.

"But the energy of such a giant goes hand in hand with his slowness, and that is why you played so slowly."

He questioned her, too, about the village where she was born, and she described the vista of mountains between two tiled roofs, and how she knew the names of every valley and every peak by heart. She loved these hours she spent with him, so much so that, at the beginning of November, two months after her arrival in Rome, her sorrow for her lost mountains had ceased to torment her. Yet the Maestro showed her no particular affection, and she had the feeling that he undertook his questions not so much to instruct her as to prepare her for something he alone understood, just as from time to time she had an intuition that he already knew her, even though they had only met that September. One day when they were studying a terribly boring score, and she betrayed her mood by suddenly and absurdly accelerating the tempo, he told her, irritated, "That's so typical of you."

She asked him the name of the fruit of the first day, and said, "Then give me some peaches, instead."

He looked at her, still more irritated, but set a score down in front of her and said, "For his sins, this man was German, but he knew a thing or two about peaches."

As she played and renewed her bond with the ethereal scrolls of pleasure, Clara pondered what might lie behind the Maestro's irritation, that surge of feeling aimed at someone whose indistinct silhouette had drifted briefly through the atmosphere in the room. And while the days that followed were not unlike those that had preceded them, they bore the trace of this jeer directed at a phantom.

Very often the Maestro also came to join her at Pietro's after dinner. The piano was in the big courtyard room and, while they were working, the windows were left open to the cool evening air. Pietro listened to them, smoking and drinking a liqueur, but he would not speak until the lesson was over. Similarly, Petrus dozed or snored in a large wing chair until the music ceased and the silence woke him up. Clara would listen to them conversing while she read or daydreamed, then they took her back to her room; whereas they would go on talking late into the night, the timbre of their voices rising across the courtyard, lulling her to sleep. Thus, one night in late November, when the French windows to the courtyard had been closed because it was raining hard, Clara listened to them conversing while she leafed through some scores they had brought her to study. She heard Acciavatti say, "But will they ever play it at the right tempo?" and then she opened an old, dog-eared score.

In black ink, someone had written two lines in the margin next to the opening staves:

la lepre e il cinghiale vegliano su di voi quando camminate sotto gli alberi

i vostri padri attraversano il ponte per abbracciarvi
quando dormite[3]

There was a moment drained of all sensation, and Clara watched as a bubble of silence spread at the speed of waves before bursting in a soundless climax. She reread the poem and there were no more explosions, but something had changed, as if space had doubled and beyond an invisible frontier lay a country where she longed to go. Although she suspected the score had nothing to do with this magic, she went to the piano all the same, and played the piece which only brought to the room a perfume of currents and damp earth, and a mystery in the shape of wooded trails and stolen emotions.

After she played the last note she looked up and saw standing before her a man she did not recognize.

"Where did that score come from?" asked the Maestro.

She pointed to the batch they had brought to her earlier at his request.

"Why did you play it?"

"I read the poem," she said.

He walked around the piano and came to look over her shoulder. She sensed his breathing, the waves of his mixed emotions. As his surprise cast sudden light over his feelings, she was struck by the images that unreeled, transparent, from his tall person—first of all a herd of wild horses, leaving behind them an echo that remained long after they had vanished into the distance; then, in the shadow of undergrowth whose pathways were gilded with bursts

3. the hare and the wild boar watch over you when you walk beneath the trees / your fathers cross the bridge to embrace you when you sleep

of sunlight, a large boulder rising from the moss, all its angles and hollows, all its noble crevices the product of the common labour of floods and centuries, and she knew that this magnificent, living boulder was the Maestro himself, because an inexplicable alchemy had perfectly superimposed the man and the rock upon each other. At last the images faded, and once again she was face to face with a man of flesh and blood, now looking at her gravely. "Do you know what war is?" he asked. "Yes, of course you do … Alas, there is a war coming, a war that will be even longer and more terrible than any that has gone before, a war desired by men who are even stronger and more terrible than in the past."

"The Governor," said Clara.

"The Governor," he said, "and others, too."

"Is he the devil?" she asked.

"In a way, yes, you could say he is the devil, but it's not the name that's important."

As an orphan raised in the presbytery of a mountain village, Clara had already heard about the devil, and all the inhabitants of the Apennines knew of the battles that had been waged and they all crossed themselves when they heard talk of those who had perished. But beyond the stories she had heard in her childhood, Clara thought she knew where the devil's desire for war came from. Living in tombs all lined up one after the other—that seemed enough to explain the intrigue in the voice of death, and she wondered whether the Maestro, this living rock, thought the same thing.

"Wars take place on battlefields, but they are decided upon in the chambers of those who govern, men who are expert at working with fictions. However, there are other places, too, and other fictions … I want you to tell me what you see and what you hear, the poems you read and the dreams you have."

"Even if I don't know why?" she asked.

"You must trust music and poetry," he replied.

"Who wrote the poem?"

"A member of our alliance."

After a long silence he said, "I can only tell you that it is addressed to you. But I did not think you would be able to read it so soon."

At that moment, she saw that Pietro was looking for the poem on the score, and from the way he was looking at them, she realized that he could not find it.

Across from her, Gustavo Acciavatti was smiling.

Before long Petrus led her back to her room; the windows had been closed because the rain continued its stubborn percussion.

"They're not letting me do my work," he said, as he was taking leave of her.

"Your work?" she asked.

"My work," said Petrus. "They are all so serious and cold. I am here because I am sentimental and talkative. It's just that they have you playing all day long and in the evening they bore you to death with wars and alliances."

He gracefully scratched his scalp.

"I like my drink and maybe I'm not so clever. But I at least know how to tell a story."

He went away and she fell asleep, or at least she thought she was asleep until, with a clarity that cared little for walls or closed blinds, she heard Pietro say, all the way on the far side of the courtyard, "The little one is right, he's the devil."

And the Maestro's voice, in reply, "But then who tricked the devil?"

Then she fell into a deep sleep.

It was a strange night, of strange slumber. Her dreams were unusually vivid, turning to visions rather than nocturnal chimeras. She could let her gaze encompass a vista in the way one takes the measure of a panorama, and she found herself exploring the byways of a foreign land as if she were setting off along the paths of her familiar slopes. Although there were no mountains to be seen, there was a pervasive charm about the landscape, and she could feel the force of its prosperous terrain and enjoy the variety of its trees. While its gentle attraction was not like that of the lovely peaches, there was a sort of suppleness about it that was unknown in the mountains, and ultimately this conferred an equilibrium which Clara found exhilarating—a vigour without harshness, a rigour that, deep down, was benevolent. Consequently within two months she had seen the entire spectrum of geographies— neatly tilled fields, velvety peaches of pleasure and, at the opposite extreme, rugged mountains standing tall. What was more, while she was admiring the careful juxtaposition of the plots of land she became aware of a powerful, invisible enchantment that went well beyond the favour granted to more opulent regions, and which transformed the landscape of thriving trees and shady paths into a scene of foliage and love. She also saw a village that was halfway up a hill, with a church and houses whose thick walls testified to the harshness of the winters. And yet you could tell that in the spring a fine season would begin, and last until the first frosts of autumn, and perhaps it was the absence of mountains, or the profusion of trees, but you knew that there would always come a time when you could rest from your chores. Finally, she perceived fleeting shadows, neither forms nor faces, that passed by indifferently while she would have liked to ask the name of the village, and what fruit grew in its orchards.

It was like an arrow. She didn't know where it had come from nor where it went, but she had seen it flash by and disappear around the corner. However fleeting the apparition might have been, its every feature had been etched upon her with a painful precision that caused her to see that face again, with its dark eyes and sleek, yet thin, features, and golden skin with lips like a splash of blood. She searched for its trace and discovered the little girl at the edge of a plantation of trees, just as a tall grey horse approached. The entire panorama lit up, and superimposed on the frosty countryside was a landscape of mountains and mist. They did not overlap but were enmeshed, rather, like clouds; she saw panoramas coiling together but also weatherscapes merging—snow falling from a storm above a clear blue sky. And then a tornado funnelled into sight. In a blazing vision that condensed action and time Clara could see the great stormy turmoil, the evil whirlwinds and black arrows that rose raging towards the sky, while a little old woman brandished a stick above her dishevelled crown. Just as dream tipped into waking she saw another scene, where the little girl was eating her dinner in the company of six adults who surrounded her with a shimmering peaceful halo, and for the first time in her life, Clara beheld, in that halo, the material manifestation of love. Finally everything disappeared and she lay there awake in the silence of the dark room. In the morning she told the Maestro what she had seen in her dream. At the end of her story she added the name of the little stranger, because it came to her in a sudden flash of clarity.

Gustavo Acciavatti smiled at her for the second time.

But this time his smile was sad.

"All wars have their traitors," he said. "As of yesterday, Maria is no longer safe."

VILLA ACCIAVATTI
Inner Elfin Council

"Who is the traitor?" asked the Maestro.

"I don't know," said the Council Head. "We can no longer be sure of half the inner sanctum. It could be any one of the ten members. I did not get the impression I was being followed, and my tracks were erased very quickly."

"I did not see that you were followed. There is after all another bridge and another pavilion," said the Guardian of the Pavilion. "We must reinforce Maria's protection."

"No," said the Maestro. "Her powers must grow, and Clara must consolidate their bond."

"We have no idea what we are doing," said the Council Head. "And yet we are transforming our daughters into soldiers."

"To say the very least," said Petrus. "You don't leave them any time to play with dolls and you don't help them very much either."

"You wrote the poem just after Teresa's death," said the Maestro to the Guardian of the Pavilion, "and she found it today. I shall send it to Maria."

"A poem here, a score there, scarcely a glut of explanations," said Petrus. "How are they to understand who the hare and the boar are?"

"Maria saw me on the day of her tenth birthday," said the Guardian of the Pavilion, "the wild boar will speak to her. And her people are cut like diamonds. They have exceeded all our expectations."

"And Clara's people, what do you think of them?" asked Petrus. "No friends, no family, no mother. An irascible, sibylline teacher, and up to her ears in work. But Clara is the artist in your team of little warriors. You must nurture her heart and her sensibility, and that is not something that can be done by training her like a recruit."

"Clara needs a woman in her life," said the Council Head.

"When Pietro is satisfied that her safety can be guaranteed, then they shall meet," said the Maestro.

After a short silence, he turned to the Guardian of the Pavilion and said, "Did you hear her play … yes, I know, she's your daughter, and you heard her before I did … It is heart-rending … and so marvellous …"

MARIA
The Hare and the Wild Boar

After the excitement of the grey horse and the assault by tornado, life on the farm returned to its country ways, filled with the hunt, salted cheese, and walks through the woods. Now that the pattern of fine seasons had been recognized by farmers and churchmen alike, everyone could count on it serenely while contemplating the billowy snow which, that winter, would cover the land whenever they were thinking of going to fetch firewood; or while enjoying the many early mornings that were crisp as a cracker, dawn shooting its rosy fingers into skies more transparent than love; or while salting and preserving the fine hunks of game that seemed in never-ending supply; and when the villagers thought of all this, they never failed to nod and exchange a glance, before returning to work, without comment.

One evening when talking of the hunt, the father made a remark that caused Maria to raise her eyebrows. They were supping on bacon and beetroot cooked in ash, garnished with a spoonful of cream laced with coarse salt.

"The game's more plentiful, but the hunt is fairer," he said.

Maria smiled, then turned back to her steaming beetroot. The father was a man of the land, rough and taciturn; he walked with a heavy tread and always took his time. When he split logs, he did so at a tempo that anyone in the village could have surpassed, but when they saw that his regularity, together with his tenacity, were even more remarkable than his pace, the widows in the region began to turn to him, requesting he prepare firewood for them, which he did in return for a modest sum, although they were prepared to pay five times as much. He moved at the same pace in all his activities, including more private ones. He expressed no great sorrow in the face of ordeals and bereavements, although they had been terrible, for he and his wife had lost both sons in infancy. But grief kept him in its cruel grip longer than it should have. Fortunately, this was also true of joy, and Maria was a blessing late in life, although he never showed it through any demonstrative display of love; instead, he spread that love equally, in the same manner he used to rake the garden, or plough a field, without haste or interruption, and thus he took pleasure in it as in a gift that graced each year uniformly. Likewise, when he spoke he took care to ensure that his words did not disturb the equilibrium of emotions but rather embraced their contours naturally. Maria knew all this, so she greeted her father's remark with no more than a smile as it passed over the dinner like a flight of young thrushes.

But he was right: the hunt had become fairer. Anyone who might have thought that the abundance of game would lead to the pleasure of indiscriminate killing must consider the facts: this was not the case. The generosity that was flooding their woods and offering them a more bountiful catch than their ancestors had ever known also instilled restraint in the men of the village, and they chose their prey with care. Over recent winters they had stopped the boars from unearthing the potatoes; they had filled their cellars with salt meat for storing; and each had taken his share of fine victuals, but no more than what was required to replenish the body for the cost of its labour. What was more, they had the feeling they were sending the piqueurs as emissaries rather than scouts, having them order the positions with unusual gentleness, which turned the hunt into a new art of exchange. Oh, of course the men did not start their prey in the thickets by waving a white flag and politely asking the rabbits to assemble in front of their rifles, but still; they drove them out respectfully and did not do away with a greater number than was reasonable. In truth, the father's comment was inspired because that very morning they'd had to chase some hunters from the neighbouring canton out of the municipal territory. Due to a dearth of game these neighbours had come to poach from our hills, where they had found an abundance of hare and pheasant, and even a few deer, which they sniped at like savages, their rough laughter disgusting the villagers, who reacted in kind by pelting them with lead shot. But the worst of it was that this time their ploy did not elicit the virile vainglory which was ultimately its true purpose, because our men felt somehow defiled, a defilement which one of them (Marcelot, appropriately) summed up very eloquently once they got back to the farms after they'd chased out all the ruffians and checked every corner of the woods: *bloody miscreants, they've no respect for work*. Whence the father's remark; but Maria could tell that the conclusions he had drawn from the day's events surpassed indignation.

Maria did not suffer from any lack of affection, for the women in the village were as generous in lavishing it as they were in dispensing the Lord's Prayer and helpings of milk in their relentless efforts to strengthen the little girl, who was too thin (but so pretty); she could not remember ever coming back to the farm without being met with a serving of *rillettes*. But what Maria liked best of all was the cheese from their cows, and to Jeannette's everlasting despair, she who was the best cook in the six cantons, Maria was not fond of stews or anything that was prepared by mixing ingredients together. She would go up to the stove and help herself to her share of dinner in the form of separate products: she would nibble on a carrot, and they would grill a little piece of meat for her that she ate on its own with a pinch of salt and a sprig of savory.

The only exception she made to this diet of wild rabbit and twigs was for Eugénie's marvels, for Eugénie was mistress thereabouts of jams and decoctions of fine flowers. And who could have resisted her masterpieces? Her quince jam was brought to holy communion and even weddings and her humblest infusions seemed to be imbued with magic; how else could one explain the sighs of contentment that were uttered at the end of each meal? What's more, Eugénie was gifted with a knowledge of simples, and the priest often consulted her and respected her greatly, for she had a way with an impressive number of plants and therapeutic applications whose origins could be traced back to ancient times, of which

Eugénie was splendidly ignorant. She tended, however, to favour those plants that grew abundantly in the region, and that had proved their effectiveness over the years, and she had settled on a successful triad that seemed, at least on the farm, to have demonstrated its virtues: thyme, garlic, and hawthorn (which she referred to as the noble thorn or the thornapple, names which the priest had verified and which were, indeed, the most popular designations of the shrub among the common people). Maria loved hawthorns with a passion. She loved the shrub's silvery grey bark, which only turned brown and gnarly with age, and the light flowers of a white so delicately tinged with pink it could make you sob, and she loved to go picking them with Eugénie in the first days of May, taking care not to crush them, then putting them to dry in the shade of a cellar now bedecked like a bride. Last of all, she loved the infusions they made every evening by dropping a spoonful of flowers into a cup of boiling water. Eugénie swore that this fortified the soul and the heart (which has since been demonstrated by modern medicine) and that it also conferred a new flush of youth (something which has not been demonstrated in books).

In short, while Eugénie might not have been the same age or had the same eye of the Lord as Angèle, she was nevertheless a granny whom you could not try to hoodwink with impunity. And while Angèle may have worked out very early on that Maria was cut from a magical cloth, since the events in the cluster of trees, Eugénie had, with growing intensity, also perceived as much. Early one morning as she was going down to the kitchen after her first prayers, she stopped short next to the big wooden table where they had their meals. The room was silent. The other old women were feeding the hens and milking the cows; the father had gone to inspect his orchards and Maria was still sleeping beneath the big red eiderdown. Eugénie was alone next to the table; the only things on it were an earthenware coffee pot, a glass of water for a thirsty soul in the night, and three cloves of garlic left over from dinner. Her efforts to concentrate only conjured the very vision she wished to put out of her mind, then she relaxed and endeavoured to forget what she was looking at.

She can see the table now as it was the night before; she was the last to leave, after snuffing out the lamp; she enjoys the silent peace of the room, still warm, where a happy family had its dinner not long since; her gaze lingers in the dark corners which the dim lighting adorns with a few jewels of brightness, before it returns to the table where there is only a glass of water next to a coffee pot and three forgotten cloves of garlic. And then she understands that Maria, who sometimes walks past the hearth at the darkest hours of sleep, came last night and moved the cloves of garlic—by a few centimetres—and the glass, too—a few millimetres, rather—and that this infinitesimal adjustment of five trivial elements has entirely altered the space and created a living painting from a kitchen table.

Eugénie knows that she lacks the words, for she was born a peasant; she has never seen a painting, other than those that decorate the church and tell the Sacred History, and she knows no other beauty than the flight of birds and the dawn in spring, or the paths through clear woods and the laughter of beloved children. But she does know with iron-clad certainty that what Maria has accomplished with her three cloves of garlic and her glass is an arrangement for the eye that pays tribute to the divine, and she now notices that in addition to the changes in the position of the objects, something has been added, as revealed to her that very moment by the shaft of sunlight, and that something is a piece of ivy placed just next to the glass. It is perfect. Eugénie may not have the words, but she has the gift. In the same way as she sees the effect of medicinal plants on the body and the quiddity of gestures on healing she can see the equilibrium in which the little girl has placed the elements, the splendid tension that inhabits them now, and the succession of filled and empty parts against a background of silky darkness through which a space has been sculpted, now enhanced by a frame. So, still without words but through the grace of innocence and of her gift, alone in her kitchen beneath the ribbons that crown eighty-six years of hawthorn tea, Eugénie, her heart full, receives the magnificence of art.

That morning, Maria went down early to cut her chunk of cheese in the storeroom. But instead of spending her time among the trees before school, she came back to the kitchen where, at her battle station, Eugénie was stirring a mixture of celery tops, periwinkle flowers, and mint leaves in a copper saucepan, to make a poultice for a young mother afflicted with breast engorgement. Maria sat down at the big table, where the cloves of garlic were still in their place.

"Did you add celery?" she asked.

"Celery, periwinkle, and mint," Eugénie replied.

"The celery that grows in the garden?"

"The celery that grows in the garden," echoed Eugénie.

"That you took from the garden?"

"That I took from the garden."

"Which doesn't smell as bad as the wild celery?"

"Which smells better than the wild celery."

"But isn't as effective?"

"That depends, my little angel, that depends on the wind."

"And isn't periwinkle melancholic?"

"Yes indeed, it is melancholic."

"Don't people give it to show when they are sad?"

"Yes, they also give it to say politely that they are sad."

"And are the periwinkles from our woods?"

"They are periwinkles from the embankment behind the rabbit hutches."

"And they're not as effective as the ones in the woods?"

"That depends, my sweet, that depends on the wind."

"And what about the mint, Auntie?"

"This mint, my sweet?"

"Where does it come from at this time of day?"

"It comes from the wind, my little angel, like everything else, it comes from the wind, which leaves it wherever the Good Lord asks it to, and where we pick it, in honour of His good deeds."

Maria loved these dialogues; they were infinitely more dear to her than the ones in church, and she initiated them for a reason that became clear in light of a new event which flooded the farm that day with its exotic fragrance. At around eleven o'clock Jeannot knocked on the door to the kitchen where all the little old ladies were assembled, busy with the same considerable chore—the end of Lent was approaching and they would soon be eating the feast that made up for all their willing sacrifices. The kitchen smelled of garlic and game and the table was crammed full of magnificent baskets, the biggest one overflowing with the first field mushrooms of the year; so many had been picked that they were spilling all around the mass of wicker, and they'd have enough for ten years of aromatic meals and fragrant jars. All this, and only the end of April.

They saw at once that Jeannot was flustered about something having to do with his position, because he was wearing his postman's cap, and he was holding his leather satchel with both hands. They hurried him into the warmth and, although they were dying of curiosity, they sat him down to a slice of *rillettes* and a little glass of local wine, because the event deserved the honours which are customarily paid with a little bit of pork fat and a glassful of red wine. He hardly touched them. He did take a polite sip but it was plain to see that he was concentrating on some serious event of great import that was now his responsibility. Silence fell over a room lulled only by the crackling of the flames under the pot, in which a rabbit was cooking. The women dried their hands, folded their towels, adjusted their coifs and, still in silence, pulled out their chairs and sat down in unison.

A moment went by, brimming like the milk.

Outside, it had begun to rain, a fine downpour—my word—coming from a black cloud that had burst all of a sudden and would provide the violets and the animals with their water for the day. The room was full of the sound of water and the whispering of the fire, muffled in a silence that was too great for the five humans sitting around the table and feeling the pulse of fate. Because there could be no doubt: it was surely fate that had given Jeannot that solemn expression they'd only ever seen when he talked about the war, where he'd also served as a courier, and where, like the others, he had been forced to inhale gunpowder and endure the misery of combat. They watched as he took another sip of wine, but to give himself courage this time, and they knew he had to muster his strength before he began. So they waited.

"Well now," said Jeannot at last, wiping his mouth with the sleeve of his jacket, "I have a letter to deliver."

And he opened his satchel to reach for an envelope, which he placed in the middle of the table so that everyone could see it with ease. The old women stood up and leaned closer. The silence returned, as vast and holy as in a primeval cave. The envelope, in the darkness from the storm, formed a little well of light, but for now all they were interested in were the letters in black ink that said, simply:

Maria
The Hollows Farm

There was also a stamp the likes of which they had never seen.

"It's an Italian stamp," said Jeannot, breaking the silence, because he saw that the old ladies were straining their eyes staring at the mysterious little square.

They all plumped themselves down again on the rush seats of their chairs. Outside, it was raining twice as hard, and it was darker now than at six o'clock. The aroma of the rabbit stewing in its wine mingled with the sound of the rain, and the interior of the farm was a single fragrant psalm in which the little company cloaked itself bending over the envelope from Italy. Another moment went by in this limbo of anticipation, then Jeannot cleared his throat and spoke, because it seemed to him that they had allowed a decent lapse of time for observation.

"Well then, shall we open it?" he asked, his voice both neutral and encouraging.

The old ladies looked at each other from under their beribboned coifs, all thinking the same thing, that is, that such an event required the consultation of the entire family, and this could only happen once the father came home from working the fields and the mother from the town, where she had been these last three days with her sister, whose youngest daughter was consumptive. (She had gone there with a satchel full of Eugénie's unguents, which the family was waiting for with impatience, having despaired of any official medication; these had had little effect, and the young woman's strength was draining away before their eyes.) Which meant, according to the calculations of our four old ladies, with their minds all suffused with Italy, in two days and two nights. A kind of torment.

Jeannot, who had been following the ladies' wonderings as well as if he could hear them, cleared his throat again and, in a tone that sought this time to be firm and fatherly, suggested, "It might be urgent."

The postal routes leading from Italy to the lowlands may be mysterious, but one can at least assume it unlikely they could be covered in less than three hours; consequently, they are not the chosen routes in times of peril. All the more so when there is no address or family name. And yet, over and above the rain and the rabbit stew, the room was suddenly shrouded in a worrying pall of urgency. Angèle looked at Eugénie who looked at Jeannette who looked at Marie, and looks were exchanged in this way until chins too entered the dance and began oscillating gently, as if each were joining in the round with a precision that would enchant the most experienced choir master. They nodded their heads for two or three minutes more, with such ever-increasing determination that they carried Jeannot with them, for he suddenly felt he was certainly up to a little serving of *rillettes*, but he didn't want to disturb the harmony of this admirable arrangement of chins. Then they decided.

"We could at least open it," said Angèle. "It's not going to matter if we do."

"Precisely," said Eugénie.

"We'll just open it," said Marie. And Jeannette did not speak, but she agreed with them. Angèle got to her feet and went to fetch from the dresser drawer the slender knife that had once opened many a soldier's letter. She took the Italian envelope in her left hand, and with her right she inserted the pointed tip and began slicing along the edge.

And everything exploded: the door flew open and there was Maria standing in the doorway, outlined against a background of storm-wild countryside; and the rain, which had been falling hard for a good half-hour, was transformed into such a powerful deluge that all anyone could hear was the pounding of the downpour in the farmyard. They had already witnessed torrential rains of the kind that can flood low-lying land in no time at all—but this! This was something else again, because the water did not sink into the ground, but hurled itself against it with a violence that caused an entire expanse of land to thrum as if it were a gigantic drum, before returning to the sky in the shape of gorged smoking waterspouts resounding with the thunder of their impact. Maria stood a moment longer in the doorway amid the general stupefaction and the terrifying clatter of the waters. Then she closed the door, walked over to the old women and held out her hand to Angèle who, without understanding what she was doing, placed the letter in Maria's palm. The world spun on itself and all of a sudden everything was the right way up again, the rain stopped, and in the return of silence the rabbit stew bubbling in its juice made everyone jump. Angèle looked at Maria who looked at Angèle. No one spoke; everyone appreciated as never before the incomparable joy of being in the silence of a kitchen that smelled of rabbit casserole, and they looked at Maria, at the new-found gravity of her expression, and they felt that something inside her had metabolized into an unknown framework of the soul.

"Well, my girl?" said Angèle eventually, her voice quavering.

Maria murmured, "I don't know."

And as no one said a word, she added, "I knew the letter was for me, so I came."

What is one to do when the pulse of fate beats faster like this? What is so fine about the kind of naïveté concentrated in that farmhouse kitchen bubbling with wine stew is that it accepts what it cannot control. Maria's words befitted the age-old belief that the world was older than its inhabitants and, consequently, it stubbornly resisted any exhaustive human explanations. All anyone wanted was for the wee girl to be all right, and while Eugénie began preparing some hawthorn tea, they all sat down again on the chairs they had so abruptly left when the fury was unleashed, and they waited quietly for Maria to open the missive herself; this time it did not breathe a word in response to the offending knife. Once she had unsealed the envelope, Maria took out a sheet of paper folded in four, its texture so fragile that the ink had seeped through to the other side, though the lines had been written on one side only:

> *la lepre e il cinghiale vegliano su di voi quando camminate sotto gli alberi*
> *i vostri padri attraversano il ponte per abbracciarvi quando dormite*

Maria knew no Italian, but just as she loved Eugénie's echoing answers because they brought with them a distillation of the world that made it more lyrical and pure, so now, simply by looking at them and without understanding a thing, she could sense the breath of these lines vibrating in her ear like a canticle. Until now the most beautiful hymns had been those of the violet and the hawthorn, hymns that Eugénie sang in her capacity as gatherer of plants; and if they got mixed up with rabbit hutches and celery from the garden, Maria did not find this made them any less divine— on the contrary, it made faith far more intense than any Latin in the church ever could. But from these Italian words, which she could not even pronounce, was emerging a new terrain of poetry, and an unprecedented hunger was being hollowed out in her heart.

And yet Maria was close to the religion of poetry every day, whenever she climbed a tree or listened to the song of the branches and foliage. Very early on she had understood that other people went about the countryside as if they were blind and deaf, and the symphonies she heard and the tableaux she embraced were, to them, mere sounds of nature and mute landscapes. When she wandered through her fields and woods she was in constant contact with a flow of intangible but visible lines which enabled her to know the movement and radiation of things, and, if in winter she liked to go to the oak trees in the combe in the neighbouring field, it was because the three trees liked winter too, and made vibrant sketches whose strokes and curves she could see as if they were an engraving given form in the air by a master's hand. Moreover, Maria conversed not only with matter, but also with the creatures of the land. She had not always known how to do so with such ease. The ability to see the past in images, to discern the suitable arrangement of things, to be warned of a remarkable occurrence like that of the letter's arrival and the imminence of danger if she did not open it herself and, finally, the ability to talk to the animals of the pastures, hollows and shelters, had increased after her escapade to the eastern clearing. Although she may have always seen the grand magnetic glittering of the universe, it had never been so sharp, and she did not know whether this sharpness came from the revelation of the fantastical wild boar or from something in her that he had changed that night. Perhaps the shock of learning the secret of her arrival in the village had enabled her to acknowledge the existence of her gifts to herself, or perhaps the magic of this supernatural creature had blessed her with new talents and transformed her into a new Maria whose blood now flowed differently. What was certain was that she could speak to the animals with an ease that grew with each passing day, and, as with the trees, this was made possible through the capture of vibrations and the currents that emanated from the creatures themselves; she could read these emanations like topological reports, and distorted them slightly in order to make her own thoughts heard. It is difficult to describe something one cannot experience oneself; in all likelihood Maria played with waves in the air the way others fold, unfold, bring together, tie and untie ropes; thus, the force of her mind warped the lines in which her perception of the world was caught, and this produced a breeding ground of unspoken words that allowed for an entire range of potential conversations.

Of all the animals, Maria liked conversing with hares best of all. Their modest radiance could be easily shaped and their light-hearted conversations provided information to which other more pretentious creatures paid no heed. It was to the hares that she turned for news about the grey horse, after the day of the black arrows, and it was with them that she had begun to suspect that a form of protection had been lost—how and why, she could not say, but the hares spoke of an ebbing of the seasons and a sort of shadow which, at times, came to drift over the woods. Above all, they had not been able to tell her how the horse had come there, but they had perceived his distress at not being able to go to her. And in answer to her cry—*What is your name?*—they had no response either, but they sensed that the horse had been prevented from revealing his name by a force that was neither good nor, alas, powerless.

And more and more often Maria could see the traces of that force in the lovely countryside. One evening in the fallow field when she was lying on her belly in the grass, letting her thoughts wander to the rhythm of the cantos which rose here and there on that March evening, she suddenly sprang to her feet, as lively as a spooked cat, because the music of the trees had stopped abruptly and yielded briefly to a great icy silence. She could have died from it. Worse still, she was sure that it was not natural, that there was a hidden and very determined power behind it, and that this power burned with the desire to carry out a very dark and deadly plan: what had lasted hardly three seconds would happen again, with still more force. Maria also knew that she was too young to understand the rivalry between great forces, but she could perceive the stirrings of an imminent panic that everyone had clearly hoped lay further in the distance. She could not penetrate the substance of this intuition that sent her to the woods in search of a hare with whom to share her helplessness, but she was certain that a disturbance in the firmament of powers was provoking these never-before-seen occurrences.

It was during this time, this spring season that was not quite as splendid as the previous ones (where it did not rain exactly when one wanted it to, and froze slightly later than necessary for the apricot trees in the orchard), that Maria had a dream from which she awoke with mixed feelings of elation and dread.

The Italian poem had already been the cause of considerable emotion. There was no one who could translate it, and the priest had been very perplexed, because although his knowledge of Latin enabled him to guess certain words, he could not understand the intention of the whole any more than he could fathom the circumstances of its arrival by post. He weighed the decision to present the ecclesiastical authorities with a range of facts that neither reason nor faith could explain satisfactorily, but in the end he resolved not to write to them; for the time being he would keep to himself the list of the astonishing events of this period. Instead, he sent to town for a fine Italian dictionary; its red cover, the texture of petals, brightened up the clerical austerity of his tired old desk blotter. The beauty he discovered in the sounds of that language far exceeded in beatitude any verbal trance he had ever known—including that of Latin, for all that he loved that language tenderly. No matter how he pronounced the Italian, his mouth filled with the same taste of clear water and moist violets, and before his eyes he had the same vision of cheerful rippling on the surface of a green lake. Long after he had translated the poem and pondered its arrival at the farm, he went on reading words in the dictionary, and within a few months he had acquired the rudiments that enabled him to understand the quotations that sometimes accompanied the definitions—especially since at the end of the volume there was a summary of conjugations, and, although it caused him some difficulty, it did not dampen his enthusiasm. In short, in six months our priest was speaking Italian—hesitantly, with turns of phrase that in Rome might seem unusual, and with an accent that did not conform to conventional pronunciation, but also with the solid foundation of knowledge one acquires when one studies hard and cannot practise elsewhere.

He had shared the results of his translation and no one could draw any conclusions beyond mere nods and conjectures; they believed the letter had not arrived there by chance and it was indeed intended for Maria; they wondered what the hare and the boar were doing in the landscape; and if you went walking under the trees, well, my goodness ... There were sighs all around. But helplessness is not tranquillity, and all this unfolded in silence in the hearts of those who wondered what the next hurly-burly would be, and whether the little girl was still safe.

So Maria, who knew all this, said nothing of her dream. A big white horse came towards her in the mist, then went by, and she was walking beneath an archway of unfamiliar trees along a path of flat stones. The music began. How many singers there were, she could not say, or even whether they were men, women, or children, but she could hear the words quite clearly, and she repeated them fervently to herself in the darkness of dawn. A tear slipped down her cheek.

the rebirth of the mists
the rootless the last alliance

At the end, when the choir had fallen silent, she heard a voice repeating *the last alliance*, then she woke up under the spell of music and the sadness of that voice which was neither young nor old and which contained all the joys and all the sorrows. Maria did not know why she had wanted to know the silver horse's name, but for a few minutes it had seemed to her to be the most important thing in the world. Similarly, there was nothing that counted more that morning than hearing the voice of pure silver once more. And while the prospect of having to leave her village one day filled her with a grief that was all the greater because she sensed it would come before the time when children normally leave the place where they have been loved and protected, the impact of the voice on her heart's desire also showed her that she would leave without hesitation—no matter how heart-rending the parting, no matter how many tears were shed.

She was waiting now.

LEONORA
So Much Light

Following the discovery of the poem in the margin of the score, and the revelation of an obscure betrayal threatening a strange girl named Maria, several days passed before Clara once again saw the Maestro, and it seemed that Pietro must have gone with him because he reappeared at the villa on the evening they informed her that her morning lessons would begin again the following day. Clara was surprised by how glad she was to see him again, although they still abided by their laconic contract established on the first day, whereby they exchanged hardly a word before going to their rooms. But there was something familiar about the voice and gestures of the tall, slightly stooped man, something that made her feel as if she were at home again, and she was surprised that in such a short amount of time, interspersed with such rare displays of tenderness, the only two gentlemen she ever saw in Rome had become dearer to her than all the people she had lived with until then. This was not the richly coloured glow that enveloped the people who gathered around the table at the farm, but the wild horses and rocks in the woods engendered a gentle affection which resonated all the way to Pietro Volpe. The following morning she went to the practice room, and the lesson began in the same way as all the previous ones. But just when she should have been on her way, the Maestro sent for some tea.

"Have you had more dreams?" he asked. She shook her head.

"True visions do not come by chance," he said. "Those who want to see them, control them."

"Can you see Maria?"

"I am told where she is and what she is doing. But I don't see her the way you saw her in your dream, or the way you could see her simply by deciding to."

"How did you know that I could see her?"

An expression came over the Maestro's face, and all her cells of flesh and blood cried out to her that it was an expression of love.

"I know because I know your father," he said. "He has great powers of vision, and I believe that you do, too."

A bubble of silence like the one on the evening of the poem burst painfully in her chest.

"You know my father?" she asked.

"I have known him for a very long time," he said. "He wrote the poem on the score for you. Once you had read it, he led you to Maria."

For a long moment the bubble formed again then burst, a dozen times.

"Are the boar and the hare our fathers?" she asked.

"Yes."

She felt breathless.

"But I don't know what I am supposed to do," she said finally.

"You see things when you play the piano."

"I see landscapes."

"Music connects you to places and beings. These landscapes exist and Maria is real. She lives far away, in France, in a place where we thought she would be protected for a long time. But time is pressing now, and you have to trust in the powers of your people, and in the powers of your art."

Then he stood up, and she understood that her time in the practice room was over. But he stopped in the doorway and added, "This evening I'll introduce you to a lady called Leonora. She reminded us yesterday that your eleventh birthday was in November, and she asked me to invite you to dinner."

In the evening, they set off towards another hill. The Maestro himself greeted them on the steps outside a fine villa, at the end of an avenue lined with tall trees of a kind she had not seen before in Rome. As darkness had fallen, she could not make out the garden, but she could hear the bubbling of a stream, its stones composing a melodic motif which aroused in her images of fluttering fireflies and mountains in the mist. She looked at the Maestro and it seemed to her that another man entirely was standing there before her, a man who was neither her music professor, nor a man to whom phantoms gave the face of passion, but rather a man whose soul was shot through with emotion that coursed like arrows in one direction. Then she saw her, dark-haired and very tall, hiding in his shadow; her hair was short and her eyes were immense; she wore a plain outfit that you might even call austere; no make-up and, on her ring finger, a very fine silver band.

Age had added wrinkles to her magnificent sobriety, as if to enhance the pure lines of her appearance. You had to admire the slope of her shoulder, clad in a smooth, plain silk, and the pale colour of the cloth, the even stitching around the collar, her bare, pearly skin; and the dark gleam of her unadorned curls made you think of a seascape where expanses of shore and sky call to one another in a refinement of muted colours that only the most pared-down masterpieces could achieve.

Who was Leonora, then, in addition to being Pietro's sister and the Maestro's wife? The house of Volpe was an old dynasty of prosperous art dealers. Before Clara went to live with them, Pietro used to host grand receptions at the villa, but now he had given them up so that Clara might remain hidden; similarly, the leading artists of the era were received by the Acciavatti family, and from their very first visits they fell into the habit of stopping by every day for lunch, or after supper for conversation. So Leonora Acciavatti, née Volpe, had never lived alone. The constant flow of guests in the family home had followed her to the house she shared with the Maestro, and she continued to receive her guests in the same singular manner as in her own home; no one walked behind her through the galleries but rather according to a geometry that knew nothing of straight lines: you adapted to her curved trajectory; similarly, you didn't sit *opposite* her, you were seated around her according to geodesic coordinates which imprinted the contours of an invisible sphere upon the private space. Thus, while the guests dined, their gaze followed the network of curving lines embraced by her gestures, and when they left they took away with them some of Leonora's grace; she may not have been beautiful, but they found her sublime, something which, in this place of art, was highly unusual, because she was not a musician, nor did she paint or write, and she spent her days conversing with minds more brilliant than hers. But despite the fact that she did not travel and did not like change, and that many women of similar station were merely women of fashion, Leonora Acciavatti was a world unto herself. Though born to the role of bored heiress, fate had made a daydreamer of her, gifted with otherworldly power, so that in her presence you felt as if a window had been opened on infinity, and you understood that it was by delving into yourself that you escaped imprisonment.

In every person, even those who have never been graced by caresses, there is a native awareness of love, and even those who have not yet loved will know of love from the consciousness of it that inhabits all bodies and all ages. Leonora did not walk, she glided, leaving behind her the wake of a riverboat, and with each gliding motion that parted air as silky as the sand on the riverbanks, Clara's heart came that bit closer to the knowledge it had always had of love. She followed Leonora to the dinner table and answered her questions about her piano and her lessons; there was a wonderful meal and a joyful celebration of her eleventh birthday; and finally they parted on the steps outside the villa, in the strange music of the stream, and it was time for Clara to go back through the cold night to the solitary courtyard room. But she felt less alone in Rome than ever before, because in Leonora she had sensed the familiar pulse of her Abruzzo mountains, the same pulse that throbbed continuously from its rocky, steep terrain. For a long time she had not known it in any other way. But after the blue musical score in the church, she had perceived the same vibration as she went along her pathways or played beautiful pieces of music, a vibration that came not only from the places her eyes or her piano connected her to, but also from her mind and her body, illuminated by her playing. And now this combined frequency of earth and art could be found in Leonora's eyes and in her gestures, so much so that while Roman society may have found it perfectly natural for the Maestro to ally himself with this member of the elite, Clara alone understood what he had truly seen in her.

They did not meet again all winter, however. Clara worked hard under the Maestro's direction, for he kept asking her to increase her powers of vision. But she saw nothing, neither during her dreams, nor during the day. He did not seem impatient for all that, and merely made sure that she continued to play scores which seemed to her as dead as the stones of the city. He never replied when she asked him why he chose these pieces that bored her to tears, but she had learned to discern the elements of an answer in the question he asked her the second she finished. Thus, one morning when she was asking him about a piece that made her yawn continuously, he frowned and asked her what it was that made a tree look beautiful in the light. She changed tempo, and the piece took on an elegance that, initially, she would never have suspected. Another time, when she was falling asleep over a piece that was so pointlessly sad that she could not even weep as she played, he queried her about the taste of tears in the rain and, by making her fingers lighter, she could feel the pure melancholy buried beneath the academic nature of sobs. But the most important conversation came about one April morning when, exasperated at having to practise a hollow score, she simply stopped playing.

"There's nothing to see," she said, "there are just people chattering and walking by."

To her great surprise, he motioned her to get to her feet and join him at the table where he was having his tea.

"You are very gifted, but all you know of the world is your mountains and your goats, and what your priest has told you about it, and he knows even less than the goats. And yet the old housekeeper and the shepherd—they told you stories."

"I listened to their voices," she said.

"Forget their voices and try to remember the tales."

And as she was looking at him, failing to understand, he added, "Where I come from, people are not interested in stories, either, provided there is the song of the earth and sky." Then, after a slight hesitation: "There is a painting in your room, isn't there? It was painted a very long time ago by a man who came from my country and who, like me, was interested in stories. Look at the painting again this evening and perhaps you will see what the earth and the landscapes have been hiding in your heart, despite the old housekeeper's tales and the shepherd's poems. Without the land, one's soul is empty, but without stories, the land is silent. You must tell stories when you play."

He told her to go back to the keyboard, and she played the talkative piece again. She had not understood what he meant, but now she heard a deeper voice beyond those voices holding forth and then passing by.

She looked up at him.

"Remember the stories," he said as he got to his feet. "They are the intelligence of the world—of this world, and of all the others."

That same evening, he came to Pietro's to work with Clara. It was the end of April, and the weather was very mild for the time of year. There were roses in abundance, as well as lilacs already in bloom, their fragrance rendered all the more sublime by a brief shower before dinner. When Clara came into the piano room, she was surprised to find Leonora there.

"I've just come and I'll be leaving again," she told her. "But I wanted to give you a kiss before your lesson."

She was indeed dressed to go out, in a gown of cascading black crepe, illuminated by two teardrops of crystal which made her hair and eyes seem even darker. It was difficult to imagine a more absolute refinement than that flowing gown and those dangling pearls of motionless liquid; add to this the arabesques that gave Leonora's movements a certain rhythm, and you no longer knew whether you were looking at a river, or a flame curling upon itself.

"I know no one tells you much, and you are made to work in solitude," said Leonora. She turned to Gustavo and Pietro. "But I trust these men. So I have come to share with you my blindness and my faith, and ask if you would kindly play for me."

Her aura wafted into the evening as if it were a rare and light perfume, and she continued, "I would like to hear the piece you played in the church the very first time, the one in the score Alessandro gave to you at the end and which was blue, I think."

Clara smiled at her. If the truth be told, in eleven years of a life with neither conflict nor torment, she had not smiled more than four times. Although she had long been inclined towards nature, she had never penetrated the domain of human affinities. Leonora saw her smile and raised a hand to her chest while Clara went to sit at the keyboard and the men, in turn, sat down. She had not played the blue score again since the day of the great nuptials. She recalled what the Maestro had told her about stories, and now, superimposed upon the piece's song of silent lakes, was a strange thread which she followed like a trail. Something coiled in the air then uncoiled inside her. It was more than a fragrance but less than a memory, and on it there floated a hint of the earth, the soil, and of the heart, in the form of a story of nocturnal discoveries that her fingers now wanted to tell.

So she played the piece as she had played it on the first day, at the same tempo and with the same solemnity, but her hands were charged with a new magic that could open up the realm of dreams in the waking hours. An oil lamp lit the table where the family were eating their meal. What crystals did this vision pass through? Clara knew it was no daydream, but the actual perception of Maria's world, far to the north. The more she played, the more she felt a connection to an immense kaleidoscope, where her heart recognized a familiar iridescence, and her gaze swooped down like an eagle, increasing the details of the scene with every beat of its wings. She was able to examine the faces of these men and women she had seen only fleetingly at the end of the first dream. They spoke little while they ate, and they were sparing with gestures that were governed by the same choreography of everyday life, by the same peaceful supper where the bread was cut in silence, where they made sure the little girl always had enough to eat, and if the father came out with a remark, there was a brief burst of laughter before everyone returned to their soup. Just as she was about to play the last bar, they all laughed uproariously, and the mother got up to fetch a bowl of apples from a dark corner of the room. Then Clara stopped playing and the vision dissolved.

She looked up. Leonora had laid her hand on the dark wood, and her cheeks were streaming with tears. On Pietro's face there was also the trace of a sob, and Petrus seemed as moved as he was awake. But the Maestro had not wept. Leonora came over to Clara and leaned down to kiss her on the forehead.

"I'm leaving now," she said, drying her tears, "but I thank you for what you have given us this evening."

And turning to the Maestro, she added, "Now there will be many more hours."

Later, in her room, Clara did not fall asleep. She felt the breach within her that had opened when she was playing for Leonora, and she wanted to go back to Maria's farm once again. For a long time she gave herself over to the silence and let her mind wander aimlessly among the snatches of stories that her old housekeeper used to tell, and after a while, she was bathing in a liquid layer of reminiscence, in which all of history was contained in the little stories of the Sasso. She did not try to follow them, nor truly to piece them back together, but she saw now that she could transcribe their texture into music—an unusual kind of music where, added to the sound and the tonality of forms, there would be the same layer of apprehension that sometimes emerged from her dialogues with the Maestro, and which she had perceived on the first evening as she stood by the painting in her room: the stories that blended with the intoxicating colours. She saw the old housekeeper sitting and darning while she told her a story of children lost in the mountains, or shepherds who had strayed in the combes, and she felt herself following the thread of a meditation that had neither direction nor consequence, its melody carrying beyond the temporal and the physical. And then more stories, more lands were set ablaze, and the same radiance kindled earlier by the score now flooded her mind without her having to make any effort to maintain the light it cast. Oh, so much light! Night has fallen, too, over the little world of the farm, and in the silent room the last embers are dying. She can feel the power of the stones, encircling and protecting the people, and the power of the wood spreading its limbs invisibly through the walls. In spite of the darkness, the mineral and organic vibrations weave a luminous web; Clara is enchanted as she deciphers the outlines, for Maria is there, in the strange brightness, gazing motionless at the table where there is an earthenware pot, a glass half filled with water, and some garlic cloves left over from the meal. Then, in the endless, blazing suspended moment while the little French girl's hand moves the glass and adds a piece of ivy, there is a redeployment of the entire universe, and Clara can hear its titanic creaking, the shifting of ice floes—then everything grows still and falls quiet and embraces the spirit of blissfulness. And so it was on the night of the great beginning. Clara followed Maria through the sleeping house to her bed, where she slipped under a large red eiderdown.

But before falling asleep, she opened her eyes wide to stare at the ceiling, and Clara took her gaze right into her heart. Was this the magic of the link between music and stories? She was as touched as she might be upon a first intimate moment with a person who expected nothing from her in return, and in the silence of her courtyard room, for the second time that day, she smiled. Finally, just before sleep, she had her last vision of a farmhouse table, where the precise tension between a glass, an earthenware pot, and three cloves of garlic graced by a piece of ivy, captured the magnificence and barrenness of the world.

"I saw her when I was playing," she told the Maestro the next morning, "and I saw her again during the night."

"But she cannot see you."

He listened while she described the dinner, and the men and women around Maria, their shared laughter and the stones that were alive and protective. Then they began the lesson with a piece which seemed more flat and dreary to her than the open plains.

"Concentrate on the story and forget the plains," said the Maestro. "You're not listening to what the score is telling you. Travel is not just through space and time—above all, it is in the heart."

She made her playing slower, more delicate, and she felt that a new channel was opening inside her, overflowing the landscape of the plain, tracing a network of magnetic points around which a story was wound, a story that only music could unwind. And so she found Maria again. She was running beneath clouds so black that even the rain was dark silver.

She saw her fly like an arrow across the farmyard, fling open the door then stand for a moment facing the dumbfounded company of a postman and four little old ladies. Finally she went in, held out her hand and took hold of the letter. Clara saw the downpour suddenly retreat skyward and evaporate in the return of silence and sunshine, and Maria read the two lines that were inscribed on the paper in the same manner as on the musical score from the courtyard.

la lepre e il cinghiale vegliano su di voi quando camminate sotto gli alberi
i vostri padri attraversano il ponte per abbracciarvi quando dormite

Clara felt the emotion that Maria had yet to discover in the poem, then she looked up at the Maestro and held the two perceptions together in a union through which she could see both here and elsewhere, the practice room in town and the foreign farm, like motes of dust in a beam of light.

"That is your father's power," said the Maestro after a moment's silence.

She felt something brush by her, light but urgent, an unaccustomed presence.

"Do you see what I see?" she asked.

"Yes," he said, "I see Maria just as you see her. Whoever sees also has the power to make others see."

"Was it you who sent the poem?"

"It establishes the connection between you," he said. "But the poem means nothing without your musical gift which connects souls in search of one another. The wager we are making may seem mad, but every new event seems to confirm that we are right."

"Because I see Maria."

"Because you see Maria outside the Pavilion."

"Outside the Pavilion?"

"The Pavilion where our kind can see everything."

Then she asked one last question, and a strange ripple went through her before disappearing like a dream.

"Will I see my father one day?"

"Yes," he replied, "I hope so. I believe so."

A new era began. Clara spent her mornings working in the practice room, then went back to the villa with the courtyard for lunch, which was always followed by a siesta; after that, Leonora came for tea and to listen to her play. In addition to her Italian friend she now felt an affection for the little French girl and her incredible elderly aunts, for the vision of Maria was constant now, and living with her had become as natural as breathing. Thus the hours spent with the Maestro's wife were combined with the hours on the faraway farm in a blaze of light that rendered the old ladies from Burgundy as familiar as the high-society lady from Rome. All day long she followed them from kitchen to garden and from chicken coop to storeroom, as they prayed or saw to their sewing, as they concocted a meal or hoed a border, and as she studied their sorry faces eroded by age and toil she learned their names, softly repeating the unusual sounds to herself. It was Eugénie she liked best of all, perhaps because she talked to the rabbits while she fed them in the same way she spoke to God when she prayed; but she also liked the father with his fierce silences, and she understood that the trust that bound him to Eugénie and to the little girl extended far below the surface of their land, like a subterranean affinity spreading beneath the fields and forests that might one day re-emerge into the daylight through the soles of their feet. Where Rose, the mother, was concerned, however, it was quite different: she spoke a strange language of the sky and clouds and she seemed to be somewhat estranged from the little community on the farm. However, it was first and foremost Maria whom Clara followed from dawn to dusk and far into the night. Maria opening her eyes wide in the dark and looking at her without seeing her; Maria who touched her heart as she walked through her countryside, making it shine with an ineffable glow.

Then the new year came, and with it a very cold January, gripping Clara with painful apprehension. On a dawn so bleak that she thought, darkly, it suited the dead stones of the city perfectly, she ventured to share her feelings with the Maestro, while they were working together.

"Our protection is holding," said the Maestro.

He looked again through Clara's vision and, wiping his brow, gave a sigh and seemed suddenly very weary.

"But perhaps the enemy is stronger than we imagined."

"It is so cold," said Clara.

"That is his intention."

"The Governor's intention?"

"The Governor is merely a servant."

Then, after a pause, "In ten days we will celebrate Leonora's birthday and several friends will come to dinner.

I would like you to choose a piece and prepare it, to play for us that evening."

Clara did not see Leonora again before the evening of the birthday dinner, but she thought of her every second of the day, devoting half her time to the piece she had chosen to play, and half to Maria, who seemed to be feverishly striding across her pale landscapes. She worked at the villa with the courtyard, and did not go to the practice room, all the more alone in that Pietro, too, had vanished, and did not reappear even on the day that she was escorted to the other hill. All morning she had been suffering from the same painful premonition, and it had grown so pressing that it felt almost as hard to breathe as on the day of her arrival in the city. All this time Petrus, unswerving in his habits, had snored away in his armchair with little regard for her torments. But just as she was getting ready to leave for the Villa Acciavatti, in a confused and mainly anxious mood, he appeared in a black suit that was in sharp contrast to his ordinarily slovenly attire. He noticed her look of surprise.

"It won't last," he said.

And as she was still looking at him, taken aback, he added, "The clothes. It's a strange thing, all the same. I don't know if I'll ever get used to it."

It was even colder than on previous days, with an insidious drizzle that got under your skin. The road wound its way through the night and she heard the song of the water, elevated by winter to its highest melodic level. For some unknown reason, her chest felt even tighter but she did not have time to think about it, because they had reached the steps, where a man with familiar aquiline features was waiting for them.

He was extremely elegant, wearing a formal tailcoat with a silk square tucked in the pocket, but the nonchalance of his distinguished gestures seemed to relax his clothing, making it seem like a second skin despite its grandness. It was obvious that such grace must be inborn, a source of great ecstasy and endless ardour, and Clara knew he was handsome because he breathed the way trees do, with a fullness that gave him both airiness and stature. It was through this solar breathing that he was wedded to the world, with a fluidity that human beings rarely attain, and that he entered into a harmony with air and soil that made him a magnificent artist. Then came his fall, when he was judged by a species with little understanding of the fervour of great gifts; but that evening Alessandro Centi—for it was he—was again the man he had once been.

"Well, my little one," he murmured, "here we are together, such perfect timing."

And he led her away, beginning to tell her a story whose words she did not hear, for she was lulled by the elation in his voice. Behind them, Petrus was mumbling enigmatically but she had no time to understand why, because they had arrived in the grand candlelit drawing room, and her chaperone made a beeline for a tray filled with amber goblets. Gustavo and Leonora were talking to a dozen guests, who kissed Clara on the cheek when she was introduced as Sandro's niece and also as a young virtuoso pianist. Clara liked the people gathered there. They were close friends, who all seemed to have known Alessandro for a very long time and were pleased to have him among them again; from the snatches of conversation she heard here and there, she understood that most of them were artists. She was surprised to learn that

Alessandro was a painter, and several times she heard people suggest that he ought to take it up again and stop being afraid of the dark. The wine they served was golden, there was laughter and conversation, a mixture of seriousness and whimsy in which Clara felt herself gradually drifting off into a blissful sensation she could not recall ever having felt ... the grandeur of communities built around shared interests, added to the protective warmth of primitive tribes ... men and women bound by the shared awareness of their naked fragility and a collusion of desire that brought them together in the exaltation of art ... and it was the same waking dream, the same abysses and the same appetites that had convinced them one day to write down their stories with the ink of colours and notes.

Leonora came to speak to her and the guests clustered around them to listen to Clara's answers to the questions she was asked about her piano and her time spent working with the Maestro. But when Gustavo came and asked her to play, she stood up, her heart pounding, while the premonition that had haunted her all day long now overwhelmed her a hundredfold.

"What are you going to play?" asked one of the guests.

"A piece I composed," she replied, and she could see the Maestro's surprise.

"Is this your first composition?" asked a man who was himself a conductor.

She nodded.

"Does it have a title?" asked Leonora.

"Yes," she said. "But I don't know whether I ought to tell you."

Everyone laughed and Gustavo raised an amused eyebrow.

"This is an evening of great indulgence," he said. "You can tell us your title if you play the piece afterwards."

"It's called, *For His Sins, This Man Was German*," she replied.

The assembly burst out laughing and Clara understood she was not the only intended recipient of the Maestro's witticism. She saw he was also laughing wholeheartedly, while at the same time she could detect that same emotion he had shown when he said to her, "That's so typical of you."

She played and three things happened. The first was that all those present at the dinner were held in thrall: Clara's playing transformed them into pillars of salt. The second was the amplification of the sound of rain on the stones in the garden, which blended so perfectly with her composition that she understood she had been living in this music from the moment she had first heard it. And the third was the arrival of an unexpected guest, suddenly outlined in the doorway.

Handsome as an angel from the great dome, Raffaele Santangelo was smiling, looking at Clara.

PAVILION OF THE MISTS
Inner Elfin Council

"She knows that the stones are alive. Even in the city she doesn't forget it. And she plays miraculously. But she is still too much on her own."

"Leonora is there, and Petrus is keeping watch."

"He drinks too much."

"But he's more dangerous than a whole cohort of abstinent warriors."

"I know, I've already seen him drink and fight, and win over phalanxes of hostile councillors. And Clara's powers are growing. But how much time do we have? We may not even be able to save our own stones."

EUGÉNIE
All during the War

After the eventful month of April with its letter from Italy, there were a few months on the farm as flat as a loaf without yeast. One season passed, and another came to replace it. Maria turned twelve and it had not snowed. The summer was unusual. They had never before seen such unpredictable, chaotic weather, as if the sky were in two minds about which path to take. The Saint John's Day storms broke too early. Warm evenings followed upon autumn twilights during which you could sense the season was changing. Then summer came back with a vengeance, and the dragonflies arrived in hordes.

Maria continued to converse with the animals in the woods. Rumours of shadows intensified in the community of hares: these creatures seemed more sensitive to them than others. But the stags, too, spoke among themselves of a sort of decline in supplies. These were being spoiled by something, though it was impossible to know how. For the time being, the village carried on with everyday life regardless, but Maria noticed a surprising paradox: the countryside was indeed in decline, while the old women's gifts were intensifying.

Proof of this came at the end of January, on the evening of Leonora's birthday. All day long, Jeannette had not so much as stepped away from her stove, which had been transformed into an alchemist's laboratory, because that evening they would be hosting one of the father's brothers, Marcel, and his wife, Léonce, who had arrived from the far south. The dinner consisted of a truffled guinea fowl set amid a liver terrine, and *pot-au-feu en ravigote* (all of it garnished with cardoons that had been so well caramelized that the juice still ran down one's throat, despite the *vin de côte*), and it was a dazzling triumph. When the meal was brought to a close by a cream tart served with Eugénie's quince jellies, all that remained in the room was a row of bellies all as happy and stupid as can be—before the onset of indigestion.

But on the stroke of two o'clock, there came from Angèle's room, which she had given to Marcel and Léonce, an unholy racket that awoke the entire farm. People groped their way through the dark, lit candles, and hurried to the room, where they found Marcel writhing in pain from a liver attack and a violent fever, and they feared he might be taken from them that very hour. Eugénie had lain dreaming continuously of deep caves where the sediment of a sticky yellow substance was collecting, and her relief upon awakening from one nasty situation was soon erased by the discovery of another one. She staggered slightly, and tried to adjust her nightcap, which had slipped down over her ear, but the sight of the sick man on his bed of suffering woke her with a start, and she stood bolt upright in her thick woollen socks. She had already treated the entire lowlands for various ills, prescribing a considerable array of potions, dilutions, tinctures, syrups, decoctions, gargles, ointments, unguents, balms and poultices of her own confection, some of them for patients whose chances of recovery were slim, and whose funerals she subsequently attended, much saddened. But however strange it might seem, this was the first time she found herself in the presence of a sick person at the critical moment. The crisis was all around them and there was no getting away from it. And in any case, she had no intention of fleeing. On the contrary, she was fully convinced that all the paths she had taken in life had been leading her to this little room full of suffering.

Unlike Angèle, Eugénie was not a woman with a rich inner life where the embers were gradually dying. She saw the world as a collection of tasks and days whose existence alone sufficed to justify them. She got up in the morning to pray and feed the rabbits, then she made up her remedies, prayed again, sewed, mended, scrubbed, went off to pick her medicinal plants and hoe her vegetable garden, and if she managed to do it all in good time and without impediment, she would go to bed content, without a single thought. But acceptance of the world granted to her had little to do with resignation. If Eugénie was content with a thankless life that she had not chosen, it was because she lived in constant prayer, inspired in her at the age of five by a mint leaf in her mother's garden. She had felt the green and fragrant sap of the plant running in her veins, and it was not just a substance that was marvellously attuned to the texture of her fingers and her sense of smell; it also told a story without words, and she gave herself to that story as she would to the flow of the river. It had brought her incredible clarity, commanding her through images to perform a series of actions that she had carried out with a pounding heart; only the exclamations of the adults who sought to prevent her from continuing interrupted her—until they discovered that she had been stung on the cheek, and they understood that by rubbing her face with the moist peppermint leaf she was applying the very remedy that could quell the pain. She had not been aware of it, she had not even suspected that others might not be lulled by the same prayer, which had initially come to her in the form of delightful songs she heard during her contact with nature, and which then was filled with meaning when she was taken to church, where the spirit of these psalms was given a face and words; she had simply written the words onto the stave of the score she already knew, and the splendour of the mint had conquered both doctrine and God. In a way, this perception of nature's hymns came closest to Maria's own perception, and if Eugénie had been struck by the composition with the cloves of garlic that had rendered the room in the farmhouse so sublime it was because she had already been initiated into the order of invisible reasons that made her happy, even though she was born poor.

But the greatest tragedy in her life had been the loss of her son to the war; his name was carved on the village monument. During all the battles that rent the skies of France with their poisoned wound, it crushed her to see the violets continuing to wither as exquisitely as ever, and when she lost her son, it seemed to her that the beauty of the woods was an inexplicable disgrace, even in the pages of the Holy Scripture, because it was inconceivable that such a magnificent world could exist alongside such agonizing pain. The death of her husband, while it had greatly afflicted her, had not been a comparable tragedy, because he had departed as all the living depart, as the irises fade and the great stags die. But the war set the lines ablaze and burned reality to the bone; everywhere people were coming up against walls as high as cathedrals that elevated death above the beautiful plains; and the fact that all this was happening amid the limpidity of spring blossoms was a paradox that touched her in the very place that hitherto had made her live, the place of sacred affinity between the living and their earth. Prior to her son's death she had already lost her appetite; but once they informed her that he would never return from the faraway fields, and that they would not send his body back to her because there had been so many losses and such terrible fires that they could only draw up lists of those who had not returned, Eugénie could not even recall the meaning of desire.

But one morning not long before the end of the war they brought her a child from a neighbouring village who had been sick for months, coughing to exhaustion from morning to night. The boy had such a wrenching, racking cough that she imagined the pain could only be assuaged if she were to place her hand on his torso and try to feel the path the illness was taking; when she discovered that his lungs were clear, she understood in a flash that he was suffering from the same ailment she herself was slowly dying from. She increased the pressure of her palm on his poor naked chest, where the powers of war were hollowing out a crevice of sorrow and rage, then she caressed the boy's cheek, applied a bit of clay sprain ointment and said with a smile, overwhelmed to be feeling the floodgates opening inside her and releasing an incredible rush of flotsam, opening inside her and finding the dawn again in spite of all the wounds and the hatred—she said to him with a smile, *It will be fine, my angel.* Two days later the mother told her that the cough was gone, and while the little boy didn't speak, he smiled all the time, and Eugénie was able to resume her familiar life flushed with the singing of the pastures and the oaks. But she had incorporated the knowledge of evil in the form of a wound, and henceforth she would feel its black hole every day, devouring her allotted amount of substance and love. Oddly enough, it meant that she was better able to detect the deep origins of illnesses, but she also felt that part of her gift was blocked, and the accuracy of her diagnosis was in inverse proportion to her ability to heal. Something had grown, something else had fallen away, and although she was no philosopher, she felt this cross she constantly had to bear impeded her activity as a healer.

Why do the paths of destiny suddenly appear like letters forming of their own accord in the sand on the shore? After the conflict, life went on, and the men returned to the fields where, during the massacres, only women and old men had worked. There were new harvests, new winters, and more autumnal languor, and the survivors mourned their dead while the horror of the carnage left them forever inconsolable. And yet they were alive, and they smiled at dragonflies in summer, while the countryside crumbled beneath the weight of grey stones carved with one word doomed to condemn them all. *Remember! Remember! Remember that crushing fate still begging for alms of remembrance, through the curse of love that was lost to steel!* Upon entering the little room where

Marcel lay dying, Eugénie felt Maria touch her shoulder, before withdrawing silently into the shadows. And only then did she return from the war. The paths of fate: a garlic clove is moved one millimetre and the world is utterly changed; the slightest shift disturbs the secret position of our emotions and yet it transforms our lives forever. Eugénie sensed all this as she observed the sick man's ordeal, and was astonished to discover that thanks to the little girl's touch she had crossed a trifling space, but found herself far removed from the suffering she had just left behind. Several decades of struggle swept to one side of her old woman's shoulder—and a dying man who was not belligerent but merely made of flesh and blood; Eugénie went up to the untidy bed and placed her hand on her godson's forehead.

In fact Marcel, who rued the guinea fowl and the bad things in his life—in particular a duck he had once stolen—was little more now than a colossal infection. The contamination had begun in his stomach and in two hours had built a little mound of pus; then, pleased with what it had done, it had called on its legions to advance at once. His body had begun to undergo the ordeal that the gangrene had restrained until such a time as it would be invincible, and in the sudden agitation of radiating pain, had spread the decline beyond his vessels and tissues. This was the principle behind all warfare, and it had become obvious to Eugénie for a reason she only began to understand when Maria, by touching her shoulder, stirred an awareness inscribed on the genetic map of her old peasant carcass, and which informed her that the only reason she could see the ravages of war so well was because her fate demanded she become a healer.

The world was growing older. After decades of evil, of constant invasion, there remained nothing more than one fortress amid the chaos of warring rulers, and each time it would confront the resistance of violets. Fleetingly, Eugénie felt sorry it had taken all this time for things to become clear, but she also understood that one cannot give orders to the battalion of gifts, that they must still learn compassion and love, and that the illumination of souls requires the work of grief and mourning—yes, solace is very near and we cannot seize it, it takes time, it takes years, and perhaps, too, the forgiveness of others.

It is after three o'clock in the morning at the farm and two women have entered together into a territory that requires still more magnanimity and sorrow, while the life of a man who only ever stole a duck lies in their twelve- and eighty-seven-year-old hands, hanging by the thread that joins them in the trance of battle.

Eugénie closed her eyes and, as if she were five years old again, lying intoxicated by her mint leaves, she watched as the succession of steps in the healing appeared on the screen of her inner gaze. She opened her eyes again, and did not need to speak, because the little girl left for the kitchen at once, then came back holding a handful of garlic and sprigs of thyme cupped in her palms, their pungent scent filling the room. Eugénie took the little jug from Angèle's night table, crushed the garlic into it, added the thyme and lifted the preparation to the dying man's nostrils; he seemed to breathe more easily and half-opened one yellowed eye, shot with clotted, black blood. She brushed his lips with some of the sticky paste. He gagged once, then she gently opened his mouth and placed a small amount of the remedy inside.

Do you know what a dream is? It is not a chimera engendered by our desire, but another way we absorb the substance of the world, and gain access to the same truths as those the mists unveil by concealing the visible and unveiling the invisible. Eugénie knew that neither the garlic nor the thyme could heal an infection that had spread this far, but she had grown up with the wisdom whispered in the ear of those who have left the battle: there are no limits to our powers to accomplish and our natural spirit is stronger than anything. She also knew that her gift as a healer called forth another vaster and more awesome gift and that Maria—standing in the shadows because she was a steward of higher causes—was the realization of the miracle.

She turned and called to the little girl, who stepped forward to touch her shoulder again. Eugénie swayed, startled by the violence of the shock. She felt energy and rebellion surging through her, waves and tempests. She gulped in surprise as she sensed herself drifting away on the flow of energy the little girl spun around her, then she was restored to her healer's elation and set sail in search of the ebb and flow of her dream. She discovered it in an image that stood out against a hazy, shimmering background, and the rhythms and sensations slackened to let her move slowly towards a red span between two shores shrouded in mist. What a beautiful bridge it was … One could sense the noble wood beneath the deep velvety carmine paint, and before long there followed a procession of absurd, unintelligible thoughts, but they all led to the sense of peace granted to anyone who cared to look at the red bridge between two clouds of mist. Yet this was a peace that Eugénie had always known, of the sort that united trees and people and caused plants to speak the language of human beings, and the bridge radiated a power of conciliation that revealed the ways of nature with an intensity and harmony she had never before experienced. Then the image was gone. It had lasted only as long as a sigh, and in that time she heard voices more beautiful than all of beauty itself.

Peace … What else had she aspired to all these years? What else can one desire when one loses a son, when his guts explode under a sky of honour? With a sharpness that would have still been painful that very morning and now felt like a caress in her memory, she saw again a summer evening in the garden, when they had set the table for the repast after Saint John's Day, decorating it with the big solstice irises. She could hear the insects buzzing in the warm air, sounds mingling with scents, the aroma of a pike simmering with little vegetables from the garden; and she saw her son again as she had not seen him in many years: he was sitting across from her and smiling sadly because they both knew he had already died in those same fields where so many of our husbands and sons had died; so she leaned forward slightly and, looking at him tenderly, said in a voice veiled by neither sadness nor regret, *Go, son, and know for all eternity how much we love you*. Eugénie could have died in that moment, in perfect, idiotic bliss, the way the poppies and dragonflies die in summer. But she had a godson to tear from death's clutches, and she was not one of those otherworldly souls intoxicated forever by a hymn. She knew that the vision and the singing had appeared to her so that she could accomplish her task—that was why she had adjusted her nightcap, crushed the garlic between her fingers, and seen her son again in the winter night.

At that very moment, the little girl removed her hand from Eugénie's shoulder, and the old woman felt, understood, and recognized everything. She focused on the sick man's body and saw that he was infected with the sticky yellow substance from her dream, and that the air was saturated with the same odour as all through the war—it was a gangrene that sought only to destroy and defeat, invading and gradually sucking away everything that lived and loved. For a moment she was overwhelmed by the evidence that the enemy was far superior to anything that a poor country healer might pit against it— her limited means and unworldly knowledge. But she had the strength of a new illumination that had entered her when Maria touched her shoulder.

Wars ... We know they dictate their laws of retribution, and drive the just to the battlefield. But what would happen if everyone sat on the grass in those fields, and in the pure dawn air put their weapons down beside them? There would be the sound of the angelus ringing from the nearby steeple, while the men woke from their dreams of horror and darkness. Suddenly, it would start to rain, and one could merely succumb to the prayer that brings with it a life full of violets and abundance. How futile it was to hope to triumph over the attack by sacrificing three soldiers—what could they do against hordes and cannons ... What was healing, in the end, if not the making of peace? And what was living if it was not for love?

Important decisions are made by those who are invisible, by the humble people. The dark army was building its bastions, piercing the sick man's very skin with spurs from which they could suspend their web of infection. So, instead of sending them to the front, Eugénie made her soldiers sit down. Her gift visualized the path the garlic and thyme would take through the sick man's bowels and blood, and her dream increased its viscosity tenfold, oiling the walls so that it would be harder for the enemy to plant its barbs. Her dream became stronger still, and she coated the base of the existing hooks until they were swept away by the crushed cloves and the needles of thyme and, at the same time, their healing properties filled the holes the enemy had drilled, and set about closing the wounds with their beneficial active ingredients.

She was filled with enthusiasm. It was so easy to use the medicinal plants in this way, and to apply them directly to the substance of the illness, and so miraculous to see how one could work towards recovery by using the magic of the dream to hasten processes that were themselves quite natural. But she also felt that her gift drew upon declining reserves, and she could tell the moment was approaching when the energy of her dream would have drained away and she would have to renounce her efforts. Then she caught a glimpse of an iris. She did not know where, it was there and it was nowhere; she could look at it but it was invisible, and it was radiating an intense presence even though she could neither locate nor grasp it. It was smaller than the irises in the garden, its white petals streaked with pale blue, and it had a deep purple heart with orange stamens. It emanated something fresh, and she could not identify the formula at first, but then she suddenly understood that it was the freshness of childhood. So …

Now she knew why the iris could not be seen even when it was so visible, and she understood how she must carry her task to fruition. She gave a start when she read the flower's message, written in letters perfumed with the joys of early childhood, then she relaxed her entire being, transported by the pure and simple acceptance of the gift.

She returned to the eighty-seven-year-old body she had forgotten when Maria had touched her shoulder for the second time, and in which she was now reincarnated, feeling alive as never before. She looked around her at a painting whose pigments had been brushed with a smooth, shining varnish. The room was silent. Angèle was kneeling on the old chestnut *prie-dieu* she had always refused to replace with one of those fine red velvet ones you saw in the front rows of the church, and she was so absorbed by her prayer that she had not noticed her nightgown was turned up over a pair of cotton bloomers with a hem of pristine braided ribbon. Léonce was sitting on the eiderdown next to her Marcel, rubbing his feet with the patience of a Madonna. Jeannette and Marie both stood in the doorway, which seemed to dwarf the two old ladies: fear had made them even smaller than age had. Eugénie took Marcel's pulse and then lifted his eyelid. His breath was weak but regular, and his eyes were less bloodshot. Just to be on the safe side, she slipped a last dose of garlic and thyme into his mouth. She suddenly felt very old and tired. Then she turned around abruptly to face Maria.

Her black eyes filled with tears, and she was clenching her fists, the focus of her heightened sorrow. Eugénie felt despondent for the little girl, whose magic could not change a heart made like all little girls' hearts, a heart that would bleed for a long time from this first distressing experience. She smiled at her with all the tenderness of a mother who would kill and die a hundred times for her child, and with her hand she made a gesture in which she placed the consciousness and majesty of the gift, in the form of the iris of childhood. But Maria's tears were still flowing and the expression in her eyes was one of bitterness and sorrow. Then she stepped to one side and the connection was broken. Besides, it was not a time for distress, while this great wave of relief was washing over the little room and they were all leaving their battle stations, including the *prie-dieu* and the down quilt, in order to embrace one another in triumph.

There was victorious reciting of the rosary beads, there was a celebration of the constancy with which Eugénie had always praised the virtues of garlic and thyme—but what was going on inside the heads of these simple country people? Over those two snowy nights there'd been no need to put two and two together to conclude that the little girl was magical and that glorious seasons and human boars do not fall from the sky every day. In fact, faith and what they had before their eyes were made to coexist, and they were convinced that the Lord must have something to do with powers of the sort where what you believed and what you saw—well, you needn't bother to try and reconcile the two. Above all, there was a more urgent task at hand now that Marcel was snoring like a baby and they had all gone down to the kitchen to drink some coffee as a reward: they must make sure that Maria was well protected, for a reason Angèle had been convinced of from the beginning, namely that the child was very powerful, and would constantly attract the attention of other powers in the world. No one had noticed that Eugénie was not drinking her coffee; she was simply sitting there, a dreamy smile on her old timeworn lips.

"What a long, or short, night it's been," said the father finally, putting down his cup, and he smiled at all those present the way only he knew how, restoring time to its regular and peaceful amble, and placing the day back on the rightful path of routine.

They heard the angelus ringing from the village steeple, while smoke rose into the sky from the chimneys of happy farms, and life went back to normal, nourished with hawthorn and love.

RAFFAELE
The Servants We Are

Oh, so handsome; so tall and blond; eyes bluer than the water of a glacier; porcelain features in the face of a virile man; a supple body, superbly unselfconscious, and on his left cheek, a charming dimple. But the most splendid thing about his remarkable physiognomy was the smile that beamed upon the world like an iridescent shower of sunlight. Yes, the handsomest of angels, indeed, and it made you wonder how you could have lived until now without this promise of renewal and love.

Raffaele Santangelo looked at Clara until she had finished playing, then turned to speak to the Maestro when silence had returned.

"I've invited myself, how thoughtless of me," he said, "and I'm disturbing a friendly gathering."

It was the same voice Clara had heard in the past, resonating with the same violence that paved the road to death.

"I wish to pay my respects," he said to Leonora.

She stood up, and held out her hand for him to kiss.

"Ah, my friend," she said, "we are getting old, aren't we?"

He gave a quick bow. "You are as beautiful as ever."

When he had come into the room, all the men had stood up, but they did not greet him, and they had continued to stand there in a position of feigned deference, while their expressions belied any friendship. Acciavatti had gone to stand closer to Clara, but the most remarkable change was in Petrus, who had had time to do justice to the moscato then collapse into an armchair; the arrival of the Governor had not roused him from his seat, but now he had sprung to attention like a watchdog, his lips contorted in an evil grimace, accompanied by the occasional hostile growl.

The moment the Maestro's gaze met the Governor's, the piano room exploded in a spray of lustrous bronze stars; Clara was so surprised that she leapt up, and the space was resplendent with a shining dust, a double cone of light dancing with fragments unknown to memory—originating in each of the two men, then converging where their powers were concentrated. Alone of all the guests, Petrus seemed to have seen the cone, and he emitted another hostile growl, his nose in the air and his suit dishevelled. But the Governor was looking at the Maestro, and the Maestro was looking at the Governor, and neither one of them seemed to be in any hurry to speak; not to mention the fact that the little group of friends also remained silent, admirably motionless and mute, despite their fear. But on Alessandro's face there appeared a fresh light, which rendered him younger, sharper, and Clara liked what she saw although it simultaneously filled her with fresh anxiety, like a foretaste of the pain of important things and final resolutions.

"A joyful company," said Raffaele at last. But he had stopped smiling. He made a sweeping gesture—oh, how graceful—as if he wanted to call a friendly brotherhood to witness, and he added, "One hopes there will be more, and that they will form alliances among themselves."

Gustavo smiled. "Alliances are formed naturally," he said.

"Alliances are forged," answered Raffaele.

"We are merely artists," said the Maestro, "and our only guides are the stars."

"But every man must find courage," said the Governor, "and artists, too, are men."

"Who can judge the destiny of men?" responded the Maestro.

"Who can judge their inconsequence? Stars have no courage," said the Governor.

"They have wisdom," said the Maestro.

"Only the weak invoke wisdom," said the Governor, "brave men only believe facts." And without waiting for the Maestro's reply, he went up to the piano and looked at Clara. "So here we have another little girl …" he murmured. "What is your name, young lady?"

She did not reply.

From deep within Petrus's armchair came a growl.

"A virtuoso and a mute, perhaps?"

The Maestro put his hand on Clara's shoulder.

"Ah … the order had to come," said Raffaele.

"My name is Clara," she said.

"Where are your parents?"

"I came with my Uncle Sandro."

"Who taught you to play the piano? Painters are obviously good teachers, but I didn't know they could make the stones sing."

In the cone of light there was an image of a pathway of black stones, lined with overhanging tall trees; the Maestro's words—*the Pavilion where our kind can see everything*—came back to her; then the cone's projections were once again unclear.

The Governor looked at her thoughtfully and she could sense he was troubled.

"What dreams are you chasing, given that you are all crazy?" he said.

"Troubadours feed off dreams," replied Gustavo amiably.

"The carelessness of spoilt children," said Santangelo, "when others work so that they might continue to dream."

"But isn't politics a dream in and of itself?" said the Maestro in the same smooth, urbane tone.

The Governor gave an adorable laugh, resplendent with the cheer of lovely things. Looking at Clara, he said, "Take care, pretty miss, musicians are sophists. But I am sure we shall meet again soon and we shall converse at greater leisure about this silliness that music inspires in them."

There was a menacing sound from Petrus's armchair.

The Governor turned to Leonora and bowed to her in a way that made Clara's blood run cold. This courtier's gesture betrayed no respect, only a cold hatred, fleetingly visible.

"Alas, it is time for me to leave."

"No one is keeping you here," said Petrus, his voice only moderately clear.

Raffaele did not look at him. "Thus you surround yourself with dreamers and drunks?" he asked the Maestro.

"There are worse companions," said Gustavo.

The Governor gave a joyless smile. "To each his own," he said.

He made ready to leave but, as if it were staged, Pietro Volpe entered the room at that very moment.

"Governor," he said. "I thought you were elsewhere, and now I find you in my own house."

"Pietro," said the Governor, with a touch of the same hatred he had displayed towards Leonora. "I'm pleased to have surprised you."

"You're outnumbered, I'm afraid. But you were about to leave?"

"My own family is waiting for me."

"You mean your troops?"

"My brothers."

"Rome is speaking of no one else."

"It is only the beginning."

"I don't doubt it, Governor. Let me see you out."

"Always the servant," said Raffaele, "when you could reign."

"Like you, my brother, like you," replied Pietro. "But time will reward the servants we are."

Petrus gave a snort of satisfaction.

Raffaele Santangelo glanced one last time at Clara and shrugged his shoulders with the nonchalance of a ballerina, as if to say, *We have plenty of time*.

"Adieu," he said, and vanished in a movement of great elegance which gave a glimpse, beneath his black clothing, of the perfection of his fighter's body.

As if there were a gem of light in a dark crystal-clear water, Clara sensed a strange aura lurking behind the angelic servant of the state before he left and took his shadows with him. But like a trace left on the retina long after the image has gone, one of these shadows struck her and, as she recalled the encounter with Raffaele, she saw again the expression that at a certain point his face assumed as she played her composition. And just as she had been frightened by the contrasts in the voice of death, now she was submerged by a wave of beauty that was instantly destroyed by a wave of ugliness. There was so much nobility, so much rage and pain in that fleeting gaze, and so much splendour in the image that invaded her inner perception …

A stormy sky rose over a valley of mists, and gardens of stones could be seen beneath the clouds that sped into the blue. On her tongue was the taste of snow and violets, mingled with an essence of trees and wooden arcades, both unimaginable and very familiar, as if the flavour of a vanished world had come alive in her mouth and by running her fingers over the exposed contours of her open heart, she had seen the blood welling there for the first time. Such a mixture of ecstasy and sorrow; an endless sadness sharpened by the blade of suffering; and the nostalgia of an ancient dream where hatred was growing, rumbling. Finally in the sky she saw birds set loose by invisible archers, and she knew that she was seeing through Raffaele's eyes what he had lost, so much so that the aversion she felt for the road to disaster and death was mixed with the rush of a feeling not unlike love.

In fact, during those moments when the two men were confronting one another, the tension had grown without words or movement, as if they were practising a martial art at such a level of mastery that the outcome of the fight required no contact, and she had seen the metabolic centre whence the same solar wave of power came, the one that taught her that they both belonged to the same world. But while the Maestro radiated an aura of rocks and riverbanks, the Governor rose up in an arrow, whose pale fletchings turned into charred feathers at their extremities, and in his heart there was a distortion that distanced him from himself and resembled an open wound where once there had been magnificence.

After the Governor's departure, the Maestro's friends continued to converse into the night, and from their discussions Clara was able to obtain a clearer picture of Rome's political chessboard. She was not surprised to learn that, although he did not have any official position of authority, the Maestro was a pillar of the city, but she was astonished to find that they all knew he had dealings with a mysterious side of reality.

"The Governor no longer has any doubt," said Pietro; "he is certain of his victory."

"But he is still trying to win you over to his side," said Roberto, the orchestra conductor, addressing the Maestro.

"It was a threat, not a request," said Alessandro. "He has already unleashed his dogs all across the country, and he is leaning with all his strength on the Council. But Italy is only one pawn in the greater war."

"Alessandro Centi, you may be a doomed artist but you are a fine strategist," said one of the female guests, with both bitterness and tenderness.

Everyone laughed. But in this laughter mingled with friendship and fear Clara detected the same determination she had sensed in Alessandro, and it both frightened her and aroused her ardour. She looked at the faces of these men and women, the suave mannerisms of those whom fortune had favoured, and she saw in them an awareness of the deep disquiet in which the flame of their art was flickering—so much so that fate hung between the soul's euphoria and exhaustion. She also saw a community of peace-loving people who concurred that the times called for battle readiness, and from this determination came a gravity that made the hour magnificent. And she understood that no one present was there by chance, that the Maestro had used the pretext of Leonora's birthday to assemble the phalanx he had constituted much as he chose her music and placed both peaches and beloved women in her path. But she wondered what it was that made them a fighting elite, because none of the members of this amiable battalion belonged to the ordinary species of soldier, those who make their way of a morning to open land that will be red by nightfall; yet they were the Maestro's field officers, forming a family with weapons and powers hidden beneath the table where they dined. Proudly, she felt she belonged to that family, too.

"The first battle is behind us," said the Maestro, "and we have lost it. We have no more influence on the Council; they will hand over their powers before the end of the winter."

"We must make ready," said Ottavio, a man with white hair and an intriguing gaze; Sandro had told her he was an important writer.

"It is time to find shelter for your people," said Pietro.

"What sort of protection will you provide for Clara?" asked Roberto, and she saw that they all agreed she was to play a decisive role in the war.

"Those who protect are protected," said the Maestro.

Finally, with the exception of Pietro, Alessandro, and Petrus, the guests departed.

"You are visible now, you cannot return to the courtyard," said Leonora to Clara. "You'll sleep here tonight."

Then she embraced her, and left. Pietro and Alessandro poured a glass of liqueur and sat down for one last nocturnal conversation. Petrus vanished, then came back with a bottle of moscato, pouring himself a glass with tender solicitude.

"Does the Governor see what I see?" asked Clara.

"He saw it at the end," said the Maestro, "even though I stayed by your side. But I don't think he understood it clearly."

"I saw the tunnel of light between you," she said. "There was a path of stones, with the same trees as in your garden."

"The stones are at the centre of your life," he said. "You will often see that path."

And from the sound of his voice she understood that he was proud of her.

"I listened to the singing of your stream," she said. Pietro's smile was like the smile he gave after searching in vain for the poem on the musical score.

"You will stay here from now on," said the Maestro.

"Raffaele will want to understand fully before he acts, so we still have some time ahead of us. But we must reinforce our surveillance."

"I'll deploy some men," said Pietro, "but we are overwhelmed. Raffaele was informed, in spite of our watchmen."

"Who is the other little girl?" asked Alessandro. "It would

seem that the Governor already knows about her. It's her you want to tell us about this evening, I think."

"I want to talk about her to you in particular because you will soon go to meet her. It's a long journey, and it will be dangerous."

"May we know her name?"

"Maria," said Clara.

But she did not have the chance to say more, because a powerful alarm was sounding inside her; she stood up abruptly, followed by the Maestro and Petrus, who had leapt up from his cushions.

Oh, what a night of agony! On the distant farm, Marcel wakes to his inextinguishable pain, and the entire household heads towards his sickroom. Clara watches the procession of old women on their way to the unfortunate man's bedside; Maria and her father are already there, having sensed before the others that death is in pursuit of one of their own; she sees Marcel writhing in agony and, like the others, she realizes he is about to die; and she sees Eugénie, who was shaken from her torpor by the sight of the dying man, as if she'd been slapped in the face, now standing tall in her thick woollen socks. Gone is the little old lady burdened by age and chores; duty has left a glow on her worn face, which expertise has transformed into a blade, and it is another woman who goes over to the dying man, a woman so beautiful that the little Italian girl feels a pang of anguish on seeing this vision of passing beauty, irrespective of the iron that has forged it. Then she follows each act of healing in succession, while time is suspended and the sense of danger grows ever stronger.

When Maria places her hand on Eugénie's shoulder, Clara feels herself sinking into a great magma of power, and she is afraid of drowning and becoming lost in it forever. But she knows that her place is with these women who have come to cross the border of the visible together, and she hunts feverishly for a way through the storm. The Maestro's words—*the Pavilion where our kind can see everything*—again assail her memory and she tries to cling to them as if they were a raft in the middle of the ocean. Then she sees, and her entire life is there. Such peace, suddenly … As the mists lift, a red bridge drifts towards her with the majesty of a swan; as it comes closer, she can see a figure on the highest point of its arc, and she knows it is her father, in his priesthood as a ferryman, providing passage. Then the figure vanishes, the bridge is motionless on the thread of an enchanted song and Clara controls all the visions. She can leave Maria to catalyse the powers; she has passed on the message and is maintaining the harmony of the visible.

"Prodigious," murmurs the Maestro.

Alas, before long they see the iris that Maria cannot see. Clara looks at the invisible flower with its indescribable petals of childhood; at the far end of the vision, Eugénie accepts the pact of the exchange, and in Rome two men appear out of nowhere and come into the room just as the Maestro says to Alessandro, "You will leave with them at dawn."

Then, to Clara: "She must see you now."

PAVILION OF THE MISTS
Inner Elfin Council

"Prodigious," said the Council Head. "The alliance of vision and powers in the world of humans."

"Maria is the catalyst," said the Guardian of the Pavilion, "and Clara is the ferryman, providing passage."

"There is a change in the bridge's force field."

"There is a change in the mists' force field. The configuration of the passage is not all they alter."

"But there has been an exchange," said the Bear, "and Aelius sees what we see."

"It will upset the entire landscape of the action," said the Squirrel. "It is time to move."

"So soon," said the Council Head. "I hope we are ready."

"The bridge is open," said the Guardian of the Pavilion. "You may cross."

CLARA
Let Her Take Rosaries

Beneath the red eiderdown, Maria was weeping.

For several weeks now she had felt in her gut the premonition of an ordeal much greater than any the people she loved had ever known, and this was as terrifying to her as what she knew about the grievous events still burdening them, even years later. Moreover, it was the end of January and they had hardly seen any snow. It was very cold, and the nights froze into icy dawns stilled by the sharp air. But the fine snow had not come, either before or after the solstice, and Maria wandered through the frozen lowlands, where the animals were frightened by shadows whose impalpable threat grew more acute with each passing day. The music continued to disappear sporadically, as it had done during the twilight in March, and Maria dreaded these eclipses of the chanting as if they were lethal attacks, particularly as she had seen neither the fantastical wild boar nor the tall silver horse. It's too soon, she thought, with ever-increasing anxiety, all the while yearning for a life still enchanted by the eternal etchings of her trees.

Therefore, when she went into the little room where a

feckless man lay dying, paying a hundredfold for his guinea hen, a sudden flash of intuition enlightened her, telling her that the first catastrophe had just struck. She had touched Eugénie's shoulder twice, and admired the art with which the healer went about her task. Maria knew Eugénie had seen the bridge and understood the message, and she had seen how the old woman turned her back on war and left the front to attune herself to the music of the trees. Maria had not needed to think or to concentrate—on the contrary, she had surrendered to the vibrant sensation of the new contours rippling through the old auntie's heart, and she had played on the waves like unfurled strings, first simply by untying them, a second time by spreading them wide open to all possibilities.

It was not very different from what she ordinarily did with the animals; what she merely twisted slightly when she wanted to address the hares, she had now simply stretched towards infinity, the difference being that the animals in the woods had not broken with nature the way men had, for men could not hear the grand hymns, nor could they see the splendid pictures. So she had shown Eugénie the bridge of harmony, the image that had come to her just as she had laid her hand on her shoulder. Where had that image come from? She did not know. But everything had been so easy and so quick, it had been so simple to set these forces free and go with the natural flow, and it was utterly incomprehensible that to heal and provide relief in this way was not the daily lot of human beings.

At the very moment she saw the bridge, Eugénie heard voices chanting a celestial hymn. But unlike Maria she had not heard the words.

on a day slipping between two clouds of ink
on an evening sighing in the lightest of mists

The transparency of the world in these moments of song was dazzling, and she was giddy with frost and snow, their silkiness sparkling intermittently through the drifting mists. Maria knew this canto of passing voices and clouds. It came to her at night-time, in her dreams, but also during the day when she walked along her paths. Then she would stop, gripped by such a marvellous fright that she almost wished she could die of it that very instant—then the song and the vision moved on, and she would set off in quest of a hare that might offer some comfort, for there was always an instant, after the voices had fallen silent, when she thought she no longer desired anything, apart from that song and those mists. At last the world became clear again and her trouble was eased by violets and leaves. She would set off again, wondering whether this grace she had seen was a dream, or rather another weft of reality. Similarly, as if in a dream she could see strange landscapes of fog, with day breaking over a pier above the hollows thick with trees. Access was through a wooden pavilion; its walls were pierced with large openings that made the view into splendid pictures. On the uneven oak floor, powdered with a light dust that was gilded, comet-like, by bursts of light, there was a plain earthenware bowl. Maria would have liked to caress its gritty, irregular sides. But she could not go closer because she knew it would leave a shameful imprint in the dust; so she gave up and looked at the earthenware bowl with worshipful longing.

Yes, the song had been even more crystalline, more heart-rending and expansive, and this warning had, in time, opened a diagonal perspective that was both magnificent and terrible. And because she was absorbed by her dream-like, misty trance, she had not seen the iris at the decisive moment, but she suddenly heard a hundred horns sounding a deep, powerful note, so beautiful and funereal that the surfaces of reality had trembled in unison and whirled around a fixed point that spiralled in upon itself. How had she been able to do this? How had she not known? And beneath the thick red eiderdown she wept profusely, although this brought no relief, because the iris that Eugénie had shown her could not make up for the exchange that was depriving her of love.

Then Eugénie came into her room. She sat on the edge of the bed and took her beloved little girl's hand, wet as it was with her tears as it clung to her old and wrinkled hand.

"Cry, my sweet," said Eugénie, "but don't be sad. There, there."

She stroked the forehead of the child who had come to them on a snowy night and given them so much joy that she wished she could spread her arms and fill them with a screen to view a procession of images of happiness.

"Don't be sad," she said again, "see what you have done and don't be sad, my angel."

Maria sat up all of a sudden. "What I've done!" she murmured, "what I've done!"

"What you have done," repeated the auntie.

She felt like a poor peasant without words, who could not share the miracle. In a flash she understood why the words they heard in churches united so many hearts and gathered in so many believers; she knew the gift of language which pays homage to the unfathomable and names everything that weaves and elevates, and at last she saw that she could find a nugget in herself; it might not express the striped irises, or the evenings around Saint John's Day, but it could, all the same, restore the bare roots of what she had seen and felt. So she looked at Maria, and with a smile that illuminated her whole being she said simply, "You have healed me, my love."

And she thought of how twice a child had delivered her from the violence committed by man.

Something snapped inside Maria, as if walls of frost shattered silently then came to rest on a carpet of velvet, glinting with deep shards of mercury. There were stars and flights of birds slipping soundlessly through a sky of drowned ink, and a stream carrying away the secret of the birth that had blessed her with the power to relieve old women of their burdens. Her tears dried. She looked at Eugénie, at the furrows etched by time onto her beloved old face, and, gently stroking her hand, she smiled faintly in turn because she saw the joy in the auntie's heart, and she was learning what it meant to be a soul that has been relieved of its crosses.

Eugénie bobbed her head in assent, and it made you think of an apple left to sour on the rack in the storeroom, then she patted the hand of her lovely magical wee girl. She felt light and proud, with erstwhile appetites whirling in a theatre of amiable shadows, tableaux of juicy peaches like the fruit of paradise, and afternoons spent picking flowers along embankments swept by a warm breeze. The taste of things returned to her, from a time when taste buds had not yet been altered by tragedy, and it was so comforting that she felt as if a rush of tears were washing away the debris from some cluttered inner shore, leaving her as smooth and polished as the skin on the finest of autumn's pears. Her memory coursed through the orchards where she had spent her daydreaming childhood; in the whirring of the bees it reconnected with the firmament of great hunger; and the fact that before dying she had been able to see the world again with a child's sensors seemed to her like the ultimate blessing from a God whose greatness she had never ceased to honour. Well now, it was time. Let her take rosaries and ribbons, Sunday petticoats and solstice feasts, and go off to join the great congregation of the dead; and let her sing the psalms of storms and sky before bidding farewell to the coolness of orchards. Eugénie was ready; all that was left was to bequeath what must be bequeathed and put forever behind her the era of narrow humble rooms. She stood up, went to the door, and turning halfway, said to Maria, "Mind how you pick the hawthorn."

Then she went away.

Maria stayed on alone in the silence of the era that had just begun. In this peacefulness of orchards and flowers, the world was being reorganized. She stood with her back against the wall and she gathered in the sensations that were spinning in the field of her transfigured life. She saw how the unities in which her life had been confined until now lay within an immeasurable order of size, where superimposed upon the layers she already knew were entire worlds, side by side, touching and bumping up against each other with a dizzying depth of field. The world had become a succession of surfaces that rose to the sky in a complex architecture, constantly shifting, fading away and reappearing in a new form, in the same manner as the fantastical wild boar, both horse and man, when she was ten, a manner that was both osmosis and disappearance and which used the mists as an alluring screen. She saw cities, their streets and bridges shining in early mornings that seemed to have caught a chill from the gilded fogs dispersing in successive sneezes then slowly forming again over the town.

Will I see these cities one day? wondered Maria. And she gave herself up to her visions. First she saw a landscape of mountains and lakes with beehives and orchards of sun-yellowed grass, and a village on a steep hill with houses arranged in curved seashell lines. Everything was unknown, everything was familiar. Then the vision changed, giving way to a large room with a parquet floor like clear water. A little girl was seated at an instrument which made one think of an organ, but she was playing a piece of music, and it did not sound at all like the music at a church service; it was marvellous, without opulence or vaulted resonance, of the same substance as the golden dust in which Maria had discovered the bowl that aroused her desire. But this music also contained a powerful message of sorrow and forgiveness. There was a moment when she simply let herself be taken to the story suggested by the melody, then the little girl at the piano stopped playing, and she heard her murmur incomprehensible words that sounded like a muted warning.

Finally, everything disappeared and Maria woke up.

PIETRO
A Great Merchant

Clara looked at the two men who had suddenly appeared in the room and thrown their arms around Petrus.

"Friend of long evenings!" exclaimed the first.

"I'm so happy to see you again, you old madman," said the second, patting him on the back.

Then they turned to Sandro, and the taller of the two, who had black hair and very dark skin, bowed and said, "Marcus, at your service."

"Paulus," said the other one, also bowing, and Clara noted with interest that he had ginger hair, like Petrus.

They were very different from the Maestro, even though she detected a kinship among them from certain rhythms and the intonation of their voices, and she thought their background must be similar to the Maestro's, evocative of hordes of wild horses, ample and dark in the one whose name was Marcus, and whose solid stature made him a full head taller than Pietro; furtive and golden in the other man, who was not much taller than Clara herself and seemed as light as a feather.

Alessandro, not the least bit surprised to see them, now

studied them with a curiosity mingled with a palpable liking.

"I am sorry about this sudden departure," said the Maestro.

"She is weeping," said Paulus, "but we cannot change what comes."

Clara understood that he could see Maria. At that moment, Eugénie entered the little bedroom, sat next to her little lass and, with a smile, gently took her hand. Clara's heart grew heavy.

"What is going to happen?" she asked.

"There are many things we do not know," answered the Maestro, "but there is one thing of which we are certain."

"Eugénie has no more strength," she said.

"Strength can be exchanged, but not created," said the Maestro.

"I won't see her again?" she asked.

"No," he said.

"And in the next life?"

"There are several worlds but only one life," he said.

She lowered her head.

"She has made her choice in all conscience," he added. "Don't be sad for her."

"I am sad for myself," she replied.

But he was already holding a campaign meeting. "Maria lives in France, in a village where the enemy is about to strike," he said to Alessandro.

"Will we get there in time?"

"No. You will arrive after the battle, but if she survives, you will take her to a safe place."

"Where is that safe place?"

The Maestro smiled.

"I'm not a warrior," said Alessandro.

"No."

"And you're not sending me into battle."

"No. But it's dangerous all the same."

Alessandro smiled in turn. "I fear only despair," he said. Then, again serious, "I hope that Maria will survive."

"I hope so, too," said the Maestro. "Because if she does we won't have to weep, and if we are not mad, perhaps we will be able to reverse fate."

Clara looked at Maria and tried to understand what she must do so that Maria would be able to see her. But the little French girl cast all around her the bronze of infinite solitude.

"You will find the way," Paulus said to her.

The five men got to their feet and Clara felt more bereft than a rosebush in winter. But Alessandro turned to her with a smile and said, "You can see Maria, can't you?"

She nodded.

"And can you see the people around her, too?"

"Yes," she replied, "I see the people she sees."

"Then you will see me again soon," he said, "and I will know that you are looking at me."

Before leaving the room, Marcus went up to her and reached into his pocket for something. He then solemnly held out his closed fist. She opened her palm and in it he placed a very soft little ball. When he withdrew his hand, she marvelled to find a sphere roughly ten centimetres in diameter, covered with fur not unlike a rabbit's. The fur was somewhat irregular, flattened in places and more prominent on one side, but despite this unevenness there was something joyful and pleasing about the ball.

"It is fitting for an ancestor to go with you," said Marcus. "Your father entrusted it to me at the time of the handing over. Naturally, it's inert."

This mention of her father was eclipsed by the sensations aroused in her by her contact with the sphere.

"What must I do?" she asked.

"Always keep it with you," he replied. "It must be in constant contact with one of our people, otherwise it will die."

Clara was delighted by the waves emanating from the fur. It seemed to her that a muffled voice was speaking to her, but it sounded like a baby's babbling, or a string of unclear words mingled with strange, gentle growls. Pietro came over to observe the object in her palm. So she looked up at him and their eyes met. In spite of her long months at the villa with the courtyard, they had never truly met. But as they bent over the sphere, they saw an abyss open in each other.

Pietro Volpe had lived through three decades of hell and three of light. His memories of the decades in hell were intact, but he only preserved them, piously, in order to celebrate his decades of light. Every morning upon awakening he saw his father, hated him again, forgave him again, then relived the hours of his childhood so sharply that it would have driven him mad had he not acquired the power to suffer and heal in a single gesture. He still lived in the house where he was born and grew up, and while the decor may have been changed, the walls were the same that had witnessed his hatred and confusion, and the courtyard was haunted by the ghosts of the people who had lived there. Why had Roberto Volpe failed to cherish the son he had so fervently desired? He was an elegant man, who loved what he did because he loved beautiful things and prosperous trade; and because he knew men well, his conversation, while not elevated, never lied; no doubt the entire individual was in this paradox, which meant he was neither superficial nor deep. But when the father and the child saw each other for the first time, they despised each other in a way that was total and irreversible—and if anyone is surprised to find such a young person so capable of contempt they would do well to remember that childhood is the dream that allows us to understand what we do not yet know.

At the age of ten Pietro was always fighting, like any hooligan from the slums. He was tall and strong, and he had that sense of rhythm that is akin to an exacerbated sensitivity. But it made him as invincible as he was cursed, and his mother Alba languished in sorrow, unconsoled by the daughter born to her subsequently. By the time ten more years had gone by Pietro had learned all the combat techniques from the street.

At the age of twenty he did not know whether he was a dangerous man or a furious animal. He brawled at night, reciting poetry; he read voraciously, fought lugubriously, returned intermittently to the villa with the courtyard, always careful not to run into his father, and he watched as his mother shed her tears and his sister acquired her elegance. He said nothing, but he held Alba's hand until her sobs were exhausted, then he left again, sombre, in the same silence he had walled himself up in all his life. There were ten more years of despair as evanescent as the voice he sometimes heard in his head; his mother grew old and

Leonora bloomed, looking at him in silence, and smiling in a way that said, *I'll wait for you*. But when he tried to return her smile, he froze with pain. So she would squeeze his arm, then walk away, moving according to whichever circular stride took her fancy that day, but as she was leaving the room, she cast him one last look that said, yet again, *I'll wait for you*. And her constancy buoyed him and crucified him at the same time.

Then one morning he awoke to an awareness that the lines of time had been reversed. He arrived at the villa just as a priest was leaving, and the priest informed Pietro that his father was dying and that they had been looking for him all night. He went to Roberto's room, where Alba and Leonora were waiting; they withdrew and left him alone with his fate.

He was thirty years old.

He went over to the bed where the man he had not seen for ten years was breathing his last. The curtains had been drawn; unable to see, he tried to make out a human shape, but then he felt a gaze go straight to his gut, a raptor's gaze that shone like a gem in the darkness of the end of things.

"Pietro, at last," said Roberto.

He was shaken as he recognized every inflection of a voice he had long forgotten, and he realized that suffering collapsed the abysses of time, restoring that voice to him now as clear as on the first morning. He said nothing but went even closer, because he did not want to be a coward. Ravaged, his father had the same face he had always had, but his eyes glowed with a fever that conveyed to Pietro he would be dead by evening, and there was a spark in those eyes that made him doubt it would be the work of illness alone.

"In thirty years not a day has gone by when I have not

thought of this moment," continued Roberto.

He laughed. A dry cough racked his chest and Pietro saw that he was afraid. For a moment he thought he didn't feel anything, then a wave of anger washed over him when he understood that death would change nothing, and he would have to live until the end of his own life having been the son of this father.

"So often I dreaded I would die without seeing you again. But apparently fate knows what it has to do." He was seized by convulsions, and for a long time he could not speak.

Pietro did not move, or take his eyes off him.

What room was this... Dark mists came down over the bed, whirling like evil cyclones. As he forced himself to stay still, all the upheavals of his life burst forth. He saw again the faces and the blood of his accursed combats, and lines from a poem came back to him. Who had written them? He could not recall ever having read them. Then the convulsions stopped and Roberto spoke again.

"I should have realized that fate would watch over me and that you would be here to see me die, to hear me tell you why we have not loved one another."

His face was now the colour of ash, and Pietro thought death was imminent, but after a pause, Roberto spoke.

"Everything is in my will," he said. "The events, the facts, the consequences. But I want you to know that I have no remorse. I did what I did in all conscience, and I have not regretted it even once in all this time."

Raising his hand, he began to make a gesture that was like a blessing but then, overcome by exhaustion, he could not finish it.

"That's all," he said.

Pietro remained silent. He was hunting for a tenuous note that had echoed when Roberto fell silent. The intoxication of hatred swept through his soul like a storm, and he had an irrepressible urge to kill his insane father with his own hands. Then the urge receded. Receded with a force as natural and sovereign as the desire to kill that had gripped him just moments before, and when it was over, he knew that something had opened up inside him. The suffering and hatred were intact, but in his breast he felt the other man's death working upon him.

Finally, with a gleam in his eyes that Pietro did not understand, Roberto said, "Take care of your mother and your sister. That is our role, the only one."

He breathed in, slowly, looked at his son one last time, and died.

The lawyer asked to see them that evening. Pietro was sole heir to his father's property. It was dark when they went out onto the steps outside the lawyer's office. Pietro embraced his mother, kissed his sister. She looked at him in a way that said, *There you are*. He smiled and said, "See you tomorrow."

The next morning he went back to the villa with the courtyard.

He walked through all the rooms and examined all the works of art. The servants gradually emerged from their kitchens and their rooms, and as he walked by they muttered *Condoglianze*—but he also heard *Ecco*. Every painting was speaking to him, every sculpture murmuring a poem, and it was all as familiar and happy as if he had never hated or abandoned the spirits of his ancestors. Pausing at a painting where a weeping woman was holding Christ to her breast, he knew at last what it was that he had always loved, and he could foresee, ever so briefly, the great merchant he would become. That same afternoon, Roberto was buried under a blazing sun, in spite of the fact it was November, and the funeral was attended by everyone who was a famous artist or a man of influence in Rome. At the end of the mass they greeted Pietro, and he saw that they accepted that he had taken on the legacy. There was respect in their words of greeting, and he knew that his aspect had changed. The hooligan had died overnight and all he could think of was the art collection.

But his hatred was still alive.

At the cemetery, he saw a man standing behind Leonora, very upright, looking him straight in the eye. There was something he liked about his gaze. When Leonora came up to him, she said, "This is Gustavo Acciavatti. He has bought the big painting. He'll come to see you tomorrow."

Pietro shook hands with the man.

There was a brief silence.

Then Acciavatti said, "It's a strange November, isn't it?"

Early the next morning the lawyer asked Pietro to come back to his office on his own, and he handed him an envelope which contained two sheets of paper; Roberto had stipulated that only Pietro must ever read them.

"Anyone who violates this wish will undoubtedly suffer," he added.

When Pietro was outside he opened the envelope. On the first sheet, he read his father's confession; on the second, a poem he had written. Everything inside him was reeling, and he thought he had never been this close to hell.

At the villa, he came upon Acciavatti, in Leonora's company.

"I cannot sell you that painting," he said. "My father should not have sold it to you."

"I've already paid for it."

"I will reimburse you. But you can come and see it whenever you like."

The man came often, and they became friends. One day after viewing the painting, they sat down in the courtyard room and discussed the proposition Acciavatti had received to conduct the orchestra of Milan.

"I shall miss Leonora," said Pietro.

"My destiny is in Rome," replied Gustavo. "I will travel, but it is here that I shall live and die."

"Why are you condemning yourself to a place you could escape from? Rome is no more than a hell of tombstones and corruption."

"Because I have no choice," said the young maestro. "This painting binds me to the city as surely as you can leave it. You are rich and you can deal in art in any big city."

"I stay here because I do not know how to forgive," said Pietro. "So I wander through the decor of the past."

"Whom must you forgive?" asked Acciavatti.

"My father," said Pietro. "I know what he did but I don't know his reasons. And as I am not a Christian, I cannot forgive without understanding."

"So you are suffering the same martyrdom you have endured all your life."

"Do I have any other choice?"

"You do. People forgive more easily when they can understand—but when they cannot understand, they forgive in order not to suffer. Every morning you will forgive without understanding why, and you will have to start again the next morning, but at last you will be able to live without hatred."

Then Pietro asked one last question: "Why do you feel such a bond with the painting?"

"To answer that, I will have to tell you who I am."

"I know who you are."

"You only know what you see. But now I will tell you about my invisible side, and you will believe me, because poets always know the truth."

At the end of a long conversation that lasted until dawn on the following day, Pietro said, "So you knew my father."

"It was through him that I came to know this painting. I know what he did, and I know what it cost you. But I cannot tell you yet either the reasons for his act or why it is so important for us."

Was it the magic of the ancestor, as they looked at each other? Or a new affinity, born of the urgency of the night? Perhaps one minute had gone by since Clara had looked up at Pietro, and although she could name neither the events nor the men involved, she saw what was in his heart. She saw that he had had to fight, and give up; to suffer and forgive; that he had known hatred but had learned to love, yet the pain left him only to come back again, relentlessly; and this was something she knew, because she could sense it in Maria's heart as well, Maria who could not forgive herself for having given Eugénie the red bridge and the possibility of the exchange. What lay inside a heart was as legible to her as a text in capital letters, and she understood how she could bring them together and offer them peace, because she now had the power to tell stories by playing the piano. She placed the ancestor on the left-hand side of the keyboard, and when she played the first note it seemed to her that they were in tune. Then she imbued her fingers with all her desire to tell a story of forgiveness and union.

Pietro was weeping and the Maestro placed one hand on his heart. Clara was composing as she played, and her fingers gave birth to the miraculous notes that a little mountain girl, who wanted to speak to a little peasant girl from orchards and combes, drew from her own orphan's heart. How many throats have sung it since, in the fervour of departure? How many battles, how many banners, how many soldiers in the field since that day when Clara Centi composed the hymn of the last alliance? And while Maria was discovering in her dream a little girl with features of purest stone, and hearing her play, Pietro was weeping tears that burned and healed and made him murmur the lines his father had inscribed on the sheet of paper, until he saw the acid of hatred coalesce inside him in a point of unfathomable, blind pain, and the pain he had borne for sixty years disappeared forever.

> *May the fathers bear the cross*
> *May the orphans be blessed.*[4]

---

4. Ai padri la croce / Agli orfani la grazia.

VILLA ACCIAVATTI
Inner Elfin Council

"She is remarkably mature," said the Maestro, "and her heart is entirely pure."

"But she's only a child," said Petrus.

"Who composes like a fully grown genius," said the Maestro, "and who has her father's power."

"A child who has had no parents and who languished for ten years with an idiotic priest and a backward old woman," mumbled Petrus.

"There were trees and rocks during those ten years, and the stories of the old housekeeper, and of Paolino the shepherd," said the Maestro.

"An avalanche of benefits," sneered Petrus. "And why no mother? And some light in the darkness? She has the right to know. She cannot go forward blindly."

"We ourselves are going forward blindly," said the Council Head, "and I tremble for the girls."

"Knowledge feeds stories, and stories set powers free," said Petrus.

"What sort of fathers are we?" asked the Guardian of the Pavilion. "They are our daughters, and we are sharpening them like blades."

"Then leave the idea of the stories to me," said Petrus.

"Do as you like," said the Council Head.

Petrus smiled. "I'm going to need some moscato."

"I've a tremendous desire to try some," said Marcus.

"You will experience joy," said Petrus.

"Bodyguard, storyteller, and drinker. A regular little human being," said Paulus.

"I have no idea what is going on," said Alessandro, "but I am honoured."

FATHER FRANÇOIS
In This Land

ugénie died the following January night. She went
peacefully to sleep and did not wake up. Jeannette came
and knocked on her door on her way back from the milking,
surprised not to smell the aroma of the first coffee of the
day from the kitchen. She sent for the others. The father
was chopping wood in the pre-dawn darkness whose frozen
gloom seemed to shatter into sharp splinters of ice. But he
split the logs in his regular, placid manner, wearing his fur
hat and trapper's jacket, and the cold slid over him just as
the events in his life had done, biting deeply, and he paid it
no mind. All the same, from time to time, he looked up and
breathed the petrified mass of air, and thought to himself that
he knew this dawn, but was unable to remember why.

The mother came to fetch him. In the sparkling light of
the rising day her tears shone like sombre, liquid diamonds.
She gave him the news and gently took his hand. Even as his
heart was breaking, he thought she was more beautiful than
any woman, and he squeezed her hand in return, in a way that
was worth all the words. When the time came to decide who
must go and inform the little girl they did not hesitate, and
that was proof of the sort of man the father was. André—for

that was his name—went into Maria's room and found her more awake than a flight of swallows. He shook his head and sat down next to her, in the indescribable way he had that was the talent of a poor peasant made of a king's cloth—which showed that it was not by chance the little girl had ended up in that place a little over twelve years earlier, however coarse the strange farm might have seemed. For a few seconds Maria did not move, or even breathe, apparently. Then she gave a sorrowful gulp and, like all little girls, even those who speak to fantastical wild boars and mercurial horses, she collapsed in desperate sobs, of the kind that come so easily to a twelve-year-old, and so hard to a person of forty.

The desolation was immense in those lowlands, where for nine decades darkened by two wars Eugénie had lived, haunted by two deaths and honoured by innumerable acts of healing. The mass held two days later was attended by every able-bodied man and woman in the six cantons. Many of them had to wait outside the church until the end of the service, but all of them joined the funeral procession to the cemetery, where they spread out among the graves to hear the priest's prayer. In the terrible cold of noon, high black clouds hurried above the mourners, and they began to hope that those clouds would bring some fine snow and restore some of winter's more gentle side, instead of this relentless ice that wearied hearts with its endless burning; and all of them, in coats, gloves and black mourning hats, secretly invoked the snowflakes, thinking that this would honour Eugénie better than any words the priest would waste in his Latin of crypts and naves. But they all remained silent, and prepared to listen to the truth of faith, because Eugénie had been a pious woman and they too were pious, however bred for wild freedom the people in these lands of powerful nature might be. They looked at the priest as he cleared his throat, and in his immaculate chasuble, his fine belly offered to the cruelties of winter, he paused for a moment of inner contemplation before beginning to speak. His mass had not digressed into a liturgy of texts and sermons, and he had known how to honour an old woman gifted with the science of simples, and everyone had been moved for no other reason than that it rang true.

Father François was fifty-three years old. He had devoted his life to Jesus and to plants, without ever considering them to be anything other than a part of the vows he had taken at the age of thirteen. He did not know how the vocation had come to him, or whether its Christian form, which seemed the most natural, would also be the most appropriate. For the sake of this mission he had agreed to a number of sacrifices, not least of which was to give up the intuition that had made him speak to trees and paths in a language other than that of the Church. He had endured the absurdities of the seminary, and the dismay of a servant of the Lord who can find no one in his hierarchy who reflects his own way of feeling. But he had gone through it all as if walking through a sudden rain shower, finding shelter in the faith he had in the rough men who were his responsibility. And if he had not suffered from the incoherence he detected in the speech of authority, it was because he loved both his Lord and those to whom he preached His word.

Now on this day Father François looked at the community gathered in the modest cemetery, where they were laying to rest a poor old woman who had lived all her life on a farm, and he felt something well up inside him, demanding to be said out loud. He was not unquiet, yet troubled by a feeling that was similar to the one that had kept him from writing to his superiors after the miracles of the rosary and the letter from Italy, and which had shown him that it was preferable to speak to Maria; she had repeated the same words as her aunties with impenetrable ingenuousness, and this convinced him that although she might know more, there was no place for evil in her crystalline heart. The priest looked at the little wooded cemetery, with the rows of graves of so many ordinary people who had only ever known the country and its labours, and the thought suddenly occurred to him that the people who had lived in this land of forest and silence, where one could hope for no other abundance than that of rain and apples—these people had never suffered from the terrible isolation of the heart that he had witnessed all around him as a seminarian in the city. Thus, beneath the omen of clouds as big as oxen gathering above the cemetery that was more crowded with people than with lime trees, Father François understood he had been blessed with the gift that people of little means give to those who accept their sorrow and pain, and that there had not been a single evening when, as he consigned to paper the day's work on lemon balm and mugwort, he had not felt the warmth of men who, with their hands in the soil and their brows to the sun, have nothing more and can do nothing more than know the simple glory of being among others.

The memory of Eugénie took on another dimension, as if it had been multiplied to infinity, inscribed in unknown spaces and times which his spirit now probed through the prism of the old lady and a land as harsh and limpid as the skies of the beginning of time. He did not know how his perception had changed, but he had never viewed the world from such an angle as on this day of Eugénie's funeral, an angle that was vaster and more open, imbued with the ruggedness of a terrain both barren and full of grace.

Yes, everyone was there, an entire village, an entire region, an entire canton; they had put on their mourning clothes, which cost more than the wages they gleaned from the land, because it would have been inconceivable that day not to wear their kid gloves and their dresses of fine cloth. André Faure, in a black hat, stood next to the grave, hard-dug in the frozen earth, and Father François saw that the entire region was there behind him, that he was one of those men who embody the spirit and who are steadfast, through whom a community feels more sure of its existence and arrives more easily at pride in itself than through any decree or edict handed down by those on high. Maria stood to his left, in silence. He felt the corolla of a flower unfurl in his gut. He looked around him in this February light, so harsh even for a land that was used to the hardship of winter; he looked at these proud but humble men and women who stood in unspeaking contemplation, paying little heed to the hostile wind, and the flower continued to bloom until he began to explore a new continent of identity, a dizzying extension of himself about to be born despite the confines of this primitive country cemetery. An icy gust swept through the enclosure of the dead and caused a few hats to go flying, and the children scurried to catch them as quickly as they returned to their elders' sides, and Father François intoned the beginning of the ritual prayer.

> O Lord support us,
> All the day long of this troublous life,
> Until the shades lengthen and the evening comes,
> The busy world is hushed,
> The fever of life is over
> And our work is done.

He fell silent. The wind suddenly dropped and the cemetery was silent along with him, in a rustling of piety and ice. He wanted to speak, to go on with the prayer—*Then, Lord, in Your mercy / Grant us safe lodging, / A holy rest, and peace at the last, / through Jesus Christ, our Lord*—but he couldn't. By all the angels, he could not, for the simple reason, which will also show what sort of man that priest was, that he could not remember what the Lord Jesus Christ and all the saints together had to do with the story he owed his departed sister. There was only this corolla, expanding and rippling and eventually filling an entire place in his flesh that was both tiny and boundless, and all the rest was empty. Father François took a deep breath and searched inside himself for the anchor dropped by the petals. He found a perfume of violets and resin and a wave of sadness so intense that for a moment he felt nauseous. Then it was over. Finally everything was mute again. But he felt as if he were looking at the cemetery, the people, and the trees without a screen, as if someone had washed a windowpane for him, where previously there had been all the dust of the road. It was marvellous.

As he was silent for an unusually long time, people began to look at him, astonished. André, in particular, grasped something in the priest's physiognomy that made him stare for several seconds with the unfathomable gaze of the taciturn. Their eyes met. They had little in common, these two souls whom fate had brought together in these austere parts; the smiling pastor who loved Italian and wine had little in common with the heavy, secretive peasant who spoke only to Maria and the earth in his fields; nor finally, was there a great deal in common between the religion of the educated and the faith of country people, for they only understood each other out of their need to weave together the fabric of their community. But this day was different, and their eyes met as if for the first time. Now they were simply two men, one who brought together the earthly souls whose destiny was in this place, and the other who understood this, today, and was preparing, with his words, to honour the bond of love. Yes, love. What else do you think it was about, in this hour of fierce wind and black clouds, what else could carry a man so high above his roof? Because those who love do not show much concern for the Good Lord, as was the case on this day for the priest, who could no longer find either his Lord or his saints; but by the grace of a magic he knew nothing about he had just discovered what the world is when it is illuminated by love. One last time before he spoke he gazed out at the tide of humble souls who were waiting for him to give the signal of farewell; he looked at every face, every brow and, finally, he returned to himself and found a trace of the little boy who used to play in the tall grasses by the stream—and he spoke.

"My brothers, I have lived with you in this land for thirty years. Thirty years of work and troubles, thirty years of harvests and rain, thirty years of seasons and mourning, but also thirty years of births and weddings, and of masses at all hours, because you lead a virtuous life. This is your region, and it was given to you so that you might know the bitter taste of effort, and the silent reward of labour. It belongs to you without any title deed, because you have sacrificed the sap of your life for it, and entrusted it with your hope. It belongs to you unquestionably because your loved ones rest here in peace, and they paid tribute before you through their work. It belongs to you without a cross because you lay no claim to it, but thank it for considering you its servants and its sons. I have lived with you in this country and now, after thirty years of prayers and preaching, thirty years of sermons and services, I am asking you to accept me among you, and call me one of your own. I have been blind and I beg your forgiveness. You are great, while I am small, you are humble, whereas I am poor, and you are courageous while I am cowardly. You have little, you are people of the earth, you till the soil at dawn, along many furrows, and in hailstorms. You are the soldiers of a noble mission, for you feed others and make them prosper, and you will die beneath the shoots of the vine that will give your children a good vintage—as we stand by the grave of the woman who would have me embrace dust and stone, as you would, too, I beg you one last time to take me with you, because this morning I have understood the true intoxication to be found in serving others. And so once we have mourned Eugénie and shared our sorrow, we will look around us at this land that is ours, and which gives us trees and sky, orchards and flowers, and paradise here on earth as surely as this time belongs to us and it is possible to find in it the only consolation to which my heart can aspire from now on. The time of man is coming, and of this I am certain: neither death, nor life, nor the spirits, nor the present, nor the future, nor the stars, nor the abyss, nor any creature, nothing will keep from love those who live in our land, and by our land. The time of man is coming—men who will know the nobility of forests and the grace of trees, men who will know how to contemplate and heal and, lastly, how to love. May they know glory, for the centuries of centuries. *Amen*."

And the congregation replied, "*Amen*."

They looked at each other, trying to digest the eccentricity of the prayer. They tried to remember the words in the right order, but it was scraps of the usual refrain that came instead, and they had trouble making up their minds about what had actually gone on during that unexpected flight of fancy. And yet they knew. Like every word that draws on the beauty of the world for its syntax and its rhymes, the priest's homily had caressed each of them with a powerful poetry. For all it was fearful cold among the lime trees, they warmed themselves at an intangible fire that contained the blessings of their life there—the streams, the roses and the sky's sorcery, and it was as if the lightest of feathers were gently stroking a wound in each of them, a wound they had grown used to living with but which they thought might some day be healed, when the skin closed over for good. Perhaps ... At least now they knew a prayer that was anything but Latin; it was like the warm landscapes they each held tenderly locked away inside themselves. There was a fragrance of the vineyard and a few crushed violets, and there were skies washed with ink above the solitude of the hollows. This was their life, just as this time belonged to them, and as they began to disperse, and struck up conversations, and greeted one another, and hugged, and made ready to head back home, for the first time they felt they were standing more firmly on their feet—because there are not many men who understand right from the start that there is no other Lord than the benevolence of the land.

Father François looked at Maria. As the corolla reached the innermost recesses of his heart, it confirmed the news: it was thanks to this little girl that they had flourished and known their good fortune, thanks to her that any obstacle obstructing the flow of the stream could be avoided, and thanks to her, finally, that there were seasons that wound around her in a spiral of transfigured time. He looked up and saw black clouds moored to the wharf of the sky as surely as any ship's cordage.

When André placed his hand on the priest's shoulder Father François felt a magnetic flux go through him, and through it they agreed that events were occurring to which their reason could attribute no meaning, but their hearts could, without a doubt, and all their love as well. André withdrew his hand, while the stunned crowd of peasants looked at these two brothers who had just found one another, and they waited, trembling, to see what would happen next. They, too, took a good look at the clouds, and to all of them it seemed that the clouds were saying something unfriendly, but what was happening at the cemetery was worth any danger they might face. And yet it looked as if it were all over, because Father François was blessing them, and motioning to the gravediggers to begin shovelling the earth. Maria, next to her father, was smiling; he had removed his hat and was looking skyward, his eyes half-closed, like a man whose face has been warmed by the sun when there is still a hard frost. Then the little girl stepped towards the grave, and from her pocket she took some pale hawthorn flowers; they fell slowly onto the coffin, and the wind did not carry them away.

André Faure, however, did not seem ready to leave the cemetery. He motioned to the priest; Maria was also looking at the sky as it grew strangely darker—the clouds were not obscuring the light but making it dark and dazzling. The priest turned around and looked in the direction André was pointing. On the southern horizon, beyond the wall of flat stones, a black column of smoke or rain was forming. It was moving slowly but in unison with the clouds as they sank lower towards the earth, and it was as if the horizon and the firmament were drawing in, and they would all have been surrounded were it not for the village backing onto the little mountain: they could still escape that way if the sky continued to fall upon the fields. Maria stood closer to her father and they exchanged a look. What did he see there? No one could say. But it was clear that there was no more time for wondering—the hour had come to learn to prepare for combat. The men—at least those who, in these parts, had a certain authority—formed a circle around André, while the rest of the assembly waited in the wind. Father François stood to his right and this meant, or so everyone understood it, without surprise: *I support him*. André began to speak, and they knew these were serious times.

A few minutes later each man went on his way, to carry out his prescribed task. Those who were headed north, east and west hurried down the road without a backward glance. The others split up among the farms, or congregated in the sanctuary of the church, where before long they were brought mulled wine and thick blankets. Finally, a dozen or so men escorted the little girl, the mother, and the three old ladies to Marcelot's farm; they thought it might be more defensible because there was a wall around it, and it was set high in the village and afforded the best view over all the surrounding countryside. They sat the women and the child around the same table to be found in every farmhouse, and they busily began to cover it with everything that might ensure the business of their physical and spiritual recovery.

The hour before battle is a short one, and Maria knew this, and smiled at Lorette Marcelot. She was an imposing woman who bore her stoutness proudly before her, with a majesty that came from the slowness of her gestures. From her splendid youth she had kept an unlined face, and copper hair arranged in a chignon that caught everyone's eye like a beacon, and one never wearied of gazing at this fine countrywoman; her muted, endlessly rolling gait was restful to hearts that were cut to the quick by the boundless hardship of the land. Maria loved to cling to her petticoats and breathe in the lemon verbena Lorette carried in little pouches sewn under her skirts; it wafted a romance of trees and pantries, enough to make you wonder what more you could possibly desire in the way of refinement round these parts, for all that they were filled with simple folk.

"Well, little one, that was a fine funeral," she said to Maria, giving her a smile.

Those were the appropriate words which, when spoken by that pale smooth-skinned face, calmed the sorrow and thereby erased its darkness. Lorette set before Maria a hunk of cheese from her cows, and a bowl of steaming milk. Maria smiled back at her. The room smelled of coffee, mingled with a predominant aroma of roasting fowl; the men had stayed outside while the three old women and the mother recovered in silence from the day's emotions; they looked at La Marcelotte who rounded her shoulders as she prepared to slice the bread, with a languor that made every movement more valiant and proud. It was a time for women. The time for women who know what men must find at home before the fight. So they inhabited every inch of space in the home, they embraced every joist, every deepest recess, and they brought in reinforcements until the home was nothing more than a throbbing breast where one sensed the purest elements of their sex. And the farm was filled to bursting with this womanly radiance as they stretched their bodies to the very ceiling beams, which seemed rounder and more welcoming as a result; the farm at last came to life, and all who entered would know that woman was sovereign there, and offered all the pleasures and joys on earth.

ALESSANDRO
The Pioneers

At dawn following the night of the great healing, Alessandro, Paulus, and Marcus set off together for France. Clara had not slept. It was Eugénie's last day on earth and it was raining in Rome when they all said farewell. On the steps outside the house Leonora embraced Clara sadly. Pietro, by her side, was silent and impassive. Petrus seemed more rumpled than ever.

"I don't know what you will find in the village," said the Maestro, "but along the way you must be invisible."

"Invisible when all of Rome is under surveillance?" asked Leonora.

"Pietro's men are waiting for them outside," he replied; "they will leave the city in secret."

Everyone embraced. But before leaving, Sandro knelt in front of Clara, and, his eyes level with hers, he whispered, "Some day I'll tell you the story of a woman I knew called Teresa." He looked up at the Maestro. "I wonder…" he murmured.

They went away in the rain. But before they disappeared around the corner of the lane, Alessandro looked back and waved. Was it the power of the ancestor? It seemed to Clara she was seeing him for the first time.

Clara stayed at the villa with Petrus; ordinarily, he would doze off the moment they were on their own. But that morning he looked at her dreamily and she thought he was more sober than usual.

"Who is Teresa?" she asked.

"What do you know about ghosts?" he asked in reply.

"They live with us," she said.

"No," he answered, "we live with them and we don't let them leave. For that reason, we have to tell their story properly."

She didn't reply. Something about him had changed.

"I can't tell you about Teresa today," he said, "but I will tell you a story that will lead to hers." He sighed. "But first of all I need a little drink."

"Maybe it will be better if you don't," she said.

"I don't think so. Human beings fall apart when they drink, but I become stronger." He got up and poured himself a glass of a deep red wine. "I must be the only one whose gifts are revealed by amarone," he said. "Why is that? Mystery and mists."

"But what are you all?" she asked.

"What do you mean, what are we?"

"The Maestro, Paulus, Marcus and you. You're not men, are you?"

"Men? Of course not," he said, dismayed. "We are elves."

"Elves?" she echoed, stunned. "There are alcoholic elves?"

He looked hurt.

"I'm not an alcoholic, I'm just intolerant of alcohol. As

are we all, anyway. Must I, for all that, deprive myself of something that is good?"

"Does everyone drink in your world?"

"Of course not," he said, looking rather lost. "That is why I am here."

"You are here for the moscato?"

"I am here for the moscato and for the conversation of human beings."

"Don't elves have interesting conversations?"

"Of course they do," he said. He wiped his brow. "It's more complicated than I thought," he said.

"What do you elves do during the day?" she asked, in a noble effort to help him.

"A lot of things, of course, a lot of things … Poetry, calligraphy, walks in the woods, stone gardens, fine pottery, music. We celebrate twilight, and mists. We drink tea. Rivers of tea." This final remark seemed to fill him with sadness. "I cannot tell you how much tea we drink," he concluded, drowning in melancholy.

"And conversation?"

"Conversation?"

"Is it like with the Maestro?"

"No, no. Most of us do not have such lofty aspirations. We are ordinary elves. There are feast days, too. But it's not the same."

"What isn't the same?"

"No one tells stories. We recite pages of poetry, we sing hymns in abundance. But there are never stories about ghosts or truffle hunting."

He seemed to find new vigour in the reference, made the

previous evening, to an endless story, begun by a kitchen boy, that was set in the forests of Tuscany.

"So you're here for the wine and the stories about truffle hunting?"

"The Maestro made me come because of the stories. But wine also helps things along."

"Were you bored up there?" she continued.

"I wouldn't exactly call it *up there*," he muttered. "And I was a little bored, but that was not the most important thing. For a long time I was a good-for-nothing. And then one day the Maestro asked me if I wanted to come and be among you. I came, I drank, and I stayed on. I am made for this world. That is why I can tell you Alessandro's story. Because we are brothers in dissatisfaction."

"The Maestro asked you to tell me Alessandro's story?"

"Not exactly," he replied. "In fact, I'm the one who suggested we tell you your own story, which implies a lot of other ones, too, and if you would just stop asking questions, I will start with Alessandro's."

And elegantly sitting himself down in the armchair where normally he would be snoring, he poured a second glass and began his story, while an unusual steeliness was visible beneath the roundness of his features, and his voice took on a velvety-smooth tone she had never heard.

"Alessandro's story begins a little over forty years ago in a fine house in L'Aquila, where he lived with his mother, a singular woman who was born for travel and who was wasting away from the sadness of having no horizon beyond her own garden. Her only joy came from her youngest son. Because Alessandro was more handsome than heaven and earth. In all the province no one had ever seen a more perfect face, and it would seem that the boy's character reflected his looks, because he learned to speak splendid Italian, with a phrasing no one had ever heard in that region, and from earliest childhood he displayed a natural talent for music and drawing that far exceeded what the teachers usually saw. By the age of sixteen he could learn nothing more from them. When he was twenty, he left for Rome with his mother's hopes and tears, and went to stay with Pietro: he had heard about him through his late father, who sold the Oriental carpets brought through Abruzzo by the northern route to rich Romans."

He paused and poured a third glass.

"You are good at telling stories," said Clara.

"Better than your old housekeeper?"

"Yes, but your voice isn't as nice."

"It's because I'm thirsty," he said, taking another sip of amarone. "Do you know the secret of a good story?"

"Wine?" she ventured.

"Lyricism and nonchalance with the truth. However, one must not trifle with the heart."

Then, looking affectionately at the ruby colour of his glass, he continued: "So Alessandro headed for Rome, in the fire and chaos of his first youth."

"I can see an image," she said.

"Can you see into my mind?"

"I can see what you are talking about."

"How extraordinary. And without drinking."

"It is my father's power?"

"It is your father's power, but it is also your gift. This

painting is the first one Alessandro showed to Pietro, who had never seen anything like it. He knew the art market and he knew that he was in the presence of a miracle. The canvas did not represent anything. Ink was tossed in elegant lines that rose towards the upper edge of the canvas like a fork with three uneven prongs, lower on the outside and connected at the base. The strangest thing was that when you looked carefully at the prongs it was possible to see that the lines could only be drawn in one direction. So Pietro saw that it was a particular form of writing, and he wondered how Alessandro had learned the language. But when he asked him, he saw that he didn't understand. You wrote *mountain* just like that, without knowing what your calligraphy meant? he asked. I wrote *mountain*? replied Sandro. He was stunned. He came from L'Aquila and had only the vaguest idea of the outside world. But he had drawn the sign for mountain and Pietro knew how to read it, because he had been to the country of these signs and he knew how to decipher some of them. Just the way all our people can decipher it, because it's a language we adopted a long time ago, and because the mountain stones are very important to us. Pietro asked Sandro if he had any other canvases. He did. And in the months that followed, he painted many more. They were magnificent.

"He had come to Rome a poor man, but two years later he was richer than his father had ever been. And everyone adored him. The women with love, the men with friendship, and he was the most charming guest and companion. I don't know when he got any sleep. You never saw him leave the dinner table. He would talk to Pietro until the early hours of the morning, and by daybreak he was at his easel, giving birth to miracles of ink and charcoal. He did not need a big studio; he lived at the Villa Volpe and worked in the courtyard room—the painting you know wasn't there yet; he only used a corner of the room, where he left his brushes and where he painted, staring at the white wall. Of course he was already drinking a great deal. But everyone always drank a lot in those circles, and Sandro was painting and laughing and no one saw any end in sight. Then he met Marta."

Clara saw a woman in Petrus's mind, a gaunt face with dark circles under her eyes; oddly enough, this gave her composure and grace. Her curls were of a very pale Venetian blond and her eyes a gentle Delft blue; in her clear gaze was a boundless melancholy.

"She was older than he was, and married to someone else. Sandro had loved many women, but Marta was a kindred spirit. In spite of her love for this splendid young man, however, she was languishing from a sorrow she had known all her life, and many people saw this as the explanation for what happened. But I don't believe the cause was what they think it was, because it was also during this period that Pietro showed Sandro the painting that is now in your room. Later he would recall how Sandro stood there, speechless, and in the month that followed, he did not paint. He shut himself away in his studio and never picked up a brush. It was as if he no longer believed in what he was painting. At night, he drank."

He suddenly seemed to remember that he, too, was thirsty, and he poured another glass.

"After he saw Pietro's painting, Sandro did paint one last canvas," he continued. "It was the colour of flax, and on either side of a big splash of ink there were two horizontal lines made with a scarlet pastel crayon. In some places the ink was very black and dull, in others it was brown, almost lacquered, and certain powdery, shifting reflections made it look as if the dust of a forest bark had been added."

Although this canvas was as abstract as the first one, neither representing anything nor suggesting any form of writing, in the motionless journey of ink deployed in depth and not over distance Clara recognized the bridge she had already seen when she had plunged into the waves of Maria's power, and she was astonished that a dark spot with neither contours nor features could also be a red bridge suspended between two shores. "The bridge," she said.

"The bridge," Petrus said, "which focuses the powers of our plan, and connects our Pavilion to this world. Sandro had recreated its soul as surely as if he had crossed it, even though he had never seen it. How could this be? You can see it because you are your father's daughter. But Sandro? Just as he had written the sign for mountain without knowing it, he had captured the quintessence of an unknown place with the silk of his brushes, and those who knew the bridge were stunned by this miracle that recreated it without representing it.

"Then Alessandro burned all his canvases, and everyone thought he had lost his mind because two women he loved had died in the space of two days. Marta had thrown herself in the Tiber, and at the same time we learned of the death of Marta's sister, Teresa, whom Sandro had loved with a friendship as intense as any that can exist between two flesh-and-blood creatures. Later on I will tell you about the circumstances of her death. The fact remains that Sandro burned his entire oeuvre, then he left Rome and went to his brother, the priest in Santo Stefano, where he stayed for a year, and after that he became a recluse in his aunt's house in L'Aquila, where he lived up on the third floor until the piano brought him to you, nine years after his return to Abruzzo. How are we to explain it? Sandro had only ever loved, or been loved, by weeping women, and that same melancholy lies in the heart of the sons of weeping mothers who then go on to love other weeping women. But I don't think experience is as important as who we are inside, and I think that Sandro's true story is not one of a man who has been burned by love, but rather of a man who was born on the wrong side of the bridge and who has been seeking to cross. This is what his first and last canvases tell us." He sighed. "No one understands better than I do the feelings of people who are unsuited to the world into which they have been born. Some have ended up in the wrong body, others in the wrong place. Their misfortune is blamed on a flaw in their personality, when in fact they have merely gone astray in a place they shouldn't have been."

"Then why doesn't the Maestro make him cross the bridge?"

"I don't think he can," said Petrus. "We are pioneers, and we must forge new alliances. But the bridges must be built in the right place at the right time."

"Do elves paint?" asked Clara.

"Yes," said Petrus, "we are calligraphers and painters, but we only depict what we see before us. Just as we only sing or write poems to move our souls—something we do very well, I might mention. But that is not enough to transform reality."

"What does it take to transform reality?"

"Stories, of course."

She observed him for a moment. "I thought elves were different," she said.

"Ah, yes, elves, fairies, wizards in folklore, all that sort of thing. I suppose even the Maestro does not correspond to your idea?"

"A bit more. Tell me about the world you were born into."

"What do you want to know?"

"What does it look like?"

"It's a world of mists."

"You live in a fog?"

"No, no, we can see perfectly well. The mists are alive, they let us see what we need to see and they change according to need."

"Whose need?"

"The needs of the community, of course."

"The community of elves?"

"The community," he echoed, "the elves, trees, stones, ancestors, animals."

"Everyone lives together?"

"Everyone *is* together. Separation is a sickness."

Then, sadly pouring another glass, "Alas, that paradise is lost now."

With his eyes slightly crossed, he added, "I'm good at telling human stories, but I think the Maestro will do a better job explaining the life of elves to you than I can."

She shrugged. "What I feel doesn't seem to interest him," she said. Imitating Acciavatti she added, "Come now, play, play, I'll turn the pages."

Petrus burst out laughing. "High-ranking elves are not

known for their sentimentality," he said. "But he is more concerned about you than you know." He paused for a moment, as if thinking about something. Then he gave a quiet laugh. "I'm dead drunk now," he said. And after a moment's silence, "But I've done my job."

She wanted to ask him some more questions, but he stood up, and struggling somewhat to stay on his feet, he said with an enormous yawn, "Let's go and rest. The days ahead will be turbulent."

Clara did not sleep all day. The rain fell relentlessly over the city, and on the far side of her dreams she was keeping watch over Maria. I won't see Eugénie again, she thought, and she summoned tears which did not come to unburden her, either that day, or in the evening, when they ate a light meal at the villa before, drowsy and lugubrious, they endured the night. Early the next morning, she did not rise until Maria's father went to his daughter's bed—she knew, without being told, why he had come. But the tears still evaded Clara even as she followed the little French girl's wanderings through the cold rooms and the hard icy fields. Then it was again bedtime, after a day of idleness to which anything would have been preferable, even battle. Another day lost between two eras passed, more long hours when she was alone again, and even Petrus did not show up; but at dinner, which she ate with Leonora, the Maestro put in a brief appearance.

"The funeral will be held tomorrow," he said, "and you must speak to Maria."

"I cannot speak her language," said Clara.

He left without replying.

Then morning came and it was time to consign Eugénie to her grave. It was the first day of February, and, on waking from a gloomy night, in which it seemed to Clara that she had neither slept nor been awake, she saw that the ancestor had disappeared. She ran first to the empty lunch room, then to the piano room. The ancestor was on the left-hand side of the keyboard. Petrus was snoring in the wing chair. The Maestro was waiting for her.

"He was here when I arrived," he said, pointing to the ancestor.

In silence, they followed the preparations on the farm for the funeral. Then everyone set off for the church where the coffin of their beloved friend was waiting. Clara was impressed by the crowd gathered outside the church, how many they were, how quiet and thoughtful. During mass, she could hear a little bit of Latin, but above all she saw in the people's gazes that they were pleased with the service, and she discovered a growing interest in the character of the priest, whom hitherto she had thought was made of the same stuff as her own priest. Father Centi was a scrupulous and dreary man: you were grateful that he was not bad, yet you couldn't exactly thank him for being good; in his dealings with everyone and everything there was something missing, which left him incapable of meanness but did not make him capable of greatness. Now on seeing Father François preaching from his pulpit with unsuspected frankness and simplicity, she was surprised by an intuition that made her follow him with her gaze when he walked at the head of the funeral procession, and she went on observing him when he stood before the tombstones and the country people and began the homily, competing with the icy onslaught of the wind. The Maestro translated his words for her, and in his speech she sensed a familiar music which had as little to do with her own priest as the monotonous musical scores had to do with the generosity of peaches and steppes.

"There's a man for you," said the Maestro, with respect in his voice.

Those were the words that best described the emotion that was continually growing inside her. At the same time, André made a gesture towards the good priest which precisely transcribed their feeling, and Clara said to herself again, *there's a man for you.*

"*A loro la gloria, nei secoli dei secoli*, amen," translated the Maestro.

Then he fell silent. But after a time during which they watched people greeting each other, speaking effusively, the Maestro said, "There will indeed be surprises before the end, and there will be unnatural allies."

Then, his voice now graver, "Look."

And she saw the black wall.

"The first battle," he said.

She peered at the gigantic wheel slowly advancing towards the village.

"A storm?" she asked. "There aren't any soldiers?"

"There are soldiers to the rear, but they don't really count."

"Is Raffaele's leader commanding the clouds?"

"Yes," said the Maestro, "the clouds and the elements of the atmosphere."

"And can you do that?"

"All our kind can do that."

"Then why are you leaving Maria all on her own?"

"We have always protected the village. But if we want to know her strength, we have to refrain from intervening in the battle. It was a difficult decision, but necessary, if we are to gauge her powers. They have never yet been dissociated from our own."

"And if she dies?"

"If she dies, it will mean that we have been wrong from the start, and there will be little hope that we can survive this war, either as individuals or as a species."

Clara looked one more time at the monstrosity lurking on the horizon of the southern lands.

"It's a colossus," said the Maestro, "but it's only a very small part of what the enemy can create. We were right to think they would not take our wager seriously."

"But there is a traitor informing them."

"There is a traitor who followed one of our people and who learned about Maria."

"Who followed the grey horse."

"Who followed the Head of our Council, who appeared as a grey horse, because in this world we can only keep one of our essences. He's a grey horse, but he's also a man, and a hare."

"Why did the Head of the Council want to see Maria?"

Then, although she did not understand why, she knew the answer.

"Because he is her father."

"And your father's power of prescience is great," said the Maestro, "and goes hand in hand with his power of vision. Now look at the enemy's power, try to understand its nature and its causes."

"It is distorting the climate."

"And each of its distortions feeds off the others. Marcel was meant to die. When forces are distorted, changes in balance are created. Even when the intention is pure, as was Eugénie's."

"But how are we to resist if we cannot use the same weapons?"

"That is the whole point of the alliance."

Silently, they observed the men who gathered around Father François and André, then dispersed in orderly fashion, some helping their families into a cart, some leading women and children into the church for protection, and some heading along the road to the Marcelot farm with the men from the first circle. The farm was bigger but also more cluttered than that of Maria, who was greeted by a woman with copper hair whom Clara immediately took to. They sat down around a big table spread with bread, honey, and the summer's plum jam, and, while La Marcelotte and her daughter prepared the meal, time became sluggish and seemed to contract.

Outside, the men were deep in conversation, and saw their defeat looming larger, but inside, it was as if a gentle mood hung over them in the form of a floating reminiscence, stitched with old embroideries and faint smiles, a serpentine stream of tall grasses, and tombs no longer graced by flowers. What trail am I following? wondered Clara, her gaze riveted to the slow gestures of the woman with the flaming hair. She could have spent her life there and never tired of this wonder; then, when she saw Lorette's gesture as she placed a glass of warm milk in front of Maria, she understood the nature of her wonder, because the gesture had the same texture as Leonora's when she placed her hand on Clara's on her eleventh birthday.

"One day you will go back to your community," said the Maestro. "I am sorry you were taken away from it. But the women are waiting for you and will welcome you among them."

Long minutes passed while the village prepared for the siege.

"What must I say to Maria?" asked Clara.

"You will find the words," said the Maestro, "and I will translate."

"Whom does the Governor serve?" she asked again.

"One of our kind."

"Where does he come from?"

"From my own house."

"What is his name?"

"Unlike men we do not have names we are given and which we keep. But since our friends have a fantasy about ancient Rome, let us say that his name is Aelius."

"What does he want?"

And without waiting to hear his reply she said, "The end of human beings."

PAVILION OF THE MISTS
Inner Elfin Council

"Petrus is going to have to sober up a bit."

"But his storytelling is never better than when he's drunk."

"There is no doubt that he is sharpening Clara's clairvoyance. What a terrifying wager."

"But the powers of both of them are still growing. And the people to whom we entrusted Maria are impressive."

"Father François grew up in one day."

"He's been an ally from the start."

"Their sense of the land is as fierce as their courage."

"The two go hand in hand."

ANDRÉ
For the Land

In the distance the wall was growing. From the farmyard the men could see more clearly what was on its way to confront them, and it was a thing they would never have thought possible: the horizon had been transformed into a mountain connecting earth and clouds, and it was coming towards them, rumbling, swallowing up the fields and trees. André was silent. There is no courage without a difficult choice, no character that is not forged by the act of choosing even more than by victory. He looked at the monster striding over the land to destroy his daughter's power, and the shafts of evil coiling in tight eddies, all in a line to form the avalanche, and he did not want to think what would be left of the land by the time the tempest stopped roaring. But André also sensed that the enemy was losing speed as it came into contact with Maria's magic, and the uncertainty of the situation convinced him of the need to act swiftly.

Someone behind him shouted out. It was Jeannot, pointing into the distance to a spot expanding on the surface of the fields, and they understood that it was water, and that the valley was flooding, the waters rising towards the village as fast as the racing horses of the storm. And although the lowlands, despite their name, were located above the high valley, they suspected, since none of this was natural, that the tongues of water lapping at the land to the south might well advance as far as the houses and cut off any retreat, and this worried André and the others—fellows you might not be able to count on to make a psalm sound spiritual, but who well knew how to avoid being cornered like rats.

The men standing on the mound at Marcelot's farm all knew how to drink the wine at a battue because the life they led was a hard one from the moment they saw the dawn, and they had learned from both their labour and their years. And André's first lieutenant, Marcelot, epitomized all the qualities with which the lowlands fashioned their liegemen. When he took a wife, he defied those who warned him that his heart's delight was ten years older than he was, and that she'd already been married to a man whom she had loved and who had died young of the fever. But Marcelot had persisted with that mute form of obstinacy which conceals all the treasures of intuition, because he knew that this woman was destined for him above all others; he knew with an almost mystical knowledge when he was enthralled by her slowness as she made her way through the world, for his days were transformed into an epic of splendour.

Marcelot had not had his head filled with neat ideas and words at school, of the sort which enabled you to express what the body was feeling so that you could share it with others; and he would have been stunned if someone had explained to him that he loved his Lorette because she slowed the natural flow of things, and through the seeming indolence of her ways she offered him the leisure of admiring them to the full. He was not, however, silent and contemplative like André, far from it, and he was appreciated above all for the maxims with which he qualified events and chores. You had to see him uncork a bottle from his cellar, always a fine vintage, the way he'd sniff the cork while dishing out the day's dictum with a mixture of seriousness and derision, the hallmark of a pure heart. He knew that words have a weight that goes beyond their author and, consequently, he both respected and mocked the words he uttered; in the same way, he would take his woodcutter's knife and hew slices of saucisson so enormous that a guest would take no fewer than three bites to swallow them, and he would dish out his precepts, punctuating his speech with papal nods of the head followed by a childish laugh (*fear doesn't avoid danger*, his favourite, gave half the people in the country a headache, however, because they weren't sure of having fully understood). Then he'd slap a guest on the shoulder and away they'd go in a conversation that would last as long as their desire to drink and tell hunting stories which, as everyone knows, lack all plausibility or proper conclusion. But at regular intervals he would look over at Lorette as she transcended the space in the room with her slow sleeping dancer's movements, and at the intersection of the raw nerves in his body he could sense the magic that turned him to crystal, however mud-grimed his feet or calloused his huge hands might be. Love, again; will anything else ever be the subject of these pages devoted to the rebirth of a world that was lost with the ages?

Marcelot, baptized Eugène, commonly known as Gégène, took his eyes off the flood and looked at the sky behind the farm. André followed his gaze. They glanced at each other, then the lieutenant said to his commander, with a meaningful air: "That sky looks full of snow."

André nodded.

A sky full of snow. It was time to decide. No father wants to endanger his child. But André knew that it was futile to imagine he could protect the little lass by keeping her within the four walls of the farmhouse, and he sighed the sigh of those who love and must resolve themselves to letting a child grow up. Then, both resigned and hopeful, he sent for Maria. There was not much time left. The black wall had stopped just beyond the big fallow fields, and you could sense it was just waiting for an order to leap forward. It was a fortress. It was made of rain, whirlwinds, and storms, and for all that they were liquid, they seemed as solid as rock; at their base, the water, dark and bristly with spikes, had spread half a foot above the earth. And it was all keening in a way that pierced your guts, because you knew what was brewing in that evil soup was a hateful cry that, in time, would cause the most resolute souls to weaken.

Bundled up in several layers of warm clothes and wearing a big felt hat stuffed with a scarf, Maria went to join her father, and gazed at the enemy with a strangely impassive look. Her own expression grim, Angèle pulled her heavy cape tighter around her. The entire surface of the land seemed sticky with ice. They watched as the temperature dropped, as the cold stirred the invisible air so the movement was perceptible to the naked eye. But just as the abominable rains smelled of death and evil floods, the cold air, crueller with every passing second, pierced the skin with the poison of unnatural ice. André ordered blankets to be handed out, and they all wrapped themselves up thoroughly, then gathered around Maria and Angèle to form a delegation; at its heart stood a little girl not yet thirteen years of age and an old lady who was almost a hundred, and if a bird had happened to fly over Gégène's farmyard that day, it would have gazed down at twelve tiny dots facing a dark rampart of a thousand feet. Marcelot nodded his head in turn as he scanned every corner of the sky, and he summed up fairly well what the others had already thought when he said: "Seasons against seasons."

And they knew he was referring to the seasons of the devil, and those of the Good Lord.

As for André, he did not believe the struggle had anything to do with matters of faith. He called to Father François and asked him to go back and look after those who had stayed in the church. The priest kissed Maria and wondered if he would ever see her again in this orchard life, which he at last knew was eternally theirs, and he blessed the old lady, putting all his heart into providing some comfort, if nothing else. Then he set off for the church, placing himself in the hands of fate. The men waited, not saying a word, observing the column of destruction as it grunted and growled like a dog, and God knows what they were thinking, every single one of them, men who'd never set foot outside their own region, and had seen no more of life than the one or two fields mowed into windrows. But André was looking at Maria. He had known that her vision went beyond the visible, ever since one dawn when he had welcomed a survivor as a daughter into his arms, and he had felt a strange tingling that initially blurred his vision then burst into a field of images where he could see scenes from the past as sharply as if they had just occurred. Similarly, he had glimpsed the paths of the future in such great quantity that he could not make out any one of them clearly, but later some returned to his memory, the day when what they depicted actually happened—such as when the little girl placed her hand on Eugénie's shoulder in the room where Marcel lay dying.

"I need to see," he said to Maria.

She pointed at the dark wall, which had fallen silent.

"You don't need a miracle," she said.

André nodded, accepting a new piece of the puzzle that had been taking shape for nearly thirteen years, and which echoed what the earth had been telling him on that day when their fortune was being decided. So he placed his hand on his little girl's shoulder and, instilling in his silent, regal gaze that depth of feeling that is called the grace of fathers, he said, "Don't be afraid, I just want to see."

She went closer to him and put her hand on his shoulder. Like Eugénie before him, the father reeled from the shock. Such were the powers of the little girl, who exercised the forces of nature to catalyse her own strength as a human being. Her gaze took in the territory of the struggle with a masterly understanding, of the sort no commander-in-chief, all through the history of armies, had ever possessed, and André saw everything within a huge radius, every detail finely drawn, as if crafted by a demented miniaturist. Then Maria withdrew her hand and the contact was broken. But he had seen. It was enough. He called to Gégène and the men tightened the circle, while Angèle went and sat to one side, keeping watch with her eye of the Lord over the manoeuvres of the storm-clad devil.

He told them what he knew: "In the fallow field to the east, there are strange horsemen, perhaps a hundred of them; to the south, something is lying in ambush behind the wall, and that's the real danger; but behind us there is also some odd movement in the sky."

Gégène scratched his nose, which was as frozen as the icicles hanging from the drainpipes. "Strange, how?"

"I don't know what they're riding."

"Odd, how?"

"A lot of mist."

"That is where I must go," said Maria.

André nodded.

"The church?" asked Gégène.

"In the firing line of their first strike."

"Your orders?"

"Four lads to defend it, two will stay here, the three others will go to the clearing with Maria and me."

"Where do you want me to go?"

"To the church, if you can leave your wife with Jeannot and the mayor."

"Done."

Then André turned to Maria. "Your orders?"

And she answered, "No one is to remain indoors."

"General evacuation," said André to his men. "Let's go."

They split up, as agreed. But before going any further, it is time to tell who these warriors were, as they set off to force an entire region to leave their farms behind, because if you believe this is little more than mere happenstance, you have been failing to grasp something they know as surely as the sky is about to fall on their heads. In reality, there is only fiction, there are only stories, and even then, one has to know how to separate the noble wheat from the chaff. As it happened, their kind obstinately smelled the good wood of the forest and the grass steaming in the early hours of virgin dawns, and it was not only that they had received the legacy of a countryside that had been preserved, that had seen the last of the blood heirs, but knew nothing yet of the lackeys of money: they were still conscious of the fact that what they owned surely deserved to be told in a story somewhere. Let others try to make sense of it. Gégène summed it up fairly well on bidding Lorette farewell, once he'd made her and the others leave the farm; he kissed her and said, *It'll be worth a song, at any rate*.

So, there were ten men.

There was Marcelot, who hunted, tilled the fields, drank, feasted, and jeered like any man forever protected by the sanctuary of love, and in that respect he was basically just one of those great mystics with his feet planted on the ground; let's watch him as he pats the priest on the shoulder and conveys the orders of Maria's father, and we'll see a man who would make a fine soldier—yet his mind is somewhere up in the stars.

Then there was Jeannot, who was reminded of another war and who was discovering inside himself the roots of a mad hopefulness that made him want to believe that the present hour might appease the torture of memories, and he could again see the paths of his life opening up before him, paths that had come to an abrupt end the day he saw his brother die. Every morning he got up to face this wound that no one could see, and he drank his wine and laughed at stories, and his soul was more bare than a rosebush in winter.

Then there was Julot, born Jules Lecot not long after a first great war and long before a second one, from which he was saved in the nick of time by the age limit; he was the mayor of this lost, enchanted village. He was in charge of the region's roadmenders, and everyone agreed that you'd be hard put to find a better mayor, for a reason that was even more elementary than the first days of creation, namely that he was the best piqueur in the six cantons, and that fact alone—for the position requires perseverance, cunning, enthusiasm and the patience of a saint—was enough to propel a man into the mayor's office, it was obvious, because those were the very qualities you needed to govern a place. Add to that his intimate knowledge of every corner of every thicket, and he was clearly the most excellent man for the job, and all that was still required was an appetite for freshly drawn wine and the venison from after Lent—and didn't he have that as well? Need one say more.

There was Riri Faure, André's third brother, who was a forester, fraternizing with every tree and every horned, furry, or feathered creature, and people liked him because he was discerning when he ordered the cutting of the trees, and maintained a balance between poaching and the law, for in this country that cared for neither rigid nor offhand behaviour, that balance was more sacred than the Good Lord's commandments. So under his surveillance people conformed to the pleasures of covert hunting, without threatening the principles which preserved the beauty of the forest, and as he knew that any rabbits stolen from the state would have caused greater harm still by spoiling the barley and the wheat, he had decided to turn a blind eye to minor misdeeds, in order that no major ones would ever be committed.

There was Georges Echard, known as the Chachard, and he could be found deep in a workshop that was darker than a cow's bottom, smelling of leather and the grease he used to soften his harnesses and saddles. He lived above his workshop but he rarely went up there; instead, you'd see him burst out from the back of the room, his day's work done, to head out into the forest to go hunting until Judgement Day. He had never taken a wife, for he was too terrified at the idea he might have to stray from the line that led straight from his saddler's den to the paths of his beloved game, but he was the best of companions, one of those who smile at the crack of dawn, when you can breathe in the lovely light of the coming day, and delight in a flock of thrushes taking off amid the murmur of men who are not yet fully awake. Now he whistled as he headed briskly towards his thickets, and he kept his rifle wedged tightly against his shoulder on its strap so that he could have both hands free in his pockets; this made Maria smile, because she liked such unions of nonchalance and swiftness.

There was Ripol, whose real name was Paul-Henri, and he served as blacksmith in the neighbouring village, but had been born in this one, and came back at decisive moments. He had married the most beautiful woman in Burgundy; when she passed by, others would look on with all the deference owed to Mother Nature's finest craftsmanship, but without any excessive covetousness either, because she was reputed to be a mediocre cook and baker, and this aspect, although by no means the be-all and end-all of love, did count for so much in the hearts of the men of the lowlands that they were easily consoled for her blue eyes the moment their own wives—and with a smile, if you please—set down before them a beef stew with carrots that would melt in your mouth more easily than all the ice at the end of March.

Finally there was Léon Saurat, who was always called Léon Saurat, because there were so many called Léon in these parts that this was how you had to go about distinguishing the one from the other, and this Léon had the biggest farm in the canton, and he worked it with his two sons, one of whom was also called Léon, out of a special sort of stubbornness that serves these hard-working regions well; the other was called Gaston-Valéry, out of an admirable desire to make up for the brevity with which both father and elder son had been sanctified. These two fine young lads looked after the farm under the leadership of their irascible old man, and they were joyful and solid as rocks; it was a wonder to see two such affable characters being watched over by a commander whose granite self sporadically crashed and shattered at the foot of these cliffs of joyfulness, his own sons. At the end of the day, if you happened to stop by the farm, where the mother and the women had set the table for twelve starving farmhands, you might surprise an indefinable smile on the patriarch's sullen mug.

So those were the nine good men who had rallied around André during the council at the cemetery, men who'd been forged the way iron is heated and worked, placed between the hammer and the anvil, with all the respect that blacksmiths have for the substance they are working with, and then set out to cool, to be shaped and sculpted into a noble form. Subsequently, as they had only ever known the roe deer and the hollows, their iron had not rusted, but had been preserved by the very thing their religion forbade them from mentioning, namely, the simple and powerful magic of the natural world, to which could be added the arrival of a little girl who could multiply its essences—so much so that what resonated in their minds, as they hurried to their battle stations, was a thing that had been born unbeknownst to them, born from the deepest waves that emanated from André and which Maria catalysed, a thing that now resonated in every mind as they prepared for battle, and that took the shape of these words of magic and wind: *For the land or die!*

Thus an entire region was wrenched from its places of refuge. The men tried to find spots that offered as much protection as possible from the wind and the first strike, and everyone tried not to look at the dark wall, while they shivered from a chill that was like nothing they'd ever known. And yet everyone obeyed a feeling which, in the slack hours of that apocalyptic day, acted like a little brazier flickering in that part of the self that is called the core, or the heart, or the middle—it hardly matters, in fact, the name hardly matters as long as the thing exists, and that was the deep understanding of the bond cementing the men and women in these lands, the bond that was spreading its invisible order and strength throughout the region. They felt they owned the wisdom of things that go the way they must go, and they knew they were being commanded by capable leaders who knew how to make decisions by counting ploughed fields rather than chimeras. They did not know, at least not with any knowledge that can find its way into speech, that this certainty came from the fact that André, who had lived fifty-two years in exaltation of the earth, amplified its song in each of them. But even if they did not know it, they felt it, and drew their strength from this infectious proximity to fertile furrows and valleys.

Jeannot and the mayor had stayed at the farm, and stood ready to dispatch little couriers, namely those young people in the canton who ran faster than rabbits, to keep the other officers abreast of anything deserving of their attention. Marcelot, Riri, Ripol and Léon Saurat had gone to the church, where they shared an understanding with a certain priest who had become one of them, and with whom on that day words were as useless as a cotton parasol. André, finally, had set off on the path to the clearing, with Maria, Chachard, and the Saurat sons at his side. This was what the pulse of destiny had led to: these men and this little girl hurrying towards a clearing more frozen than the ice floes, observing how everything had succumbed to the desperate silence of an entire transformed forest. But on they went, and soon they reached their goal.

A strange goal, or so André put it. While only a short distance away the forest pathways were numbed with icy silence, a sudden rustling of sounds and vapours greeted them the moment they crossed the line of the last trees. Stunned, they stopped and gazed out at the sight. The cold that had been gnawing at their bones seemed a touch less biting under an open sky, and they wondered if this was the effect of the mists floating in an abnormally shaped space. André had stopped the three men behind him in their tracks; he looked at Maria then again gave the order to move ahead. They carried on to the centre of the circle where the mists were coiling upon themselves in a slow, thick, but still transparent dance. It was astonishing: the banners of fog were as opaque as walls and yet as clear as water. You could see through invisible whirlwinds, and yet in spite of that they were more impenetrable than stone!

Finally, the whispered murmurings in the central opening seemed to them to be the fairest thing in this life. A confused sensation came over them—that voices were slipping into the hollow of these light pulsations, but they could not actually distinguish them from the vibrations that were causing the rustling in the clearing. Chachard, who had climbed up the hill at a good pace, like some dandified woodsman, never taking his hands from his pockets, now came close to tearing the linings of those pockets when he suddenly drew out his fists—such a scene, he could hardly leave them in his trousers—and, unusually for them, the two Saurat sons' jaws dropped as if granting to gravity all the honour of their stupefaction. But as for André—he was looking at Maria; his gaze did not turn away, or coerce.

She was standing motionless in the middle of the clearing, and the mists had begun to choreograph a strange, complex dance around her. At last she could see what had once been only a foreboding, what she had been expecting all these long months since the letter from Italy and the dream with the white horse.

She saw.

She saw the furore to come, and the arrows of death.

She saw departure, if she survived the attack.

She could distinctly perceive voices that others could only guess at.

the rebirth of the mists
the rootless the last alliance

Something tore inside her and split the firmament of her inner vision with streaks of ink that slowly diluted then disappeared in a last pearly wash of light.

She could feel the waves of her power billowing and rushing forward.

She could hear the voice of the little pianist from the night of healing.

Maria
Maria
Maria

The men were waiting. They were still cold, but not as cold as they had been in the valley, and they looked at the mists swirling around the wee girl petrified by a cold that did not come from without.

Maria
Maria
Maria

There was an explosion of such violence that they all flung themselves to the ground. The enemy was acting at last. The dark wall bore down upon them with a roar, striking with all its might at the last houses in the village and at the church. As it struck, it shattered, and the extent of its deformity became visible. Worse yet, the advancing tide revealed the mortal ambush that was yet to come, and seething tornadoes, charged with deadly rains, opened the way for the black arrows, as they shrieked and fired their lethal blades and ice.

The roofs collapsed.

The first seconds were the most terrible. It was as if all the plagues of the Antichrist had converged at the same time upon the villagers, stripped as they were of any shelter or protection. The rain fell hard and heavy, with drops that wounded like fragments of stone, leaving gashes that did not bleed but seemed to stab the skin with needles of pain, and into those gashes slipped an icy, abnormal chill. The wind swept away the roofs, not in the usual way, which was to carry them off, but by causing them to implode, and Gégène and his men blessed Maria for protecting them from this fury. Finally, the most terrifying assault came from the black arrows: they sped like lightning over the first part of their trajectory, slowed down halfway and now, suspended in the tempest, seemed to be endlessly readjusting their sights, preparing to take aim. Then they rushed forward and the nightmare began: they did not touch their victims, but exploded nearby, flinging them to the ground with the force of a shock wave that shattered bones. Several villagers fell. But almost all of them had already been lying down when the attack began, and, with the frail ramparts of their bodies, the stronger tried to protect the weaker, while wind and arrows made the waves in the air as dangerous as landmines. Worse yet, the water level was rising, and they watched as, impossibly, the waters climbed the slope for no other reason than the fact that an evil power had willed it … alas … an entire region flooded by the assault of the missiles of hatred, turning the elements of life into weapons of torture and death. The villagers lay flat on their stomachs on the surface of the universe, and they felt like rats on a sinking ship.

Everyone had flung themselves to the ground, except for two men who, despite the fury, refused to submit, and it was something to see, the priest and the yokel standing proud in the tempest, while the whirlwinds and arrows seemed to spare them, miraculously, even as the charge overwhelmed the entire valley. Minds prone to hasty conclusions will say that this was either courage or folly, but it was simply the fact that when the arrows exploded in the storm, the good father and the peasant were enlightened by an understanding that showed them what weapons they must take up in this war. In truth, Gégène and Father François sensed this was as much a battle of mind as of matter, and they knew they must fight with their hearts as well as their rifles—indeed, the arrows seemed to be ignoring the two valiant souls, who did not bow their heads even when everything around them was collapsing. Moreover, when they saw this, Riri, Ripol, and Léon Saurat, who had never felt so heavy from his old rheumatism, nor so intoxicated from the sudden burst of energy that set his sixty-nine-year-old self on his feet, now stood up as well, and began organizing the defence, remarking that the arrows were locked onto targets on land.

Just as there are certain days when soldiers must be made to sit, there are some battles which require one to stand and face the salvoes: without a word, the five men rallied like sheep-dogs around their herd, and in no time they had driven those who could still walk to the centre of the square, where they made them line up, back to back, in a tight circle; the arrows seemed to abandon the head-on attack, although they continued to explode all around the church. There was a moment's respite. But they knew it would not last for long, because the waters were approaching, and Gégène lifted his head in the direction of his farm, then the woods, looking more worried with each passing minute as he wondered what Maria was doing, and whether his Lorette would survive.

The nave of the church collapsed with a crash, as if struck by a cannonball, and fragments of stone flew in every direction. At the Hollows Farm, where Maria's mother had stayed behind, the frost united with gusts of wind strong enough to sink a ship at sea, and although the roof was still intact, the walls of the stable had begun to give way, and the farmyard was submerged by gravel tossed here and there on the rain. In the woods the animals had gone to ground, but the cold was even more biting beneath the foliage than on the open plain. All through the land the ravages of nature reduced to nothing the mildness of days it had once woven, hurling to the ground everything that used to stand proud under the sky, and it made you wonder how long anything could resist a tempest which, in mere minutes, had destroyed so much of what human genius had taken centuries to build.

And yet still they hoped, because they had a magical little

child on their side, a leader who knew greatness, and a land that had never betrayed those who served it, and once the initial panic that reduced everyone to an animal state had receded, they even felt a growing sense of indignation, because—no matter how poor—they were not used to being treated like this, and into their rebellious selves they welcomed a reserve of courage, inspired by the long winter hunts and by their poaching and toasts to friendship, and that courage fortified their hearts in the storm. In fact, it seemed as if they owed this bravery to the land, for the land could not harm those who knew how to honour it—and all the cataclysms had come from the vast sky, after all; their surge of courage provided a moment's respite in the course of the disaster, and the wind and rain could go no further, because they had been thwarted by the strength of the land.

Yes, the strength of the land. In the clearing where the other battle was taking place, the battle in Maria's heart, André could feel that strength with all the vigour of a life spent standing tall on the marl of his fields, could feel it with all the age-old peasant knowledge that flowed in his veins. He did not know how, but he knew it was by some magic, and all that concerned him now was this anchoring, with its knots and lines on the geological map of the lowlands, offering to his loved ones new reserves of determination born of the bare roots of the earth. He also knew that the fleet was doing battle up there at this hour and could not be overcome by the mere weapons of the earth.

He looked at Maria and said, "The sky is yours."

TERESA
The Clemente Sisters

Clara and the Maestro watched Maria as she set off with her father to the clearing in the mists, while the other three brought up the rear as if they were escorting Our Saviour Jesus Christ himself. The two young lads were as handsome as autumn pheasants, and you could sense in them the vigour of personalities never prone to torment of any kind. The oldest one, his hands in his pockets in a manner that bespoke the jubilation of being free, wore a face furrowed as much by a constant urge to laugh as by maturity. But all of them expressed the same determination, born of their awareness that they were caught up in something much greater than their simple brains could comprehend. When they left the cover of the trees to enter the clearing, Clara was struck by the calligraphy traced by the mists. Like Alessandro drawing characters in ink without knowing the language, the mists told a tale, and she was unable to interpret its idiom. But she was concerned above all about Maria, and worried about the new set of her features since the night Eugénie cured Marcel. She could read sorrow there, and fear, as clearly as if they were carved in stone, and she supposed it

215

was the same on the faces of officers who had undergone the loss of their men.

Petrus had not stopped snoring noisily since early morning, and now he yawned repeatedly, and hauled himself out of his armchair with some difficulty. He exchanged a look with the Maestro, and something seemed to set him back on his feet.

"I need a drink," he muttered.

But when he saw the battle through Clara's vision, he let out a whistle under his breath.

"It's not going well," he said.

"She's thinking about Eugénie," said Clara. "She's afraid of losing more people she loves."

"A sad experience of command," said the Maestro.

"She is not giving commands," said Clara, "and these are her parents."

"Rose and André are not Maria's parents," said Petrus.

In the east clearing, Maria had swung around to face the sky of snow, and the men had followed her example, looking up at clouds more opalescent than milk.

"There are many orphans in this war," said Clara after a pause.

"There are many orphans in the world, and many different ways of being an orphan," said the Maestro.

There was another pause. In the look Petrus levelled at the Maestro, Clara could detect a hint of reproach. Then he poured himself a glass of moscato and said, "We owe you that story as well. The story of the Clemente sisters."

In his mind she could see two young women sitting side by side in a summer garden. One of them she already knew, her name was Marta, and she had been Alessandro's great love, but as she looked at the other young woman her curiosity was tinged with a sweet sensation, luminous with the sort of hazy clarity you can find in the air on a hot day. She was dark-haired, fierce; she wore two drop earrings made of crystal; her face was a pure oval tickled with dimples; her skin was golden; and her laugh was like a fire in the night. But on her face you could also read the concentration of a soul with a rich inner life, and a mischievous gravity which acquires a silver patina with age.

"Marta and Teresa Clemente," said Petrus. "You cannot imagine two sisters more dissimilar, and yet more united. Ten years between them, but above all a rift of pain. The Clemente family gave receptions, and Marta's sorry little face would wander through them like a ghost; everyone thought she was so lovely, yet so melancholic, and they loved her sad poems—you could have sworn they were written by the hand of an adult, from the heart of an adult. At the age of twenty she married a man with as little talent for love as for poetry, and she used her married life as an excuse no longer to attend the soirées. Another little girl was there now, whom they also found very lovely, and very joyous, and she was a young prodigy of the type one rarely encounters. At the age of ten she had a skill and a maturity that was the envy of pianists twice her age—and on top of it she was as mischievous as a magpie and as stubborn as a fox when she did not want to play the pieces they gave her.

"Alessandro had become her friend long before he met Marta, and he often said that she offended the rule according to which artists find consolation for their pain, because it is that very pain that allows their art to take flight. But he was also aware of the dizzying well inside her, and he knew that her laughter had never, not even for a single day, betrayed her mission, which was to delve deep into her art. Sometimes she would look at the clouds and the Maestro could see the shadow of the mists passing over her face. Then she played, and her soul seemed to rise even higher. Marta listened to her and grew vibrant with the love of her younger sister. Then she left again in the evening, after a kiss as she waltzed Teresa around the room. But once the older sister had vanished around the corner of the lane, the little girl sat down on the steps outside the house and waited for her pain to subside, the pain of seeing a loved one suffer so much. She expressed all this in her playing, her talent for extraordinary happiness, and the pain of loving a sister who had chosen to lock herself away in sorrow. I do not know the migrations of the heart between those who share their blood, but I believe that Teresa and Marta belonged to a guild of pilgrims united as a noble sisterhood in an identical quest. Their parents fluttered around them, busy with their grand dinners, which boiled down to nothing more than their fantasies of the privileged class, and they were as unable to understand their daughters as they were to see the human wood for the trees of their drawing rooms.

"So the Clemente sisters grew up among their servants and two ghosts who wore tailcoats and organdie gowns; they lived on an island, and in the distance you could see the ships sailing to their destinations, never stopping to call at the pier where people lived, loved, and went fishing. Perhaps Marta, because she was born ten years before her sister, had absorbed all the indifference of her mother and father; consequently the strength that came from their lineage, from an ancestor, perhaps, or from more ancient times when money had not yet corrupted a taste for the gentle life, had been embodied in Teresa's tender flesh where, shielded by the older sister's melancholy, that strength had been able to blossom. But in return, this created an alliance in which Teresa's vital principle took its source in the sacrifice that Marta had agreed to make of her own life force, and it was no surprise that the death of one sister was closely followed by the death of the other—whatever the circumstances that made it so difficult to determine the causes and the machinations. Indeed, I would not be surprised if, in the end, we find out that we are all the characters of some meticulous but mad novelist."

Petrus fell silent.

"You play the way your mother did," said the Maestro, "and it is your playing that invokes her ghost—a ghost to whom I have not yet been able to tell the story properly. Do you know the reason why a man cannot find the words inside himself that would free both the living and the dead?"

"Sorrow," she said.

"Sorrow."

For the first time since she had known him, she could see the imprint of pain upon his face.

"It was already an era of unrest and suspicion, and your father often came to the villa during the night," he continued. "One evening Teresa was there, playing a sonata."

The Maestro fell silent and Clara immersed herself in his remembering. They had left the windows open onto the balmy summer air, and it was the same sonata, the one where she'd found the poem in the margin of the score, the one that united hearts and pierced the space of visions. When she had played it two years earlier, on the evening that had taken her in her dreams to Maria, there had been a perfume of currents and damp earth in the air, but she had not been able to decipher the story told by the score, and the poem had curled up into a bubble of silence. She listened to the young woman playing, and the same bubble formed in her chest. Then a man appeared in the room. He had come out of nowhere and he was focused intensely on a place inside himself revealed to him by the music. She could see every detail of his features, transfixed as he was by the music, and on his face, luminous with youth, was the serenity of a thousand years, reflections of moonlight and thoughts of a river.

"She has the inspiration of our mists," said the man to the Maestro, as they stood facing each other in this memory from ten years earlier. "But she combines it with a beauty that comes from her land."

"Her land inspires her but the source of her gift at the piano and her intoxicating playing remain a mystery, which we commonly refer to as woman," answered the Maestro.

"Not all women play the way she does."

"But all of them possess that essence you can detect in her playing."

Then the vision passed and Clara was once again with the Maestro in the present day.

"There was a year when they were happy," he said, "and then Teresa found out she was expecting a child. It was a devastating revelation."

"Devastating for the Council?"

"Your father did not inform the entire Council. As I told you, it was the era of the first unrest, because Aelius's ambition and influence had been constantly growing, and this was a source of great concern to us. We were subjected to far-reaching internal dissent, and we witnessed betrayals of a sort we would never have deemed possible. So when we found out about Teresa's pregnancy, we decided to keep the secret of this miracle to ourselves, as inexplicable as the extinction of our mists, the secret of a child conceived between a human being and an elf. It was the first time, and to this date, the only time. All the other mixed marriages have been sterile."

"Teresa let it be known that she wanted to devote a year to meditation, and she withdrew to a family estate in the north of Umbria," said Petrus. "No one knew about it."

Clara saw a villa with austere walls set amid a large garden overlooking a valley of gently rolling fields and small ridges, and she heard the notes of the sonata drifting from an invisible room, embellished by a new depth, a vein threaded with silver, with summer rains.

"The day before you were born, Marta threw herself into the Tiber. Then Teresa gave birth to a daughter. Teresa died the following night. She fell asleep and never woke up. But your father had already crossed back over the bridge because another birth was calling him to us. Another girl had been born in the home of the Council Head, on the same day and at the same hour as you, and she too was proof of an impossible miracle, because although she had been conceived by two elves, she had come into the world with a perfectly human appearance, something which had never happened in

221

our scheme of things, and has never happened since. We are born in a symbiosis of essences and we only acquire a unique appearance when we leave our own world. But this little girl, no matter which way you turned her, no matter which way you looked at her, this girl resembled every other little human being. We were in the presence of two impossible births, on the same day and at the same time. Therefore it was decided we must hide them, for clearly they were part of a powerful plan, and we knew we had to protect them from Aelius's camp."

"So you sent us far away from our roots," she said.

"Alessandro had once told me about the village where his brother lives," said the Maestro, "and so I had you sent to Santo Stefano. Maria's journey was more complicated, for she went through Spain, and ended up on Eugénie's farm. But she must learn of it first, so we won't share it with you now."

"Does she know she was adopted?"

"Your father showed her how she arrived at the farm," he said. "She had to know it, too, in order for her powers to be released."

"Of the two of you, you are the one with a human part," said Petrus, "and that is why you create bonds and build bridges. You have your mother's gift for the piano, but you have an added strength that comes from your father's power. You can see, the way your father does, but you also have bonds that take their source in your mother's humanity."

Clara was overwhelmed by a vision. Its texture was finer and more vibrant than the reminiscences in her mind, and she knew she was looking at Teresa's face as she was playing the sonata threaded with silver and summer showers. Upon the final note, her mother raised her head, and Clara was overcome by the dizzying awareness of a living woman's presence.

"The ghosts are alive," she murmured.

And for the first time in twelve years spent with neither tears nor laughter, she began to laugh and, at the same time, to cry. Petrus noisily blew his nose into a giant's handkerchief, then the two men waited in silence until she had dried her tears.

"In all these years, I have been so sorry that your mother never knew you," said the Maestro. "I watched you grow up with that crystalline quality and courage that many brave men would envy, and I have often thought of how fate had prevented the two of the most remarkable women I have ever had the fortune to know from meeting. I saw the legacy of her strength and her purity, and I have found it in you again, so many times, but I have also seen what is yours alone, and I know it would have left her spellbound."

Clara saw her mother sitting in the half-darkness of the garden in Umbria. She was laughing, and the crystal teardrop earrings sparkled in the evening. In the ten o'clock light, a silver languor passed over her face, slipping down her cheek like a glinting river fish.

"If it's a girl," she heard her say, "I want her to love the mountains." Someone must have replied, for she smiled and said, "The mountains, and orchards in summer." Then she vanished.

"Alessandro told me that the orchard at the presbytery was the place in Abruzzo he liked best of all," said the Maestro.

"This story taught me to trust the signs left in our path. To trust the poems a father has written in the hopes that his daughter will read them; the calligraphy of the mountain, traced by an unknowing brush. I knew that you would come back to me from Abruzzo some day and, just as I sent you there because of the sign of the orchard, you took the road to Rome because of the sign of a forgotten piano."

She heard Sandro saying, *there are transparent plums there, and cascades of shade*. But what was as luminous to her as fireflies in the night was her mother's voice, in which a faultline opened up to let other voices pass through. There were women and graves, there were letters from the war and gentle songs in the evening. All these voices and graves and women with their mourning veils murmuring of love along the stone walkways of graveyards ... She saw a garden of irises and a young man with bright sad eyes, while a voice was murmuring tenderly, *Go, my son, and know for all eternity how much we love you*, and she felt a tightness in her heart when she recognized old Eugénie's voice. Then she saw Rose, sparkling, diaphanous, smiling through the wings of the tempest, and her smile said, *We are mothers beyond death and the mystery of birth*.

And so, for the second time in twelve years, she wept.

PAVILION OF THE MISTS
Inner Elfin Council

"Clara is the link."
"Her powers of empathy are magnificent."
"In spite of the years of drought."
"Because of the years of drought."
"Because of the miracle of who she is, able to overcome the years of drought."
"All the women are with her."

ROSE

The Lineages of the Sky

This is what evil is.

The first to fall was one of the little messengers assigned to the rapid relaying of information between Marcelot's farm, the clearing, and the church. They sent him because they had noticed movement to the east, where André had said there were some strange horsemen on unfamiliar mounts. They sent him off just as the winds began pounding the hillside. Because the others were not moving, they were safe, but the young boy's speed precipitated him into the storm's tentacles, and he was tossed instantly into the icy ridges of its currents, then flung like a bundle against a wall of hard stone.

Everyone saw the messenger fall, and two men tried to hurry to the unfortunate lad's side, creeping close to the ground to avoid the gusts, but fate played its hand, and the enemy's horsemen appeared in the downpour, surrounding the two farms. Their appearance was terrifying. They were gigantic, made of a pallid substance that merely suggested the outline of deformed, faceless men. But it was the way they suddenly appeared all around the farm, ghostly, still, a mass of silence and rage, that made everyone's blood run cold. As for the mounts … truth be told, there were no mounts. The horsemen were straddling a void, and if all those brave souls had had the slightest knowledge of physics, they would have realized they were in the impossible presence of a source of anti-matter that reversed the mechanisms of the known world.

Still more fell. At the church, the arrows were coming thick and fast once again. There was no respite, and stones flew, while tremors left a trail of destruction. The rain smashed against the world, and the wounded crawled beneath torrents of water resembling a shower of needles. Three men perished, crushed by rubble that came loose from the base of the church steeple, and two more succumbed to the swift flight of the arrows that zinged and shattered with renewed vigour. The five men who were in charge of the refugees from the church watched helplessly as everything around them was ravaged, and with the first deaths all hope was lost that Maria's magic might be enough to protect them from the abyss. The priest and Léon Saurat ordered their flock to close ranks yet again, while the others crawled over to the victims and tried to help them as best they could. Alas, there was little they could do. And their helplessness was searing.

Oh, helplessness … The helplessness of human animals is boundless, as is their bravery in the final hours of defeat. The sky of snow was gathering behind the zone of combat and seemed to be waiting at the edge of the clearing, and the men from the church could feel it, as could those who were defending Lorette's farm or waiting with André in the forest, because that sky of snow, in that moment where everything was faltering, conveyed to each of the men the fragrance of an old, long-forgotten dream.

Naturally it was Gégène who was first to rally the men. It should be said that his dream, as will be revealed anon, was hardly the least significant of all those ephemeral and sublime dreams, but the fact remained that on that day he was still the same man of duty and derision as always; and once his initial stupefaction at the enemy's raging fury had subsided, along with his dismay at discovering how powerful and vile they were, he felt that they had wasted too much time pussyfooting around, and now they must pay their tithes to a life of good wine and love. Moreover, the prospect of drowning or being crushed by a stone from the steeple was hardly to his liking: he was prepared to die honourably, but could not see where any honour was to be found in slithering like a snail under the clouds. Therefore, whether it was the devil or the hand of some other evil power that was arming the storm was of no greater concern to him than his wife's recipes when she was serving up his dinner. In addition, he was beginning to grasp what was more and more obvious: behind the mountain, there were archers firing the deadly black arrows. He motioned to Riri and Ripol to go with him to join Léon Saurat and, cupping his hands around his mouth, he yelled, "Everyone to Chachard's workshop!"

It will soon be told what he intended to do there, but you see, already their helplessness has moved on and will not return. And there were other reversals up there, outside the farms surrounded by a hundred shadowy figures.

*

So it was Rose who was of the sky, when all the others were of the earth, and she fed off the waves in the air and the streams in this land of pastures and reaping—whence her unassuming manner that was stronger than steel, and that evanescent texture as transparent as flowing water. When Maria kissed her mother goodnight, she could sense the sadness that, in her father, had become a sediment of silt and clay, but in her mother flowed like a river sweeping its dead along until it dissolved in her liquid breathing, and no one suspected the force of its flow. But while André slept peacefully, although he had a premonition of his daughter's destiny, it was because he knew the nature of Rose's power, however fragile she might seem at first.

You could stare at that self-effacing peasant woman, and neither her face nor her gestures nor her voice nor the texture of her skin aroused the slightest interest, and you would be endlessly surprised that such an absence of verve could give birth to such a whirlwind of beneficial, amiable impulses. The only word of love that André had ever said to her, early one morning in winter when they were still lying in bed looking at the stars, was like water one could hold in one's hand as if it were a pebble or a flower. Naturally, it had been exceptional, because André Faure was not accustomed to making pronouncements, and he always shared matters of moment with his wife with an economy of means that bordered on genius and which was facilitated, it is true, by the genius which love confers on gazes and gestures. But nestled at the heart of this parsimony was a name that had escaped the scarcity of his utterances, and when he looked at her he simply murmured Rose, because he alone could see the blade sharpened on a crystal thread as it sparkled, deeply and terrifyingly beautiful, in moments of love.

Thus, together with Jeannette and Marie, Rose had gone out earlier onto the steps in front of the Hollows with the intention of joining Lorette at the neighbouring farm. But the tempest had already unleashed its frontal attack and it was impossible to cross the courtyard where loose flying boards and terrified hens were dancing the tango. Rose and the two old women retreated to the south wall of the stable which, for the moment, was withstanding the gusts, and she waited there while through the gale she could sense Maria's dismay, and her entire life came back to her upon the wind.

It all began with the fact that her parents, who were illiterate, had wanted a better life for her. But the little her mother had seen of cities had convinced her that there was no virtuous life to be had there, and while she accepted the fact that they were poor, it was on the condition that they belonged to themselves alone. So while others from her village found positions in town as nannies or maids, she did not want to see her little girl lost in some big manor house. Instead, they took her once a week to the convent near the neighbouring town, and it was there that, along with their dogma, the sisters taught the poor girls from the canton how to read and write. It took two hours to get there, and at dawn Rose's older brother would seat her in the cart and drive her to her lessons, then wait for her in the kitchens until they were over.

As the weeks went by, Rose stopped listening to the litanies and sermons because she was euphoric, completely absorbed in the books the sisters handed out after Vespers. She wept as she read the poems of streams and skies, which showed her the only world that was truly her own, or the tales that lay beneath clouds more palpable than the clay in the fields, where one could make out the word of God in a beguiling reflection. Later, Father François gave her travel tales to read, where mariners navigated by the stars and sailed the pathways of the wind, more intelligible than any network of roads, and the call of sea voyages and constellations was even more precious to her than God's celestial scriptures. But as far as Rose was concerned, this natural symbiosis, which enabled her to identify with the liquid elements, had little to do with an awareness of the physical universe, and one would have to look beyond the tangible world for the principle that connected her to currents and clouds.

Certain women possess a grace given them by virtue of an increase in the female essence—as the result of an echo effect which, by making them simultaneously singular and plural, allows them to be manifest both in themselves and in the long lineage of their kin; if Rose was a woman of sky and rivers, it was because the river of those who had come before her flowed inside her, through the magic complicity with her gender that went beyond mere blood relation; and if she dreamed of travel, it was because her vision cut through space and time and connected the border territories of the female continent—whence came that transparency rendering her light and elusive, and that fluid energy whose source was somewhere far beyond herself.

Through an inexplicable mechanism of memory she could see herself as she was on the morning of her wedding, wearing a white skirt and bodice and, in her hair, a gauze veil embroidered with lace. Her brothers had escorted her because all the young people had come to André's village, taking shortcuts the carts could not manage, and for that reason she still had her clogs on her feet, holding in one hand the immaculate shoes she would put on once they were at the entrance to the church. The men were making their way along the path in their suits of black woollen cloth, their brows pearling with sweat, and they picked flowers from along the path that they would give to the girls in the village. All the while, Rose's heart was beating wildly in the splendour of the sunshine.

She had met André only once before he'd come to ask her father for her hand. She had seen his gaze from a distance, as she was going through the gate on her way to the Saint John's Day bonfire, and the feeling of evanescence she experienced when she withdrew into herself was transformed into a brilliant cascade that he, too, could see. Similarly, she could discern how his awareness of the earth had left dark ridges in his soul. They were not laid out in parallel furrows, but were elevated, and elevated him in turn, towards the sky, and she knew then that it was his power amid the fields and the earth that made her own language of water and sky decipherable to André.

Then the wheel of memory turned and she saw Angèle again with a newborn baby in her arms, wrapped in white swaddling clothes. She had parted the folds of embroidered cambric and taken the infant as her daughter, with a joy that resembled an ether shot through with indecipherable traces of light. She received the message from these glimmerings, just

232

as, in the crystalline lapping emanating from the child, she had read of an annunciation: that two worlds would coexist. Which worlds? She did not know, and yet they existed.

The memories stopped.

The rain was falling like an axe. She heard a new clamour from the village, even as the wind blew ten times harder. She looked behind her, beyond the stable roof, at the sky of snow that was waiting for Maria. And then she cast her whole heart, as a woman and as a mother, into the wind.

Meanwhile, Gégène's men had gone to fetch rifles from Chachard's workshop. This gentleman of the forest hunt had masses of them; the care he had lavished upon them was as loving as any caress he would have given a wife had the plumage of a partridge not been more desirable to him than a kiss; so now each man was able to choose the weapon that suited him, and stop for a moment to listen to Gégène's instructions. They were more like conjectures that, given the situation, he might as well make, because they had to do something after all.

"We have to go through it," he said, "and I don't see why the rifles shouldn't give us the upper hand."

"So you think there are men waiting to ambush us round the back?" asked Riri.

"How can we get through?" asked Ripol.

"We can do it," said Léon Saurat. Apart from the real distress he felt, he was secretly jubilant that the day was proving to him that he still had what it took for action and no one was about to bury him yet. "But we can't stay here," he added, pointing to the roof.

It would be wrong to imagine that this conversation took place in hushed tones in the comfort of the workshop, smelling sweetly of seal blubber and handcrafted leather. Even there they had to shout, and they had to leave soon; Maria had given them the order, and they knew it full well after having seen their church decapitated against the sky. But it was impossible to speak out of doors, and Gégène ventured to stay on a bit longer because he wanted to be sure the men had grasped the truth of what he was trying to ram into their brains.

"What do we do when we want to shoot a partridge in full flight and there's a fearsome wind?" he shouted.

That was an easy one, and they did not even need to give him the answer.

"And how do we go about shooting game with a bow and arrow?"

That was an easy one, too, but what was not so easy was to connect the two trains of logic that in Gégène's head were clear, apparently. Despite the prevalence of hunting and battues, it was traditional in the region to favour a form of hunt that was nominally forbidden because it encouraged poaching, but for all that, it was considered a finer method than the others. There were not many of them who practised it, for lack of material or know-how, but three or four of them would gladly set aside their rifles for the bow and arrow, and they were much respected, because at this game only those who had sufficient knowledge of their prey could excel, and they had to adjust their aim well enough not to miss, and have at their disposition an elaborate repertory of all the tricks required to approach their quarry, including awareness of terrain and winds. (For what is the point of being a stone's throw away from a deer if the breeze suddenly blows one's tobacco breath right into the animal's nostrils?)

In short, ancient natural forces joined in this game at which the true squires of our regions excelled, forces of men and of forests which once again for a day of pursuit had become the same fundamental matter. The bows they used had neither sights nor any of the accessories that have flourished in an era when hunting has declined to the status of a mere pastime; these bows resembled those used by savages and, because they lacked any precision instrumentation, they required so much more from the archer. They could also be used as paddles, or as walking sticks, because their simplicity required a combination of elegance and solidity, and the instrument was valued because there was no harm in it being so versatile and useful. But every attention was paid to the quality of the arrows, which had to be fashioned so that the trajectory and the impact could be calculated to perfection, and they were carried in their quivers with all the delicacy excellence requires. (For what would be the point of finding oneself a stone's throw away from a wild boar only to miss the charming beast?)

The other men were actually beginning to see the light, and they could almost hear Gégène's voice resonating under their scalps, in that sententious, mocking way he had, the only difference being that they were not all on the verge of uncorking a bottle, cutting some slices of saucisson, and raising a toast to friendship. But the terror of the moment did not manage to extinguish the spark of excitement that had flared ever since they had opted to act rather than let themselves be crushed like cockroaches, and they could easily do without the plonk and the pork, provided they understood the order of the day, which was there before their eyes as clearly as if Marcelot had said it out loud: *Go closer, take aim, and shoot into the wind*. All in all, the furtive procedure of things was now clear to these men, who were used to spending their Sundays in the forest: they would be cunning, and they would anticipate. That they did not quite know how did not prevent them from seeing the beauty of their plan, and they felt revitalized as they recalled that the grace of the land belonged to them.

"Straight into the wind and head for the fallow fields!" shouted Marcelot, and they nodded vigorously, feeling for their rifles.

They went out into the wind and hail; it seemed to have grown even stronger while they'd been conspiring indoors. But the roof had held. And they made headway. Despite the lashing rain and the flooding, they advanced slowly and surely, as if their courageous determination offered less purchase to the gusts and made them somehow invisible to the enemy.

Up at the clearing the first act of fate was being played out at last, while the years materialized into a whirlwind of revelations brought forth by the inhospitable shrieking of the wind. The preliminary storm vanished beneath the icy onslaught of rain, and with every passing second the drama became more terrible and more apparent. Maria stood motionless for a long time, in spite of the tragedy unfolding in the village. All around her she could feel friendly presences waiting behind the sky of snow; she could hear the voice of the other little girl murmuring her name, and she saw a landscape she had already seen in her dreams. Access was along a passage of flat black stones beneath a canopy of chiselled trees until one reached a wooden pavilion with windows that had neither glass nor curtains, then finally across a wooden pier over a misty valley. But she could not determine how she was to use this vision when there were men who had perished, and in the ice was murmured the beloved name of Eugénie.

A succession of images caused her to hesitate. First she saw a country road where young men in tight Sunday suits were picking armfuls of wildflowers, then a window in the clarity of a winter dawn, where two stars had frozen, their orbits stopped forever, and finally an unknown graveyard in the pounding rain, spray splashing and splattering over the granite slabs. Ordinarily the pictures from her dreams were as physically precise as the fields and hares, but these images were blurry and marred by distortions, and she could not see the faces of the young men as they bantered under the July sun, any more than she could read the names and dates carved onto the tombs in the graveyard. But she was astonished that the image could reach her during the battle, because she knew she was seeing it through her mother's eyes. Other images followed, emerging from Rose's memory; she had entered into a sort of communication with Rose that was unlike anything Maria had ever shared with another, not even Eugénie at the time of the healing, or André when they would gaze long and silently at one another. The images poured over her then moved on; there were trees and pathways, blazing fires on winter nights, a little shed of grey tiles where they went to fetch the firewood on a cold day, and faces whose features were blurred by memory but which, intermittently, revived in the sudden radiance of a smile. She saw an old woman whose corneas were engulfed in whiteness, who smiled as she mended a worn veil, and she knew that this was her grandmother at a time when she herself was not yet born. A long lineage of women … She caught glimpses of faces melting into a chain that was lost in time. There were graves, and women singing lullabies of an evening or screaming with pain as they read the letter from the army. In one last, spinning round of fleeting images she saw each face clearly, every glittering tear. Then they all disappeared. But in the swirling of shared memory their message had carried.

And in Rome, Clara also received the message from the women, who told Maria that she was one of them and that she must honour the lineage beyond death. Then she heard the little French girl say:

"What is your name?"

PETRUS
A Friend

"*Tu come ti chiami?*" translated the Maestro.

"*Mi chiamo Clara,*" she replied.

And he translated again. "Where do you come from?"

"*L'Italia,*" she said.

"That is so far away," said Maria. "Can you see the storm?"

"Yes," said Clara. "Can you see me, too?"

"Yes, but I cannot see anyone else. Although there is a man who is speaking French."

"I am with him and with other men who know."

"Do they know what I must do?"

"I don't think so. They know why, but they don't know how."

"It is urgent," said Maria.

"It is urgent," said the Maestro first in French, then in Italian. "But we don't have the keys."

"The revelations will not come on their own," said Petrus, "and at the moment the sky is not exactly on our side."

"Who is speaking?" asked Maria.

"Petrus, at your service," he said, in French.

"I know you."

"You know all of us. And you also know your powers. Your heart is at ease, you can set them free."

"I don't understand what I must do."

"Clara will guide you. Can you hold the tempest back a little while longer?"

"I am not holding it back. Men have died."

"You are holding it back, and we are helping you. Without you there would be nothing left of the village or the land. We are going to speak to Clara in Italian, but we won't forget you, and we will be with you again soon."

Then, to the Maestro: "The key is in the stories. Clara must know."

"What is a prophecy if it is revealed?" asked the Maestro.

"It is still a prophecy," said Petrus. "And perhaps a guiding light, as well. It should have been done earlier. But we must begin at the beginning."

In Petrus's mind, Clara could see the Maestro, thirty years younger, shaking hands with a man who looked like Pietro, then following him down familiar corridors where marble tabletops and brocade curtains blended with a heavy, toxic atmosphere. It hung over an indescribably terrible scene and cast a predatory shadow over the man's amiable face. Then Roberto Volpe opened the door to an unfamiliar room, and the Maestro stood opposite the painting Clara had seen on the very first day.

"From our Pavilion I saw and already knew the art of humankind," said the Maestro, "and I have always been fascinated by their music and their paintings. But this painting was different."

"You must understand what is happening here," said Petrus. "We are a world without stories."

"You told me that elves do not tell stories," said Clara.

"Elves do not tell stories the way people do but, above all, they do not invent them. We sing of fine deeds and great exploits; we compose odes to the birds of the ponds, or hymns to the beauty of mist; we celebrate the things that exist. But imagination never adds anything. Elves know how to praise the beauty of the world, but they do not know how to play with reality. They live in a splendid world that is eternal and static."

"From the beginning I have loved what humans create," said the Maestro. "But that day I made an additional discovery. Roberto Volpe had attracted the attention of the Council because he had done something which continues to this day to have consequences for our destiny. I crossed the bridge and I met him. And he showed me the painting. I had already seen portrayals of the lamentations of Christ, but this one was different, and the shock was enormous. And yet it was the same scene as usual, the Virgin and Mary Magdalene leaning over Christ taken down from the cross, the women's tears, the crucified man with his crown of thorns. But there could be no doubt that it had been painted by an elf. I knew it the moment I saw the painting, and later I conducted an investigation that confirmed it. One of our kind, four centuries ago, had left our world for this one, taking a human name and a Flemish identity—we believe he lived in Amsterdam—and painted the greatest fiction of humankind with a perfection that has been rarely equalled."

"What did Roberto do?" asked Clara.

"He killed someone," said the Maestro, "but we won't

tell that story today. The most important thing is that, as I stood before the painting, I made the same decision as the artist who painted it. It was the most marvellous emotion of my entire life. Prior to that, I had been yearning for human art. Now I could see the path that had been opened by this unknown painter, a passage to the other side of the bridge, and a complete immersion in the music of this world. And others besides me also made this discovery, before and after, but for different reasons."

"Some of them want the end of humankind, others want an alliance," said Clara.

"The alliance is the message of the Flemish painting," said the Maestro, "just as Alessandro's canvases speak of the desire to cross over in the other direction. It is inconceivable that we have taken so long to hear and to understand this call from the footbridge. All the more so in that, not long before this, I made another discovery thanks to an elf whom you know well, and whose perspicacity far exceeds that of great and wise men. I was still the Head of our Council, and I went to consult the ancient texts in the library of our world. I was looking for something that might help me understand the era we were living in, but I didn't find anything that day."

"You were the Head of your Council before Maria's father?"

"Yes. But another candidate ran against Maria's father, and almost won."

"Aelius."

"Aelius, whose anger you can see today in the sky over Burgundy. Now, as I was leaving the library, I had an interesting conversation with the sweeper, who seemed to be behaving very oddly."

"There are sweepers among the elves?" asked Clara.

"There are gardens all around our libraries," said Petrus, "and we sweep the paths every day at dawn and at twilight during the seasons when there are leaves on the trees. We have pretty brooms, and the moss mustn't be damaged. It is a noble task, although I have never found it very interesting, but as I already told you, for many years I was a rather uninspired elf. And besides, I always liked to read. I think I have spent my life reading. Even when I drink, I am reading."

"So the sweeper wasn't sweeping, he was reading under a tree," said the Maestro. "And he was so absorbed in his reading that he didn't hear me approach. So I asked him what he was reading."

"And I replied: a prophecy," said Petrus. "A prophecy? asked the Council Head. A prophecy, I said. In the body of our poetic texts, there is one that is different from the others. It belongs to a collection of poems and songs, most of them elegiac, entitled *Canto of the Alliance*, and it celebrates the natural alliances: mists in the evening, clouds of ink, stones, and all the rest."

He sighed, vaguely chagrined.

"But that text was different. It did not celebrate any known event, nor did it evoke anything in my memory, but it described our trouble as if it had anticipated it, and it proposed the remedy as if it had dreamt it. No one had ever paid it any attention. But when I read it, I believed that the world was being torn in half, and that a door was opening in my heart. Only three verses telling an unknown story—but after centuries spent drinking tea and listening to sublime poems, it was life as a whole that was exploding and sparkling, like after a glass of moscato."

His eyes shone with the emotion he had felt at the time.

"I read the text and I understood what the sweeper meant to say," said the Maestro. "Then I had to convince others, and Petrus showed a great deal of talent for this. Since that day, the prophecy has been our guide in war."

When he recited the poem, the ancestor trembled and Clara thought she could see a silvery glow flash through the soft fur.

the rebirth of the mists
through two children of November and snow
the rootless the last alliance

"It is the only text of fiction ever written by our kind," said the Maestro. "For that reason, we think it is prophetic. That it depicts a reality that is still to come, but that might save us. For the first time in our history, our mists are declining. Some think that men are responsible for this decline, and that their negligence has weakened nature; others, on the contrary, think that the trouble stems from the fact that we are not sufficiently united. If I consider the paintings inspired by our alliance, this Christ painted by an elf—and who has for all that never seemed more human—and Alessandro's last canvas, which exalts the bridge of our world without showing it, then I know that the art of humankind has given us stories we could not have conceived of, and in return our mists transport them beyond their lands. It is time to invent our destiny and to believe in this last alliance; there are too many footbridges showing the desire we have to cross the same bridge together."

"Are we the two children of November and snow?" she asked.

"Yes," said the Maestro.

"There are other children born in the November snow."

"There are no other children born elfin and human in the November snow. But for all that, we do not know what to do with this miracle."

Clara thought of the men haunted by bridges and by mountains that could save them from being born far from their heart, of those elfin painters, sweepers and musicians, who were fascinated by the creative genius of humans; she thought of those footbridges crossing between two worlds through a vastness crisscrossed with art's glowing lights. And above those lights shone a more intense clarity, supplanting music and forms and inspiring them with its superior strength.

"The universe is a gigantic story," said Petrus. "And everyone has their own story, radiating somewhere in the firmament of fictions and leading somewhere into the sky of prophecies and dreams. In my case, amarone shows it to me. After two or three glasses, I always have the same vision. I see a house in the middle of the fields, and an old man on his way home after work. Do that man and that house exist? I don't know. The old fellow puts his hat on a large dresser and smiles at his grandson, who is in the kitchen, reading. I can sense that he wants the boy's life and work to be less exhausting than his own have been. And so he is glad that the boy likes to read and to daydream and he says, *Non c'è uomo che non sogni*.[5] Why do I always return to that same story? Every time, when the granddad talks to his grandson, I weep. And then I dream."

"Your powers are connected to the power of fiction," said the Maestro, "and alas, we do not understand it very well."

---

5. There are no men who do not dream.

"There are only two moments when everything is possible in this life," said Petrus, "when one drinks, and when one makes up stories."

Clara felt an ancient consciousness quiver inside her, a consciousness that resembled the connection between women that existed beyond space and time and that she had experienced with Rose. This time, however, it connected beings to the creations of the mind. A vast constellation appeared before her mind's eye. She was able to map out souls and works of art on a brilliant globe, whose projections of light went from one end of the cosmos to the other, in such a way that a canvas painted in Rome in this century led the way to hearts and minds in a distant era and a faraway place. The combined frequency of earth and art became one, uniting distant entities that were similarly attuned. This frequency was no longer limited to her perception, but crossed different levels of reality, and spread like a network that lit up as the distances dissolved. It was powerfully natural and powerfully human. Similarly, it recorded a succession of images that lasted no longer than a few seconds, but in which Petrus's empathy conveyed a story as lyrical and complex as those he had already told her, because they were both connected to this infinity of bonds in the ether, and they could see the footbridges over the void where others saw only solitude and absence.

Then she saw a little boy sitting in his country kitchen, in the evening shadows. An old man with a face furrowed by labour is placing his peasant's cap on one side of the dresser, and wiping his brow in a gesture of repose. The church tower is striking the seven o'clock angelus; the day's work is over; the old granddad smiles and his smile lights up the entire land and then, beyond his mountains and his plains, lights up unknown regions and even further still, exploding in a spray of sparks, illuminating a country so vast that no man could cross it on foot.

"*Non c'è uomo che non sogni*," she murmured.

"No one has ever penetrated my vision in this way," said Petrus. "I can feel your presence at the heart of my dreams." Then gently, visibly moved: "You and Maria are the totality of two worlds, that of nature, and of art. But you are the one who holds the possibility of a new story in her hands. And if so many men have been able to live for two millennia in a reality shaped by belief in the resurrection of a crucified man wearing a crown of thorns, it is not absurd to think that anything is possible in such a world. It is up to you now. You see souls, and you can give them their stories and their dreams, which build footbridges that both humans and elves aim to cross."

"You have to help me," she said.

"I am just a simple sweeper and a soldier," he replied, "and you are a prophetic star. I don't believe you need me."

"You were a soldier?"

"I was a soldier and I fought in my native country."

"The elves have armies?"

"The elves have wars, and they are as ugly as human wars. One day I will tell you the story of my first battle. I was drunker than a skunk. But you can do a great deal of damage by falling over."

"Have you ever killed someone?"

"Yes."

"What does it feel like to kill someone?"

"You feel fear," he said. "Are you afraid?"

"Yes."

"That's good. I am with you and I won't leave you, either in times of war or peace. You haven't had a family, but you have a friend."

She thought: *I have a friend.*

"But now it's the first battle," he said. "There's no going back."

"The snow," she said. "That is Maria's dream. The earth, the sky, and the snow."

She got up and went over to the piano where she had often played pieces whose stories she could not hear. But Petrus's dream had forged the key to her hours of work with the Maestro. Inside every score was the story from which the composer's heart was spun, and all those stories, right from the start, scrolled through her memory, taking on the colour of those dreams which, splendid or dull, were written in the great constellation of stories. So she played again the hymn of the alliance, which she had composed in a desire for union and forgiveness, but she added a new spirit and words that came to her from Maria's heart.

PAVILION OF THE MISTS
Half of the Council of the Mists

"We are withdrawing our protection. They will have to fend for themselves from now on. Soon we will find out."

"We have been getting messages. Those who are in charge of the command must stand ready."

"Must we gather by the bridge?"

"It hardly matters where we gather."

WAR

through two children of November and snow

EUGÈNE
All the Dreams

In one fell swoop, the land's defences collapsed. For Maria it was like a great undertow in the ocean, exposing a shoreline swept with sadness and desolation. She knew that the lowlands had flourished for years because of the power of the fantastical boars and the mercurial horses, but this power was so inseparable from her own, and she was so accustomed to it being her source of song and of nature's energy, that its sudden disappearance left her as blind and deaf as if she had never heard its operas or gazed at its etchings—and she knew that this was the fate of ordinary humans.

From the clearing in the east wood to the steps outside the church, there was a tide of despair, and everyone felt as if they were standing abandoned on the edge of an abyss. Father François and Gégène stood rooted to the spot; the little girl's helplessness had destroyed the very thing that had sustained them in their struggle against the storm. The priest in particular could no longer find the corolla that had spread through him, no matter how hard he looked; horrified by the degree of his blasphemy, he resolved to confess to the bishop as soon as he could, once the cataclysm was behind them. I have sinned, he kept thinking, as he shivered with cold and looked all around at a landscape that seemed as wretched as his fervour of a lapsed preacher.

But the good father was not the only one whose enlightened moments as a free man had vanished, for Gégène was now filled with the same old insidious jealousy he had once felt about Lorette's past love, and it was the same thing from one end of the land to the other: disgust and bitterness were taking hold, and every soul raged against the baseness of destiny. The men following Gégène no longer knew their own names; there were those at the church who were degenerating into swaggering braggarts, although a warning shot would scatter them like crows; and at the clearing, it took all André's remaining strength to rescue what was left of the courage of the three others. It was as if scars were reopening and old wounds they'd presumed were healed forever were becoming reinfected; they felt spite towards that baneful child who was plunging their world into such deadly chaos; people suddenly realized they owed no other fealty than to the duty taught by the priest and the Bishop of Dijon; and they believed that their duty did not include saving a stranger with powers that were bound to be sacrilegious. When all was said and done, old resentments were adding salt to their wounds, old resentments which the combined powers of Maria and her protectors had defused for a time— remorse and the legacy of guilt, meanness and fear, the litany of concupiscence and cowardly denial, and an entire string of petty acts that left them trapped within a cellar acrid with terror.

Then in Rome, Clara played and the tide turned. Maria's

sadness and desolation ebbed away and made room for a rush of memories: through the transparency of Eugénie's face came the mercurial horse, the fantastical boar, the mists that told of her arrival in the village and that sky of snow into which everyone's dreams had slipped while life opened up and you could look inside. Music and the vibrations of nature became intelligible once again. The first time, the same piece that Clara was playing had eased her heart, burdened with anguish by Eugénie's death. And now it told her a story that honed her powers.

in te sono tutti i sogni e tu cammini su un cielo
di neve sotto la terra gelata di febbraio

There was a sudden gust of wind in the clearing. The landscape was apocalyptic. The sky became a menacing, deathly lid, shot through with the light and rumblings of the storm. All that was left of the world was a feeling of immense danger.

"All fronts are alike," said Petrus to Clara. "This storm looks just like war, and what you see is what every soldier before you has seen."

The mists began a new movement, not swirling around Maria any more, but emerging from her own palms. A colossal bolt of lightning hung in the sky and illuminated the destruction of the region. Then the little girl began to whisper quietly to the sky of snow.

And then … And then from one end of the land to the other there was a flow of all the dreams, in a magnificent symphony that Clara could see on the screen of the sky, and from each soul she could see the pearls of desire embroidered on the taut canvas of the firmament, because each soul, after the despair of their earlier resentments, felt reborn and began to believe in the possibility of victory.

But it was with wonder that she contemplated Gégène's dream, how he had conjured a great enchanted land for Lorette and himself, with a wooden house surrounded by beautiful trees and a gallery that opened onto the forest. But it was not just the dream of a man who aspires to love and a peaceful existence. It also evoked the vision of a land that would belong to itself, of a hunting tradition that would be fair and bountiful, and of seasons so abundant that a soul would feel similarly elevated. Lost little girls would be left outside the doors of simple people so they might grow up amid greatness; there were images of old women rich with the austerity of their intimate acquaintance with the hawthorn bush; and there were coarse yokels drunk on the mission of ensuring a peaceful night's sleep for little girls from Spain; and in this place they lived in a harmony that does not exist in a pure state, but which dreams isolate in the periodic table of desires—and that was how the border between earth and mind could be abolished,—an abolition which, ever since the dawn of time, has been called love.

Because Gégène Marcelot was a genius at love.

This genius of his gave birth to the vision that shone brighter than all the others, through the circulating of dreams with which the sky of snow was flooding the land. Life was hard, and they were so happy! That was what every man said to himself, and every woman even more so, while the lads were marching against the devil's archers with renewed cheer, and the priest looked up at the clouds and felt strengthened by the restoration of his faith. Everywhere the same joy that came from the rebirth of dreams was accomplishing its work of courage and hope. Jeannot gazed from the farmyard out at the battlefield, and through that war for the first time he could see his brother as he had been as a child. For so many years a grimace of excruciating suffering had possessed his brother's face and prevented Jeannot from knowing the taste of happiness, but now on this day happiness took the shape of a woman's body and a white shoulder on which to weep his pent-up tears, while all his former taboos went up in the smoke of the storm. He knew then that he would soon be married and beget a son, and with that son he would talk about his brother and about the blessed hours of peace; turning to the mayor, he slapped him joyfully on the back.

"Ah, doesn't it make you feel young again," said Julot in response to his warm gesture.

The mayor was savouring the remembered poetry of the moment before the hunt, when the forest belongs to the tracker preparing it for the others. But the cold dawn paths had been infiltrated with a new magic. He saw a man with a painted brow speaking to a motionless deer, and the animal's coat radiated perfection. Finally, since all of them had the same revelation of their dreams, in the sky of Burgundy there was an almighty commotion: porcelain eyes mingled with richly coloured partridges, and with sprints through the woods and kisses in the night and blazing sunsets echoing with stones and clouds, while in the prism of every image and every wish all life could be found. So many tears held back, so many secret sorrows ... They had all known the salt flavour of tears, they had all suffered from loving too greatly or not loving enough, and locked away a part of themselves behind the protective yoke of hard work. And every one of them felt, nailed to the tender wall of his heart, a sinister burden of regret or a dusty way of the Cross, and every one of them knew what the constant hammering of remorse will do to a man. But this day was different. Somewhere deep inside they had shifted three forgotten cloves of garlic, and everyday scenes had been transfigured into pictures of beauty. Each one of them had recognized his dream in the sky and found determination and strength in it, and the most powerful dream of all, which was Gégène's, made an offering containing still more bravery and splendour, so much so that the lads who were following him told themselves that their martial quest was aesthetic, too, and that their killing would be without mercy but without rage, so that the land might regain its innocent splendour.

They reached the fallow fields in the east, then went around the hill whence the arrows had come flying over their heads before entering the flow of the storm to be transformed into lethal bombs. Now these were arrows made of good wood and feathers, and they were all glad to be doing battle with an actual real enemy whose fighters were sheltering like cowards behind the black wall. At that moment, Gégène gestured to them to position themselves in such a way that their quarry would neither hear them nor sense their approach. So they went as close as they could and dealt with the archers as if they too were archers, but with the instruments of modern hunting in their hands: they let their bullets fly out on the wind. Oh, the beauty of the moment! It was combat, but it was art, too. For a second, as they stood facing the mercenaries, they saw a vision of naked men whose breath embraced the breath of a land scarcely touched by their light stride; then each of them became clearly aware of his nobility as an archer, the honour they owed to the forests and the fraternity of trees, and they knew that for all that their fingernails might be black, they were the true lords of these lands.

Only he who serves is a lord, Gégène might have said, if it had been time to pull out a cork rather than shoot a villain. The moment passed but the awareness remained and, in the meantime, in the space of two minutes, the surprise of the attack got the better of half of the bad lot, while the other half retreated as quickly as they could and disappeared around the other side of the hill. In actual fact, the enemy bolted like rabbits, and in spite of the villagers' initial urge to give chase, they decided not to, because their main concern was to get back to the village. They cast only a quick glance at those who had fallen, and they found them to be as hideous as any mercenary had ever been. Their skin was white, their hair dark, and on the back of their fighting uniform was a Christian cross, and the lads could not rally until they had closed the eyes of all the dead. Then they tried to make their way as quickly as possible to the church. But the waters barred the roads and there were no more paths they could follow safely on foot.

In the clearing, the story Clara had given to Maria took the shape of a sentence she murmured to the sky of snow, and it spread into three tree-like branches, the three powers of her life. It was neither in Italian nor French, but only in the stellar language of stories and dreams.

in you are all the dreams and you walk on a sky
of snow under the frozen earth of February

Maria knew the earth through the man who had taken her in as his daughter on the first night, she knew the sky through the woman who loved her like a mother and connected her to the long line of women, and she knew the snow through the fantastical mists, an offering from the original story of births. But Clara's words had freed the formula of earth, sky and snow, and Maria could see her dream taking shape. The red bridge flashed in her vision, glittering with the force fields of the unknown world, whence the misty cities drew their light and their life force. An ethereal joining took place inside her. Her inner worlds reconfigured, their junctures absorbed in the birth of an organic wholeness dissolved from every layer of reality.

This reconfiguration then spread from within her, into the vast world outside. The piano fell silent and in a gesture of absolute solidarity, Maria obeyed the story gifted to her by the piano. A breach as long as the world opened in the snowy sky, and out of this glistening abyss came strange beings, who settled on the frozen ground. But what astonished the peasants was the reversal caused by Maria's magic: the sky had become the earth and the ground had taken the place of the clouds—not only that, but one could move about, living and breathing there much as usual. They even understood that it was this reversal that caused the sky to split in two, allowing their defending army to pass through. But more than that, they were astounded by the feeling they had of walking on clouds, while the combat took place beneath. André had removed his cap with its ear-flaps and, standing next to his daughter, he was torn between pride and terror, as if he had been split into two separate, equal parts.

The clearing was covered with their allies.

"Maria is the new bridge," said the Maestro. "This is the first time a detachment of the Army of Mists can fight in the human world and that the elves can implement their laws there."

The earth seemed to have recuperated, and fifty or so strange beings stood in a circle around Maria. Some looked like fantastical wild boars, others like hares, squirrels, or a massive, heavy creature that must have been a bear, but others looked like otters, beavers, eagles, thrushes and every possible kind of known or unknown animal, including—this they realized with amazement—the unicorn of fairy tales. All the newcomers, however, were composed of an essence of man, and that of a horse, and their own specific part, and the three did not meld, but swirled together in a choreography which Maria and the lads recognized. André looked at his right-hand men. They too had doffed their hats and, while they stood to attention with some swagger, they felt their blood run cold as they gazed at the strange army. But they would have died sooner than relax their stance, and ramrod-straight they awaited their orders, there amidst the unicorns and bears. There was a heavy silence until one of the newcomers from the sky stepped away from his fellows to come and bow down before Maria. He was a fine bay horse, his tail turning into a flickering will-o'-the-wisp when his squirrel essence prevailed over the others, and on his human face golden sequins prickled his grey eyes. He stood up straight again, and addressed Maria in the incomprehensible language of the fantastical wild boar from days of old.

In Rome, the ancestor escaped from Clara's hands and grew and grew until it was the size of a man, then it began to spin around the room, and with each spin an essence came loose from the ball of fur before returning, still visible, to the dance. Clara saw a horse, a squirrel, a hare, a bear, an eagle, and a big brown boar, and many other creatures, all part of the waltz, until an entire host of aerial and terrestrial beasts had appeared. Finally, the ancestor came to a halt, while the others could still be seen. The Maestro had risen to his feet and he placed one hand on his heart. Petrus's eyes were shining.

"This miracle you are seeing—we no longer dared hope for it," said the Maestro. "In the olden days, we were all ancestors. Then gradually they became lethargic, and we were born deprived of certain essences, until we only contained three of them, and we began to fear they might weaken still further in the future. We do not know what has been causing this disappearance, but it goes hand in hand with the disappearance of our mists. However, there are at least two things of which we have had a forceful premonition. The first of these is that your births are part of this change, but they are a force for the good; the second is that a certain harmony has been lost forever, but it will be possible to reconstruct it in a different way. The evil that has divided nature may possibly be thwarted by the alliance."

And she saw tears in his eyes.

In the clearing in the east wood, the emissary from the Army of Mists was speaking to Maria, and through the power of the ancestor and the revival of a time when the species had not yet been divided, the little French girl and the little Italian girl understood what he was saying and what they were saying to each other. As for the men, they didn't understand a thing, but waited silently for Maria to tell them what fate had in store.

"We have answered your call," said the bay horse, "although you don't need us in this battle. But the opening of a new bridge is a crucial event, and we must understand the hopes and powers it will enable."

"I need your help," she said, "I can't manage on my own."

"No," came the reply, "we are the ones who need the breach you have created, where the laws of our mists are in force. But you are not alone, and insofar as the battle is concerned, the sky, earth, and snow are on your side."

"You are not alone," said Clara.

"You are not alone," echoed Petrus.

"The snow is with you," added Clara.

And these words, at last, triumphed over all the others, because the snows of the beginning are like the snows of the end, they shine like lanterns along a path of black stones and they are a light in us that pierces the darkness. A familiar warmth enveloped Maria just as night was falling on an unfamiliar scene. A column of men was advancing through a lunar twilight disturbed every so often by the echoes of faraway explosions, and she knew these were the soldiers of the victorious campaign that would forever condemn them to remember their dead, while at this very moment the cold was striking down legions of these brave men that the greatest war in history had not been able to kill. One of the crucified men raised his head and Maria knew what his imploring gaze implied.

It began to snow.

It began to snow with a fine sparkling snow, a curtain that spread quickly from the clearing to the flooded steps outside the church. It was impossible to see either the sky or the ground; they had melded in a thickness of beautiful, pristine snowflakes, a miraculous warmth streaming to the ground. Oh, the caress of heat at last, on those frozen brows! Had they not all been men they would have sobbed like raw recruits. On a signal from Maria, the troop resumed its march, back down the winding passage they had climbed earlier with heavy hearts, while the snow was blowing November over February and the thaw over the icy countryside.

By the time they reached the centre of the village, the winds had dropped and the storm, calmer now, rumbled dully between the last houses and the fallow fields. But the villagers stood rooted to the spot when they saw the army accompanying Maria, and initially they did not know whether to flee or rush to embrace their little girl; and while Chachard and the Saurat boys were gloating—they'd recovered quickly from the shock, and remained nonchalantly on their feet among the unicorns—it took the others a little longer before they could look at these strange shifting creatures without panicking. Finally, once they all had their wits about them, they racked their brains to try to decide what laws of hospitality might apply to an otter with a human face, and they looked to the priest, praying he might suggest a few social graces to use with giant squirrels. As for André, he was watching as the snow grew thicker and, paradoxically, warmer and more transparent, and as was fitting, at that very moment Jeannot, the mayor, Lorette, Rose, and the old ladies arrived, for they had taken the path to the church at the first signs of the storm abating, while the enemy horsemen had suddenly disintegrated in the snow. When they saw who had been sent as reinforcements for the church assembly, Rose and the old ladies crossed themselves, over and over. As for the lads, they felt more or less the way they had the day they had first been smacked. But then the lookouts arrived with news that required urgent attention, and Léon Saurat, exhorting himself to act like a true veteran, came to report to André.

"Behind the hill there is another troop," he said, "even more of 'em, with combat rifles. Our men are on the front line but they can't retreat because the waters have risen."

Astounded he'd managed to deliver such a clear speech, he grinned like a child despite the gravity of the moment.

Maria nodded. She closed her eyes and the snow fell more heavily. Then, by means of the same magic that had infused the lowlands in those glorious seasons, that had maintained the integrity of nature's reign, the snow re-formed as an adamantine curtain and advanced towards the black wall. At the moment of impact they could feel a strange trembling throughout the countryside, a form of emotion that had little to do with any seismic order. A vibration of the same nature ran all through the detachment of elves, and it was clear that they approved of what the little girl was doing.

Finally they saw the storm subside in the same way that the horsemen of doom had collapsed into their own void: the storm literally swallowed itself up, and they were all aware that Maria's strength was vastly superior. There was a moment suspended between the memory of fear and the relief of victory; they all looked at one another, not really knowing what they ought to think or do (in fact, they'd had no time for either thinking or doing); finally, they began to weep and laugh and hug, enthusiastically crossing themselves and rattling their rosaries. Alone among them all, André maintained the same vigilance as the strange creatures and, like them, he was looking only at Maria. Beneath the fine skin on her face, in concentric circles starting at her eyes, tiny dark veins were spreading, and her features were tense with an extraordinary concentration—eliciting a new-found reverence among the newcomers from the sky. André heard them murmuring in their incomprehensible tongue, in a manner denoting astonishment and admiration, and he saw that they had clustered in groups around her the way soldiers would gather around their commander. Then she turned to André and said, "Forward march."

But before the company set off, she called Father François over to her.

Father François's life had changed suddenly with the white curtain. When the snow had liquefied and re-formed, the corolla he had felt while they were burying Eugénie returned.

Three days earlier, he had known only that this corolla had something of the nature of love, spread over a territory more vast than the prisons of the soul. But in the magical twinkling of the snowflakes a universal spirit was revealed, and the significance of his own homily appeared to him at last in all its biblical clarity. Why had it fallen to the faithful servant of the cause of the separation of earth and sky to witness the revelation—with such unprecedented force—of the indivisibility of the world? That is what Maria had acknowledged in him, and that was why she wanted him to walk by her side along with André. In a horrendous epiphany, the enormity of the conflict to come penetrated every cell in the priest's body. Loved ones would be lost; there would be unexpected betrayals; they would march against iniquitous tempests; they would shiver from inhuman cold and, adrift within the most diabolical iniquity ever whispered into a human ear, all faith would be lost, and they would know what it was to march through an icebound landscape; they would know the despair for which there was no remedy. But he had not travelled unawares over two millennia of inner revolutions to pledge allegiance to fear. A shiver went through him, then gave way to the hope of the little boy who used to play in the tall grasses by the stream, and he knew that that which had been separated would be united, that which had been divided would find harmony, for otherwise they would die and nothing would matter any more, nothing other than having wanted to honour the alliance of the living.

Thus they set off on the path to the fallow fields, and they were within a stone's throw from the hill where the gun battle was taking place. The women had stayed at the church but Father

François was walking side by side with André and Maria in the vanguard of the lines, where no one was surprised any more to be marching with unicorns and thrushes. No one was armed, but they were ready to fight with their bare hands, and they suspected above all that the allies would not be powerless when the time came to conclude the matter; and the sky of snow progressed with the company, and anyone who had any sense understood that it was thanks to that same sky that Maria was holding the enclave where the soldiers who had burst from the inverted land and sky could fight.

They reached the hill, and saw that Gégène and his three companions were in an unfortunate position, unable to retreat—even though the waters had receded by then—and surrounded by the enemy who were firing cruelly at them. When the first shots had rung out, they had flung themselves below the curve of the hill, but the hail of bullets came very close and the enemy outflanked them. Now they were four against fifty. Even though they could see that a few of the villains had fallen to the side, they knew it was a miracle that any of their own men were still alive—they caught sight of one of them on the ground, stirring feebly. In fact, they had had to show proof of heroic resistance in order not to be exterminated like woodlice and, seeing this, the reinforcements felt the surge of sacred wrath which the sight of unequal combat arouses; banking on the probability that their allies were burning with the same indignation and the same desire to redress the scales of justice, they were not surprised to see the bay horse lean over to Maria and say something to her. His gesture made his words crystal clear: *Let us finish the job*. To this she agreed.

The snow vanished.

It vanished all of a sudden, as if not a single flake had fallen during the battle. The earth was as clean and dry as in summer, and between clouds as white as doves the sky was daubed with blue of the sort to make you gasp with joy. They had not seen such a blue sky for so long, and advanced all the faster in the direction of the enemy, who now saw the extraordinary battalion at last. You might have thought that men who had shot their arrows into a supernatural storm could resist better than others the shock of that extraordinary vision, but instead they seemed to freeze to the spot, rigid with stupor and fear. One of them, however, managed somehow to drag himself from the general paralysis and he aimed his rifle at the line of advancing soldiers.

The land was transformed. It was a strange transformation, in fact, because there was no change to either its appearance or its essence, but its elements were enhanced and its raw energy uncovered, and everyone could perceive this, owing to unfamiliar sensors that revealed to them a new dimension of their visible world. It was primitive and splendid. The allies, metamorphosed as terrestrial animals, caused vibrations to course through the earth and raise it up, then spread like a subterranean tremor, mowing down the mercenaries. The eagles, thrushes, seagulls and all those connected with the sky spun the air into a turbulent field locked on enemy targets. The otters, beavers, and other terrestrial and riverine animals transformed the air into water, and with it they fashioned spears, which the men had time to admire before they were hurled at the enemy, wounding them more gravely than any weapon made of metal or wood. But while the diabolical tempest had seemed to draw its furore from the warping of natural elements, it now seemed as if the strange army had slipped harmoniously into the rhythm of nature.

"Don't stroke a cat's fur the wrong way," murmured Father François.

At his side, André heard him and a smile creased that face of his, hitherto so resolutely grave. But today he smiled like a young man at the priest's drolleries, and the priest returned his smile, adding all the new jubilation he felt at being a man, and they laughed briefly under the blue sky of victory, because they had come from opposite directions but now were bound by friendship before the same brotherly hearth.

The last enemy fell.

The first battle was over.

Gégène was wounded.

They hurried over to that good soul, and saw he could not get to his feet. He'd been hit by a bullet, and a spot of blood was spreading into his shirt, which they'd pulled away from his jacket. But he was smiling, and when they were all around him, he said in a loud, intelligible voice, "They got me, the swine, but I did for a few of them first."

Father François came over to examine him, then removed his scarf and pressed it to the wound.

"Are you cold?" he asked.

"Nay," said Gégène.

"What sort of taste in your mouth?"

"None, more's the pity."

But he was paler than a ghost, and they could see how he suffered with each word. Julot reached into his overcoat for the flask of tracker's brandy and held it to his lips. Gégène sipped, visibly content, then let out a long sigh.

"I'm thinking the bullet slipped on one of my ribs," he said. "Or else we'll find out soon enough, because I'll be dead before I see Lorette again."

Maria knelt down next to him and took his hand. But first, she addressed Clara. "I've learned," she told her simply.

Then she closed her eyes and concentrated on the fluids running through Eugène Marcelot's palm. There was no hope, and she knew that he knew this, too.

Father François knelt in turn by his side.

"There won't be any confession, my brother," said Gégène.

"I know," said the priest.

"At the hour of my death, I'm a heathen."

"That I know, too."

Then Gégène turned to Maria and said, "Can you do it, lass? Give me my words. I've never known them, but they're all in here."

With a pained, exhausted gesture he pointed to his chest.

She squeezed his hand gently. Then she asked Clara, "Can you give him his words?"

"Who are you talking to, then?" asked Gégène.

"To another girl," said Maria. "She's the one who knows about hearts."

"The priest must take his other hand," said Clara.

At a sign from Maria, Father François took the dying man's hand. Through that paw squeezed by the little French girl, Clara could hear the music of Eugène Marcelot, so like the dream she had contemplated in the sky earlier. It told her a story of love and hunting, the dream of a woman and of forests with a fragrance of verbena and foliage; it spoke of the simplicity of a man who was born into poverty and remained poor, and the complexity of a simple heart laced with mystique; wound through his music were frank gazes and ineffable sighs, bursts of laughter and religious eagerness that asked nothing of the Good Lord, and it swelled with the coarseness and generosity that had made him the representative of a land where little Spanish girls found refuge. All Clara needed to do now was play, and transmit his grace, which reminded her of old Eugénie's as she performed her exalted devotions. So, with exquisite deftness, she ran her fingers over the keyboard, until Father François in turn could hear the music telling the story of Lorette and Eugène Marcelot. When the piano fell silent, he placed his other hand on Gégène's forehead.

"Will you tell Lorette?" asked Gégène.

"I will tell Lorette," said Father François.

Eugène Marcelot smiled and looked up at the sky. Then a trickle of blood seeped from the corner of his lips, and his head tilted to one side. He was dead.

Father François and Maria got to their feet. Men and elves were silent. In Rome, the same silence reigned. Petrus had taken out his giant handkerchief.

"All wars are alike," he said finally. "Every soldier loses friends."

"Those who died weren't soldiers, they were just good people," said Maria.

There was another silence. On the hill they heard what the little girl said, and they searched inside themselves for an answer which, by definition, they knew they could not find.

But it was the bay horse who solemnly unearthed it for the others.

"For this reason we must win the war," he said. "But first you must bid farewell to your dead."

Then he withdrew to his own line, and his fellows bowed in unison to the stunned peasants. Their bow was one of respect, and of the brotherhood of old comrades-in-arms. Maria closed her eyes, and the dark wrinkles that ran beneath her skin grew darker still. Then, from the circles of her palms, the mists began to envelop the strange creatures one after the other, until they reached the emissary, who smiled and waved, then disappeared in turn. All that remained in the land was a handful of men torn between stupor and sorrow. The departure of their allies left them as helpless as children, orphans abandoned to their grief. But after a short spell they rallied: they had lost a friend to whom they owed the tribute of friendship, just as he had shown them, right up to the doors of death. So they set about carrying their fallen brother in the most dignified manner possible, in order to present him to his widow, and it was Léon Saurat who took charge and declared the battle over when he said, "They got him, that they did, but he did for a few of them before that."

When they were within sight of the church where the women and children were waiting, Lorette came up to them. She knew. Her face had been altered by the dark scar of pain, but she listened as Father François said the words Eugène would have wanted her to hear.

"From Eugène to Lorette, through my voice, but from his heart alone: my love, I walked for thirty years under the sky without ever doubting that I lived in glory; I never wavered;

I never stumbled; I was a reveller and a loudmouth, if ever there was one, as stupid and useless as the sparrows and the peacocks; I wiped my mouth on the cuff of my sleeve, tramped into the house with mud on my feet and burped many's a time amid the laughter and the wine. But I always held my head high in the storm because I loved you and you loved me back, and our love mightn't have been all silk and poetry but we could look at each other and know we'd drown all our woes. Love doesn't save, it raises you up and makes you bigger, it is a source of light inside you carved from the wood of the forest. It nestles in the hollows of empty days, of thankless tasks, of useless hours, it doesn't drift along on golden rafts or sparkling rivers, it doesn't sing or shine and it never proclaims a thing. But at night, once the room's been swept and the embers covered over and the children are asleep—at night between the sheets, with slow gazes, not moving or speaking—at night, at last, when we're weary of our meagre lives and the trivialities of our insignificant existence, each of us becomes the well where the other can draw water, and we love each other and learn to love ourselves."

Father François fell silent. He knew he had come closer to his mission, which was to serve, and which gave his life the only meaning it had ever stolen from the deafening silence of the world, and he was destined for all time to be the spokesman of the wordless. Proud and magnificent, Lorette was weeping, but the dark scar had vanished, and through her tears she was smiling faintly. Then she put her hand on her dead husband's chest and said, looking at Maria, "We'll give him a fine funeral."

*

Night was falling. They clustered beneath the roofs that were still intact and, at the Marcelot farm, they organized the vigil. Then they took the time to think. The lowlands had been cruelly ravaged and only after an eternity would they be able to return to any sort of normality. First they had to bury the enemy; the fields had been devastated and they did not know what state their crops would be in; they had to repair the houses, and the church could not wait until last to be restored, because they did not want a priest like theirs to head off to some other steeple. Finally, they wondered what would happen in the future because they suspected that while the sinister enemy might have retreated, it had outlived its soldiers, and would prepare further attacks. But they had become acquainted with fantastical squirrels and wild boars and they knew that in spite of their misfortune and grieving, they had been changed forever.

So, the next day, the second day of February, they held a council at the Hollows Farm, attended by André, Father François, Gégène's companions, Rose, the old ladies, and Maria.

"I cannot stay in the village," said Maria.

The men nodded but the old women crossed themselves. Then, looking at the priest, she said, "Three men will come tomorrow. We will leave with them."

"Are they coming from Italy?" asked the good father.

"Yes," said Maria. "That is where Clara is, and we must join forces."

The news was greeted by a heavy silence. The events of the previous day had made it clear to them that there was another little girl, but they'd had no idea of her role in the affair.

Finally, summoning her courage, Angèle asked, "Will Father François have to leave with you, then?" She seemed almost more alarmed by this desertion than by Maria's departure.

"Thing is, he speaks Italian," said Julot.

Father François nodded. "I will go," he said.

The old women made as if to mumble and grumble but one look from André silenced them.

"Will we be in touch?" he asked.

Maria seemed to be listening to someone speaking to her. "There will be messages," she said.

André looked at Rose, and she smiled at him. "Yes," he said, "I believe there will. By heaven and earth, there will be messages."

The morning of the funeral came at last, two days after they had buried Eugénie and the tempest had laid waste to the land. Father François did not say mass in the roofless church, but when the time came to bid farewell to the seven victims, he uttered a few words which resonated for a long time in those grieving hearts. Once he had stopped speaking, three men came into the cemetery. They walked up the lane and, as they went by, people took off their caps and nodded their heads. When the strangers reached Maria, they nodded in turn.

"*Alessandro Centi per servirti*,"[6] said the man who looked like a prince without a throne.

"Marcus," said the second one, and the fleeting image of a

---

6. Alessandro Centi at your service.

brown bear was superimposed upon his heavy form.

"Paulus," said the third man, and a red squirrel hopped briefly in the sunlight.

"*La strada sarà lunga, dobbiamo partire entro un'ora,*"[7] said the first man.

Father François took a deep breath. Then, with what seemed to be a pinch of pride, he replied, "*Siamo pronti.*"[8]

Alessandro turned to Maria and smiled at her. "*Clara mi vede attraverso i tuoi occhi,*" he said. "*Questo sorriso è per lei pure.*"[9]

"She is smiling back at you," said Maria.

Ever since the end of the battle, each girl had seen the other as if she were there on the edge of her ordinary perception. The permanence of this bond was a balm for Maria, and she was all the more eager for it: now that her powers, her suddenly painful connection with the elements, had been demonstrated, she felt isolated from the beings she loved most. When she had spoken to the sky of snow, she had felt the strength of every natural particle deep inside her, as if she herself had become solid matter, but she also felt another internal change, which terrified her, and she intuited that only Clara would know how to appease its violence. So she kept her fears to herself, waiting for the opportunity to speak freely with the other girl.

Immediately after the battle, Clara had placed the ancestor on her lap, and when the Army of Mists returned through the breach in the sky, it became inert once again.

"What is going to happen now?" she asked the Maestro.

---

7. We have a long way to go, we must leave within the hour.
8. We are ready.
9. Clara sees me through your eyes. This smile is for her as well.

"Maria will set off for Rome," he replied.

"When will I see my father?" she asked.

"There cannot be an answer to everything today. And you are not the only one who is on a quest for light."

"My own father," said Pietro.

"The footbridges," said Clara. "We need more of them, don't we? Will I know the other world some day?" But the Maestro had fallen silent.

For an instant, Clara thought Petrus, in his armchair, his gaze dark, looked disapproving.

Now on this new day when a funeral was to be held, all four of them had gathered in the piano room.

The Maestro turned to Pietro. "My friend," he said, "after so many years when you have accepted not knowing, I promise you: before the end you will know."

And, to Clara: "You will know the worlds that you opened for others."

Then he fell silent and looked at Petrus in such a way that she thought she could see the trace of a well-intentioned capitulation.

"Listen to this as well," said Petrus, "on behalf of the sweeper and the soldier. I would like very much to sit quietly drinking while you play amid the fragrance of the lovely roses in the courtyard. We could walk up and down the rows of our libraries and wax ecstatic over the beautiful moss, or we could go to Abruzzo with Alessandro and chat and eat plums until we die. But for the time being, that is not quite what has been planned. However, I do know from experience that there will be light amid the danger. You will know the mists and the living stones and you will also meet your dream. You will meet Maria and it will be the story of a great friendship, and you will see what it means to be in the company of men who are united in the fraternity of fire. We will go together to the land of the sign of the mountain, and we will drink tea there, but some day, and I bless our mists, you will be old enough for a glass of moscato. And on every step of this great adventure I will be with you because I will be your friend forever. Now if I am not quite the hero of the stories, I do know how to fight and I know how to live, too. And I prize friendship and laughter above all else."

He poured himself a glass of moscato, and propped himself comfortably in the armchair of dreams.

"But for the moment," he said, "I want to raise my glass in honour of those who fell in battle, and remember what Father François said this morning in tribute to a great man whose name was Eugène Marcelot: *My brother, return to dust and know for the eternity of the forests and the trees how much you have loved. This victory and this strength, I shall always maintain.* And surely it is not by chance that the motto of our mists slipped into his words."

Manterrò sempre.

COUNCIL OF THE MISTS
Half of the Council of the Mists

"**O**ur kind came under a surprise attack last night in Katsura," said the Council Head.

"Casualties?" asked a councillor.

"They all died," said the Guardian of the Pavilion.

"That means the start of a new war," said another councillor.

"We have raised a great army," said the Council Head, "despite betrayals and renegade bridges. And the armies of men are mobilizing. We will soon be fighting on every front."

"Can we wage two wars at the same time? We have to find the enemy's bridge."

"Maria is our new bridge. But no human beings have ever crossed over to this side, and we don't know how dangerous it could be for them."

"That sort of uncertainty worries me less than the present betrayals," said the Council Head. "And I have faith in my daughter's powers."

"Perhaps there is a traitor among us at this very moment," said the Guardian of the Pavilion. "But the transparencies of the path are pure, and at least we can be sure of this enclave. As for my daughter's powers, they will soon surpass my own."

"Councillors," said the Council Head, getting to his feet, "the withering of our mists does not only threaten the beauty of our lands. If they disappear, we will disappear as well. The world has never stopped fragmenting and losing its way. In ancient times, were humans and elves not kindred species? The greatest evil has always come from divisions, from walls. Tomorrow, those whose thirst the enemy is hoarding will wake up to a modern world, which means old and disenchanted. But our hopes lie in a time of alliances and we pursue the illusion of ancient poets. We will fight with the weapons of our Pavilion and of their stories, and nowhere is it written that the paths of tea and dreams cannot triumph over cannons. Our bridge is holding, strengthening the harmony of nature and uniting the living. In the little girls' wake, we see men and women aspiring to build footbridges from nature and dreams. Are Maria and Clara the ones we have been waiting for? No one knows yet. But they have been fighting courageously and we owe them the hope that enlivens us, even as the first battle has shown us the bravery and compassion of their human protectors. No matter the outcome of this war, remember their names and fight alongside them with honour. And now, after you have wept your tears for those you have lost, withdraw and prepare for battle. As for me, I will do what I must. I will maintain."

ACKNOWLEDGEMENTS

With my thanks and gratitude to Jean-Marie, Sébastien and Simona.